PASSION *and* PROPRIETY

Emilie's Story

The Golden Hearts Series

ELINA I. TROSHIN-MOROZOV

Elina Morozov Publishing
Copyright © 2020 Elina I. Troshin-Morozov
All rights reserved.

ISBN Paperback: 978-1-7357525-0-1
ISBN Ebook: 978-1-7357525-1-8

Edited by Shavonne Clarke
Cover by 100Covers.com
Formatting by formattedbooks.com
Online author education and community by self-publishingschool.com

Be who God meant you to be and you will set the world on fire.
–St. Catherine of Siena

Thank you to my dearest husband, Alex, who caught my author spark and fanned it into flames. You saw before I did. Thank you for believing in me.

Thank you to my three sons, Matthew, Michael, and Elijah, who kept asking me when my book would be finished. This kept me focused on the end goal. You are my gifts from above.

Thank you to my incredible parents, Igor and Nadia Troshin, whose life of sacrifice has brought me to this place. I would not be here if it weren't for you!

Thank you to my awesome siblings, Yuri, Natasha, Vlad, and Cristina. Your spoken and unspoken encouragement and support mean the world.

Thank you to all of my family and friends who have continually supported me on this journey. Your encouragement has been like wind beneath my wings. You know who you are.

Prologue

"You mustn't be so stubborn, Elisa. It isn't right. Father died to ensure that you and I were taken care of. I don't want to fight with you on his funeral day of all days, but I need to know that you won't do anything irrational. He *died* for our future!" Clarence contended with ever-increasing persuasiveness.

"He died of dysentery aboard a *slave* ship," Elisa retorted, not the least bit moved by her elder sister's outburst.

"Ugh! You're so unreasonable. You—" she began, when suddenly a funeral usher interrupted with a hushed knock on the door.

"They're awaiting you in the main hall, please, if you will ladies."

The two young sisters in black both shot him a sharp look, then faced one another. Elisa stood, briefly nodded to her sister, and began to turn toward the door. Now, a second beyond her sister's gaze, her eyes began to fill with tears at the woes of life. She felt so misunderstood. Father was gone, but his expectations remained. Conviction had pitted her against her family's very livelihood and continued to shape her vision of the future.

"Elisa," Clarence hissed, unable to contain her implacable disdain but still aiming to appear proper, "you must think of our future.

What if we have daughters one day? What if you have a daughter? You must think of her."

Elisa picked up her heavy skirts and stepped out the door.

Yes, I must think of her.

Chapter 1

Year: 1805.

"Emilie, Father and Momma are dead," voiced a pale, morbid Oliver.
The thin veil between reality and the dreadful existence one never wishes for tore into a million shreds. A violently trembling porcelain cup unsettled the now suffocating silence.

"I'm sorry, Lady June, but it appears tea time is over."

Unspeakable pain colored the elder's face, who could no more speak than she could move to comfort her young friend. With shaking hands and fumbling gait, however, she forced herself up across the short distance. Heaving a still Emilie into her arms, she held her delicately so as not to crush her fragile body. The young—now orphaned—woman slipped through her warm embrace onto the cold stone floor. Despair encircled like a ravenous raven; death had found them most cruelly.

What now?

Emilie was the youngest of three children, the older two being Mick and Oliver which, to a great extent, explained the fortitude of traits found in her character and mind. Growing up with two older brothers meant less time for ribbons and frills and more time for so many other things. She learned discourse and tactical discussion while observing the late-night conversations between her father and brothers. While Mother would rest her eyes by the low glow of dusk after a long day on the small estate (for they never hired but four servants: Ethan to tend the outdoors, Miss Fist the indoors, and two others to raise the livestock), Emilie would sit by Father, fastidiously embroidering (as all young ladies were expected to do), while at the same time engaging in the back-and-forth banter so common to the men. In her young mind, she was their equal. In their eyes, she was.

She was their delightful pride and joy. They would often watch their daughter's quick nature and wonder if allowing so much freedom without the expected so-called "proper English restraint" would end up harming the child. Although her mother did endeavor to impart the graces of English femininity from an early age, and try as she may have, this child would consistently question its purpose and form. And seeing their daughter's natural tendency toward the free world outside, they would allow Emilie to run with the boys.

She always had questions which, when answered truthfully, often touched upon subjects far beyond her young frame.

"Momma, why are the field workers all black?" she asked one day when the family took a brief summer trip to London, having passed several fields rife with workers.

"What's a lady?" was asked during the aforementioned trip, when an ill-tempered noblewoman reprimanded her for misbehaving at the hat shop which she and Momma visited, instructing her to "act like a lady."

"Momma, why is Lady June not married? How can she be so rich if she isn't?" came a different day, when the elder family friend had given her a most exquisite birthday gift that dazzled under even the faintest candlelight.

Such were the deliberations of an insatiable young mind that could not help but question what most took for granted. Question after question, the young Emilie learned about herself while cradled tenderly amidst the realities of a harsh world. Mother was the most trusted source of knowledge, the supplier of most of her answers. Emilie depended upon her interpretation of everyday events, and observing the singular kindness shown by both parents to consequential and inconsequential people, she acquired the propensity to see all people as worthy of friendship.

The Forthyn family, which owned a newspaper branch in the countryside of Suffolk, generally saw people this way. Although they did have connections to the city, they preferred life far from the noise of the industrializing world. Not desiring the reproach of soul permanently affixed to the slave trade so commonly practiced in the city, they chose the freedom of the lowlands and hills, where any man could prosper should he desire to. The branch employed thirty men and seven women, paying a fair wage comparable to what was paid even in London. Father periodically allocated a small percentage of profit toward the work of abolition, which they wholeheartedly upheld.

They were close to the McGrays, whose one child, Phineas, was a lifelong friend of Mick and Oliver, spending much of his time in their company. This was like his second home.

The country was the freest place in all of England for young and old alike. Dreams of a long and prosperous life were sown into its fertile soil, tended lovingly, and showered with the fullness of expectation.

At the gentle age of nineteen, however, due to a most unforeseen and catastrophic accident, Emilie lost everything. She hurt so much, she couldn't cry.

The day of the funeral, the rose garden was especially bleak. The birds chirped quietly along as the wind blew their songs away. The place was dead—even the infinitely dancing dahlias seemed downcast with grief. Momma and Father had designed this place for her, knowing that every girl yearned for a secret escape in which to dream dreams as she grew. The swing, found by following a curvy, narrow pathway lined by trellises generously endowed with rose bushes, was the favorite spot. Momma would push, and Emilie would squeal with delight to be pushed higher, at which the woman would laugh, beaming with pride at her daughter's fearless disposition.

Now, at the end of the funeral which took place beyond the garden, Emilie quietly fled to the swing, sat down in the hard-worn seat, and drew in a trembling breath. What was she to do now? Where would she go? She exhaled, letting heavy tears fall onto an ugly black dress. Who would love her?

"Em," a voice said behind her. The voice was far enough behind for Emilie not to startle. It was soft, hesitant. "I-I wanted to say I'm sorry for what happened."

Looking back slightly through tear-stained eyes, Emilie recognized Phineas standing forlornly by the trellised entrance and acknowledged him as she was able with a grief-stricken heart. She wiped the tears to focus in on him, but could not stop them. His presence was not unwelcome, though. It brought comfort. "Oh, Phin!" she whispered as a heavy sob rose from her chest and out.

Seeing her frailty, he could not help but come closer.

Head down in her hands, hair drowning in sobs, Emilie embraced the presence of an old friend and let her guard down. Here, in this moment, she cried with Phineas by her side. She did not mind; he could offer nothing but quietness and presence.

He did not understand why, when he saw Emilie head to the garden after the funeral, he followed. But he did, and now he was glad of it. She needed him.

Neither of them understood the significance of the moment at hand. Two young individuals had just lost two people who had played such an important role in their lives. They both loved them, albeit in different ways. But now they were gone.

As the sounds of people died down with the funeral coming to a close, Emilie and Phineas walked back to the house in silence. She had heard enough crying, sniffling, and whispering voices to last a lifetime. She needed quiet, and he obliged. She thanked him for walking her back, formally curtsied, and shut the door. The dark house, however, was too much to bear. She ran up the stairs, entered her bedroom where everything reminded her of the ones she had lost, and collapsed to the floor. Sorrow and exhaustion prevailed.

At this same time, Phineas, too, wrestled with an unexpected change of heart. He kept telling himself it was nothing more than sentimental emotion toward his best friends' little sister, or simply himself getting caught up in the sorrow of the shared loss. Yes, that's all it was. *Tomorrow it will all be gone*, he kept telling himself as he went in search of Oliver and Mick. But thoughts of Emilie would not leave.

Chapter 2

The following days involved all sorts of unwelcome activity. Quick conversations and decisions were being had and made irrespective of the young Forthyns' gaping wound. Emilie was nauseated by the speed with which things were being done. No one asked her what she thought about the whirlwind of plans taking place around her and on her behalf. Dazed, she wanted Momma and Father. She desperately needed to be held.

Lady June decided to stay a few days longer to provide comfort and to facilitate necessary planning. Compared to Momma, it was true that Lady June was the next best thing. She was different in that she was pristinely English-lady-like, and wholly proper. However, she too held within her spirit a fire that blazed upon the coals of wisdom and a life truly lived. Amidst perfectly refined manners and regal attire, one felt they were in the presence of supercilious royalty, yet a witty word or timely smirk would quickly betray her presentation. Her eyes twinkled delightfully. She was confident, and like Momma held her convictions close to heart. And when the time would come, she'd speak loud and clear about what was good and right in life. Unwavering conviction earned Lady June unreserved respect from many of her contemporaries, for many of them, as aware as they were of the truth she spoke, were too afraid to speak up out of concern about the fiscal ramifications of such intrepid forthrightness.

It has been wondered if the female spirit is so timidly maintained and strictly bound in society because it *can* and *does* cause such a stir to the accepted norm. Lady June and Momma both knew that a single spark could kindle a raging fire. Thus Emilie grew chasing fireflies and riding horses, an equal amongst the men, a wildflower dancing in the meadow wind. They refused to tame that fire.

Throughout the years of June's visits to the Forthyn estate, Emilie could not get enough of her stories about heroes and heroines that saved the world and stood for all things right. As she grew, she would often ask why people did such unexplainable things and why some fared better than others. She wondered about finding true love, declaring at the age of eleven that she would never marry, vowing to Momma and Father to stay with them forever, to which Lady June would smile and say, "You, beloved, are your mother's daughter."

Chapter 3

*S*uch was Lady June. Today, however, Emilie loathed the woman. She detested herself for feeling this way. But the request by the woman whom she loved dearly was too much to bear. How could she acquiesce? Grief had overtaken her young soul so deeply that she cared nothing for her personal refinement and future bliss. She wanted to stay at the Forthyn estate as long as the roses bloomed...as long as the place stood, reminding her of what once was.

But sitting by the window of her bedroom, seeing friends and neighbors coming and going with food and heartfelt condolences, Emilie realized that as quickly as their lives had gone on, hers would have to go on, too. She kept remembering Lady June's words that Momma would not have it any other way, that sending her to live with Aunt Clarence not far from London would be the best thing for her. She insisted that Emilie needed to think of her future, that life on the estate would not nurture the woman she was destined to become, and that moving to live with her aunt and uncle in Kent was the best decision to be made. As the trusted matron of the Forthyn family (by way of friendship, not legally), Lady June played a heavy hand in this decision. Emilie did not understand the severity of her persistence and struggled under the weight of her own resentment.

One day shortly after the funeral, while June sipped on afternoon tea in the four o'clock rays streaming lightly through an old window, Emilie hesitantly came down the stairs and crossed to where she sat. She longed to speak openly with the silver-haired woman. Kneeling, seeking understanding in the woman's perceptive eyes, she started, "Lady June, *why...*?" The question searched and pleaded, begging for a change of heart. "Why must I go? I will continue my studies here, a-and I'll learn to manage the estate, and..."

"Having you move in with Sir and Lady Fox is not a novel idea, my darling love," she revealed bluntly yet softly, to Emilie's astonishment. "Emilie, look at you: you are a ravishing young woman in her prime who has never stepped foot into English society. Although your upbringing here has done you much good, the future will expect more of you. Your mother and I have spoken of this moment many times, and..." Her voice broke. Holding the teacup with trembling hands, for the first time she let her pain be seen. "And we knew that this moment would come, when we would all have to embrace this decision."

She put down the peach blossom cup and let her gaze shift from Emilie to the new graveyard just beyond the rose garden. "Women make hard decisions, my darling child. For example, today I chose to let my dear friend go." She breathed softly, eyeing the fresh gravesite. "I will live on. For your sake and for the sake of your brothers. And you must choose to live, too. You *must* choose so, because one decision will enlarge your capacity to experience life beyond anything you've ever imagined...while the other will keep you forever the same. You must understand that what is being done is being done in love." And with that, June kissed the forehead of the silent child, tenderly working through her thickly braided hair.

Emilie felt Momma in these words. Lady June's vulnerability softened her, allowing what was said to be true. She felt the hand of providence in the words, though she did not understand anything at all. The sting of death was yet so tangible. She felt alone, and grieved that even if she were to move to Kent, Momma and Father would not even see her change the world as everyone always insisted that she would. Was *this* the next step? Was there a worthy cause ahead?

Today, she insisted on knowing nothing at all. Numb with the pain of loss, moved by Lady June's love, she raised herself up from the stone floor and went to be alone on the swing. In the stirring of the garden with the sun casting shadows all around, she cleared her mind to think.

The following morning when coming down to breakfast, she said that she would go to live with Sir and Lady Fox in Kent.

The room filled with mixed emotion once again. Talk about how soon and for how long ensued, though Emilie was hardly present. She knew very little about what lay in store. She nodded and answered questions, but she was not happy. Like a heroine in the stories of her childhood, however, she would go and go on. She was as principled as she was passionate, and this decision was based on principle. *A young woman needs an older woman in her life to teach her the ways of a lady*—principle one. *Fatherless brothers are incapable of raising a young lady*—two. And finally, *a young woman is more likely to be favorably married when she is out in the high society of England.*

Today, Emilie only hoped that Momma would be proud.

Chapter 4

*I*n the days that followed, much happened. Phineas hung around more. He hung around Oliver and Mick, of course, but his gaze kept following Emilie's quiet figure. She paid him no notice and continued mindlessly inside the house. It was planned that she and Lady June would ride together from Suffolk to Kent in two days' time, and much had still to be done.

Oh, what would she have done without Miss Fist? The young woman had helped her to pack four cases of *things*, insisting that she would need every single one. Petticoats, summer dresses, winter ones, undergarments, bonnets, winter hats and gloves, and a few more fancy options for special occasions which she had received over the years as gifts from June. Knowing the little that she did about the Foxes, she surmised that her cousins, Violette and Carleighla, would consistently dress to severely impress every soul that would be so fortunate as to make their acquaintance.

She began to doubt her fitness for such a life. And if she were entirely honest with herself, she began to experience a sense of visceral insecurity about the decision. What would they think of her? Would they be friendly? Would Kent change her to become like them?

These thoughts followed her hour by hour as the day of departure arrived. It did not come warm and welcome as better days did, but instead rushed in cold and quite in spite of a sleepless night. Emilie shuddered in the cold of late September, slipped frozen feet into slippers, and sat up on the edge of her bed. She gazed around the still dark room and thought of the many years spent here, in this home. Mick and Oliver shared a room next door, while Father and Momma had once slept across the hall.

It was a splendid room. She allowed herself to grieve this farewell, trembling shoulders covered, alone in a changed world. Clutching the blanket tightly, she stood and walked to the window where the first rays of day peeked assertively through. Sniffling and in spite of it, a vacant smile toyed with her lips, causing her to feel the dry face and taut skin where tears had fallen. The house began to awaken. Life was irrevocably different, but the adventure began today.

Emilie noted how thoughtfully Miss Fist had laid out a bright dress for the road ahead. She assumed it was to brighten this very despondent day and appreciated the woman's thoughtfulness. Pouring frigid water into a basin, she washed her face, not hearing Lady June (who also could not persuade herself to sleep) slip into her room with Momma's jewelry box.

"Good morning, darling," she announced with a vigorous whisper and jovial grin.

"Lady June, good morning to you," said Emilie, truly pleased to find the beloved woman there with her.

The older woman again swelled with pride at Emilie's dignified resolve to move forward today in strength, humble as it was. She knew without a doubt that this was the right decision. "Emilie, before we head downstairs, I wanted to give you something," she said as she quietly shut the door, crossed softly on the creaking floor across the room, and beckoned for Emilie to join her on the bed. She held in her hands Momma's jewelry box. "This box contains all the jewelry owned by your mother. Do you see this necklace?" she asked, pointing to a timeless piece that sparkled even at this hour of day.

"Oh, Lady June, it's *radiant*. Why have I never seen Momma wear it? Where did she get it?"

"Hm, yes, indeed you never have. Your mother saved it for you to wear on your wedding day. You know how much I loved your mother; she was like the daughter I never had. I gave it to her the day she married your father—and Emilie, was she a sight to behold. I'll never forget that day. She had made many difficult decisions at so young an age, and I was there all along, supporting her through each one. What a beautiful woman she always was. Before you were born she would say to me that if she ever had a daughter, she would save this necklace for her. So, in honor of your momma and as we embark on this journey, you and I, I give all of this to you. Wear these pieces and know that they were specifically intended for you. May they remind you of her beauty. Not just outward, mind you, but even more so inward. As you are reminded, be strengthened to remain true to yourself. Emilie, my love," she finally said, cradling her face, "you are moving to a new place to do new things."

As she listened, Emilie imagined her momma in her shoes, about to travel across the country to a new place without close family or true friend, to learn the ways of an English noblewoman in preparation for an unknown future. As the thoughts settled in, Emilie vowed to never forget a single thing about her.

"I am fully confident"—June's words penetrated her thoughts—"that all will be well." She met Emilie's gaze for a moment, gently squeezed her arms, and smiled. There was peace in her eyes. Emilie believed her.

The two women exchanged a tender embrace and proceeded to get Emilie dressed as the morning finally greeted them with its fullness: clanging pots in the kitchen; mouthwatering wafts of coffee, bacon, and biscuits; and the unintentionally rambunctious activity of men right outside Emilie's window, preparing the livestock for the day. Mick and Oliver were discussing estate affairs with Victor and Ethan, who were conveying to them the need for the purchase of two more cows and five more sheep.

June so loved the Forthyn boys. This morning, however, as she peered out the window she noted the presence of another young man in the bunch.

She had known Phineas McGray since his childhood, as he, like herself, was a constant visitor in the Forthyn home. She had taken note of his unusually kind demeanor and solid determination to make something of himself for his family name's sake. Being an only child, he shouldered many responsibilities but, June noted, rarely complained. As a young lad of thirteen or fourteen, he would take school lessons with such effortful determination that he gained entry into one of England's most prestigious educational institutions. He, however, declined the offer, feeling that at that time his mother and father would suffer greatly if he were to leave. He swore to pursue an education in law once his family had gained more helping hands and he felt could spare him. June knew that he had begun his studies just two years ago now. She admired his selflessness and was exceedingly happy that his education had finally begun. *He deserves it*, she thought.

She also noted that since the funeral, he was seen around the estate more. At first she thought nothing of it, but wise old ladies, being the mysterious creatures that they are, are notoriously good at observing and deducing certain human qualities that often easily and conveniently escape the untrained eye. It took but a glance on his part and June knew before anyone else what she had seen. Her eye confirmed with a certain contentment what her heart had known all along. *That's not the last of him*, she thought to herself, and smiled.

Breakfast was over in a rush. The table, laden with the usual fullness, was heavy with deliberate talk. The post-funeral gray had not yet lifted. Mick and Oliver affirmed that they were happy for her journey, but the sorrow in their eyes betrayed them. Miss Fist hurried about and fussed packaging food for the long journey. And even though both June and Phineas were present at the table, there was much left over, as no one seemed particularly hungry. The brothers insisted on her writing every few weeks of her whereabouts and doings and that if anyone should trouble her, to let them know immediately. Though they had never been particularly sentimental, having lost their father and mother and now losing their beloved sister, even their tears eventually fell. Phineas sat quietly by, absent-mindedly fiddling with this or that, not feeling like it was his place to talk. This was understood by the lot of them as the melancholic state of being that had overtaken many friends of the family since the funeral.

A knock on the front door expedited the transition from table to door, where a carriage awaited Emilie and June. The house was a mess. Old funeral roses filled the home with musty sweetness. Everything had been slowed to a stop the past days. The home of Emilie's childhood had visibly aged. While the men prepared her belongings outside, she decided to take one final stroll through the house. Whether this was a good idea or not, she did not know, but she needed a moment to look once more. She memorized the kitchen, father's study, mother's vanity, her bedroom, and the view from her window. *Only good memories*, she decided.

The front door had been opened and closed several times while the baggage was being loaded outside, and as it was quiet, Emilie, thinking that everyone was outside by now, made her way there. To her surprise, Phineas stood there waiting, as it were.

He straightened expectantly as soon as he saw her, releasing his hands from his pockets. His eyes were eager to speak, but his posture was helplessly stiff and reserved.

She heard her family outside the door and wondered if perhaps Mick had asked him to help her with something while they loaded the belongings. She just wasn't sure what to make of this. Did she feel him to be intrusive?

But she also remembered the solace he had offered the day of the funeral, quickly recognizing this sudden moment as the perfect opportunity to thank him. It dawned on her how much a part of her life he had been. Phineas engendered the pleasantest memories of warm summer evenings when he and the Forthyns would play late into the night, then come running home to cold milk and warm pie, hands and feet dirty from their escapades together. The pleasantness of their shared memories plucked a heart string that was finally neither unpleasant nor minor. A brief flicker of *something* shot through her, but the perplexing nature of the emotion and the unusual moment at hand pushed it away.

Aware of her vulnerability, and understanding that he too was not himself, she aloofly began on an assumption. "Phin, I don't have anything else that needs carrying... Is that why you're waiting? Did Mick ask for you to wait here? Indeed, my life fits into those four bags," she said dryly, nodding at the baggage outside and hoping to lighten the encounter which, in her mind, lacked a proper reason. Then she continued, "Phineas, but while you're here, I would like to thank you for being with me in the rose garden that day. I will always cherish your kindness and friendship. I am obliged to you. Thank you," she said, gently pressing his forearm, looking into his eyes. *How deep and distinct they are,* she thought.

"Emilie, no, no, please don't feel obliged. I was eager to support you—your family—in any way I could. I'm just so sorry this all happened. This trip—your going away, it will serve you well, I'm sure of it. To be in society with new people, and new engagements. It will help you to...forget. And I-I thought you might require something to remind you of home when you wanted to remember. Here, please accept this token of my friendship with you, a-and with your brothers and family. My only request is that you open it later, when you're on the road...please," he finished as he reached into his pocket to give Emilie a small, smooth package neatly wrapped in white paper.

As she took the package from his hand, that quizzical sensation flickered again. An unspoken exchange of certain mutual affection took place right then and there. It was in the atmosphere and shared by both. Unable to define the experience and not wishing to exacerbate her mystified soul any further, Emilie curtsied, thanked

Phineas, and remarked that it was time to head outside as she hastily proceeded past him toward the front door.

Indeed, he was a *dear* family friend.

Clutching the smooth package out of sight with fingers pulsating like drums, she stepped into the light of day, flushed. The turmoil within presented with a vengeance, and she longed for her own time and space. Phineas's behavior inflamed it.

Lady June, noting her severe countenance, took her firmly to her side and encouraged everyone that it was time they set out toward Kent, at which point Mick, Oliver, and the servant cohort embraced her and wished her farewell one by one. It was a sight to behold. So much tenderness and love lavished upon a young woman who desperately needed it.

One moment they held one another, and the next she was climbing into the stately carriage after Lady June. The black horses whinnied and grunted, kicking back their manes, displaying their grandiose impatience. Emilie felt the same. She was impatient to leave this place where what was left of her loved ones remained. Also, however, she wanted to get this chapter of her life begun and completed so she could be back here once again. As the horses began their steady trot forward, she wasn't sure what she wanted anymore. Actually, she wished things had never changed. That's what she wanted. But they had.

As the carriage prepared to turn onto the main road, Emilie looked back and waved. Try as she may, she could not hold back the tears. She smiled and let them come. They were all waving back at her. Before they were too far out of sight, she guardedly allowed herself a glance at Phineas, who stood in the doorway. He neither looked nor waved, but instead stood with hands in pockets and head leaned against the doorpost, eyes closed, sun bathing his face. He was obviously in thought. She, too, leaned her head against the moving carriage and closed her eyes. Instead of seeing visions of Father, Momma, Mick, or Oliver, however, she thought back to her encounter with Phineas. She would open the gift later.

She considered how kind it was of him, that he was likely compelled by the need for closure to provide it, and that he would likely
be out of her life the closer he came to completing his studies. He
was her brothers' friend, after all. In the steady jostling motion of
the carriage, the emotions she had been feeling over the past two
weeks descended weightily upon her in the form of deep sleep.

"Lady June," the exhausted traveler mumbled softly, "I'm so glad
you're here with me."

The older woman smiled warmly at her companion and gently
encouraged her to sleep. She understood that rest was vital in order
for Emilie to regain and maintain her spirits on the journey ahead.
Derbyshire at Kent—the destination—was no less in the forefront
of her mind because she knew the challenges that awaited her brave
Emilie. June knew that she would not be able to shield Emilie from
hardship, as she would only see her from time to time during visits,
but she also knew that Emilie would reach out to her if she required
the assistance. This gave her comfort.

The horses picked up their pace as Emilie fell into sweet sleep.

Chapter 5

𝓔milie awakened three and a half hours later drenched in warm afternoon sunlight pouring in through the carriage window. Lady June was heavily asleep, as evidenced by the occasional snore escaping her semi-lunar mouth. Emilie took a deep breath in, raising herself up for a much-needed stretch of her back. Outside lay fields of fading green with hay bales scattered about. It was not so different from Suffolk.

Thinking back to home, she recalled Phineas's gift. She reached to her right under the blanket and found the smooth package on the humming carriage seat. Before opening it, she considered how thoughtful it was and how kind the gesture, that someone would think of her at such a time when she was at her lowest and wholly negligent of others, legitimately living in a most unattractive misery. She clenched the package, thinking back to the cause of this misery, feeling a sense of guilt that she had not thought of Momma and Father recently and that this new life rhythm was already making it so hard to.

Oh, Momma, what am I doing? she thought. *I've left you and Father behind. How will I do this without you? What if I forget you?*

There was no way back. Not wanting to wake June and treasuring the solitude, she grieved sweetly and peacefully in the carriage that traversed the English countryside for her sake. This time, however, the tears held back some; the balm of time was already beginning to work. With a delicate heart she began to unwrap her gift. She found a plain notepad with a cover beautifully inscribed with her full name and with a very familiar scent. The pages were filled with dried-pressed rose petals from the garden! Emilie's heart leaped to attention, as if Momma had heard her anguished thoughts and had acknowledged them. In this moment, it was as if Momma had given Emilie the benediction to leave the past and to live onward. With bated breath, Emilie allowed herself to smile for the first time since the funeral. She couldn't believe the magnitude of the moment.

Her thoughts fell back on Phineas. She wished she could thank him. Thinking back to their final encounter, she felt a twinge of emotion deep within. It was a mixture of feelings that she had not felt before toward him.

With the clicking of the horses and before she could think further, Lady June began to stir.

"Lady June, how do you do? Are you quite alright? How was your nap?" Emilie sat up, expressing a genuine interest in the elder woman's well-being. She loved her so.

June chuckled heartily. "Nothing quite like an afternoon nap, darling, especially for this old lady."

Emilie relaxed and settled back again into her newly rediscovered sense of self. She smiled largely for her own sake, permitting herself to feel again.

Lady June most definitely noticed the change. Shifting her bottom on the hard carriage seat, stretching and yawning, she caught a glimpse of the wrapping and notepad. She began, "If I am not mistaken, something smells marvelously of home...?"

Without the slightest warning or request for consent, Emilie's cheeks flushed red. This she was not prepared for. She had been ruminating about Phineas the past hour or so, and apparently had confused her mind about his role in her heart. She could—no—she *would* not expose herself to even this woman's curiosity. She hurriedly looked down and away, gathered her unexpectedly scattered self, and focused her attention on the gift. "It was a gift, Lady June, from a…friend," she emitted levelly, hoping that this astonishingly perceptive woman would for once not perceive right through her. To her utter relief, it appeared that she did not.

Instead, Lady June only remarked of how much the scent reminded her of the rose garden and how pleased her parents would be of this most grandiose adventure. June, resting both arms on her cane and fixing a steady gaze on a point outside the quickly moving carriage, presented rather detached. Outwardly she was the appearance of the queen—head high, spectacularly composed; inwardly, however, she happily treasured the unraveling of the blossom seated right beside her. June was far too wise to frighten this delicate dove. She would wait for it to find its resting place before hearing its coos.

The two sat self-consciously by as the road moved and turned. Rather, Emilie sat awkwardly by, working through what had just happened, and June was all contented composure. At age nineteen Emilie was extraordinarily self-aware, but even so, she did not know what to make of the current happenstance. She turned inwardly to process as the mid-afternoon sunshine played atop her stressed forehead and nose. She had heard that a true English lady emanated a certain air of intrigue by her very presence. She, quite clearly, had much to learn about this art of mystery. Her golden hazel eyes and chestnut curls had not yet acquired the wise prudence of maturity, presenting instead unapologetically free. One look of her eyes or turn of her head would, without the slightest doubt, betray the contents of her heart. She felt immensely vulnerable.

The ladies were expediently notified by the carriage driver that they would be taking a break quite soon, and as such began preparations for their exit. Emilie was grateful for Miss Fist's endless fussing earlier that day, though at the time when she was in an altogether different state, she could not have cared less. Now, with the gradual return of wellness (in spite of the emotional flurry of the prior moment) she was not only hungry but also interested in the people she would soon be meeting. As the horses began to slow their pace toward a meadow abutting a lake where they could sit and eat, and as Emilie prepared to question Lady June about her cousins, all heard the wrathful snap of a whip accompanied by shouting. The grotesque display obliterated normalcy. The cohort went still, not knowing whether to begin unloading or to reroute and go.

Emilie nervously peeked out of the carriage to see a livid Englishman whipping a negro man for an ill, being defined by hysterical shouting. How deceptive the moment was: the place was breathtaking, but the image now burned into everyone's memory—heartbreaking. The experience was an unwelcome violation of her novice knowledge of the world. Her eyes cemented to the scene and would not let go. The decision was unanimous: they would keep going in search of a new resting stop. *Click, click, click*, and they were off.

Emilie noticed the deep, furrowed brow on Lady June's face. "Lady June," she whispered, "what do you think of what we just saw?" Her eyes insisted on an honest answer.

June was never short on words, but here she narrowed her eyes, squaring off with Emilie. "What do *you* think of what we just saw, Em?"

Emilie didn't know whether this was some sort of test of character or if the woman was preparing her for the disappointment of an untoward answer. In June's presence, she knew she was safe. So in full honesty, she began, "In my heart I can't imagine how any human being can treat another like that, but then I look at what just happened and see that this happens, Lady June, and I think it happens often. And I think, if it happens a lot..." She paused, pondering the next words to say, her brow furrowed with searching. "Then is it wrong? Or is it *very* wrong? Are so many people comfortable with doing such wrong?"

June softened. "Emilie, what does your *heart* say?"

And without hesitation, she plainly said, "My heart says that it's wrong."

To which June responded, "Yes, I believe your heart, child, is right. Sometimes the mind confuses the heart, and the heart the mind. Is this not so?"

The perceptive gentleness of her voice coaxed Emilie out of hiding. Taking a vast breath in and then slowly breathing out, she fully agreed with her. For her mind, too, insisted on confusing her heart, and all she could say was an absentminded albeit affirming, "Mm-hm."

June, who could guess the thoughts going through Emilie's mind, still felt compelled to continue, "The Englishman has forgotten how to listen to the heart, Emilie. It is with great sorrow that I say this. When *one* decided to make a comfortable living on the back of *another*, our great land lost something more vital than words can say. Then, when father teaches son and mother teaches daughter that this is normal and acceptable and perhaps even right, the children lose a piece of their heart. So there is much loss. Oh, of all the times to *not* listen to the heart," she exclaimed as she raised her right hand in a decisive upward swoosh to an unknown spectator, then lowered it to her mouth, as if contemplating a plea for any who would listen. Her hand trembled. She *despised* slavery.

Shifting on her seat to better face Emilie, she then asked, "Have your father and momma told you about Sir William Wilberforce?" To which Emilie responded that no, they had not. Lady June lit up. "Emilie, now there is a man of God if ever there was one. He and some others like him give me hope."

At which point the elder commenced to teach the younger about the current goings-on in Parliament related to the English slave trade. How a certain Sir Wilberforce, after having an otherwordly encounter with God, had become a political public servant with the goal of eradicating the slave trade in his lifetime. How he called the slave trade what it really was—namely cruel and unjust—and tirelessly fought in Parliament for its full abolition. How he said that England had lost her conscience. June reported that he had quite a following at this time and that many in England supported the abolitionist movement, though not all overtly.

Listening to June speak, something inside Emilie stirred. She could not forget the memory of one man whipping another. It was inhumane, or more accurately, *un*-human.

Nearing their second attempt at a rest stop about twenty-five minutes down the road, though hungry, nervous, and emotionally exhausted, Emilie allowed the workings of passion to persist within. Leaning her head against the buzzing, hard surface of the bumbling carriage, she closed her eyes and for a moment, forgetting her own pain, thought about the negro man they had seen. Was he a husband or a father? Why had he become the object of such rage? How was he dealing with what had happened today? And was this a normal occurrence?

She couldn't get his image out of her mind. For all she knew, he may have had four or five children whom he never saw. His wife may have been given away to work for a different master. *Or worse yet...* She shuddered at the thought. Sheltered as she was, she had heard about what happened with certain women out in the world. What if he came from a wealthy family? Then he was sold into this. Did someone know? Would anyone ever know how much one man could suffer at the brutal hand of another?

She thought herself into despair. The realization of undeserved pain and suffering was enormous. She looked at Lady June, who also sat with heavy brow and tense soul. Getting up from her seat across from the elder, she moved to sit next to her. Laying her head on the woman's shoulder, she cried, "Oh, Lady June, it's so horrid. I can't stop thinking about that man!"

June put her arm around her and held her close. "Neither can I, Em, neither can I. I find consolation in the fact that we are not alone in the realization of this truth. And you should, too. In fact, I do hope that you get to come across Sir Wilberforce while you're in Kent. Perhaps you will find friends that share this same mind." She stopped abruptly, hesitating to speak any further.

And while Emilie did notice the stammer, the carriage had just come to a complete stop near a sparkling river, and after being confined to the interior of the carriage, she was quite eager to finally stand on solid ground. She turned from June, opened the door, and jumped out of the carriage. She determined to continue the conversation shortly.

The crisp air was welcome on her skin. Emilie walked over to the horses and patted them gently in a gesture of gratefulness. They snorted and tossed their manes, as if expecting more than just that. They were hungry and thirsty, Emilie surmised. "You'll get your fill soon, my friends."

As the two men brought down the basket of food and blankets, June peered out of the carriage. Physically tired from the journey, her spirit maintained strength.

Emilie pulled her out, assisting her descent downward, and the two turned toward the water.

"Here, let's put the blankets here," Lady June called to George, who was bringing things over while the other took to the horses.

"Sure thing, Lady June." George and Herbert were long-time friends of June's. They were part of the cohort which tended to her traveling needs (as she did travel quite a bit).

Used to doing things for herself and determined to continue in the same fashion, Emilie took the blanket from George's full arms and began to spread it on an even parcel of grass.

George, used to a different sort of young lady, avidly insisted that she allow him to work out the details. "But m'lady," he retorted, "young ladies do not usually involve themselves in such matters. Please, *allow me*," he said, offering his arm, which would lead Emilie to a seat by the resting elder woman who was, in fact, studying the interaction between the two.

Watching Emilie interact with a man who functioned in the capacity of a hired helping hand, it dawned upon June that Emilie held about as much prejudice in her heart as would a newborn babe. To this remarkable young lady, a man was a man. She was not raised to experience people based on their social class, skin color, or occupation because her parents did not believe in life this way. Even the servants at the Forthyn estate were respected and given a fair wage. They were free to come and go, so long as the work excelled.

Emilie felt an entirely new gathering of emotions as she took George's arm. For the first time she felt an unsettling bewilderment about her new role: was she expected to grow in independence as a strong woman who possessed extraordinary traits of character, knowledge, and skill, or to be led about like this? Was this what English ladies did? By his respectful act, she felt demeaned. As she sat near June, she considered the dignified manner in which the elder woman conducted her everyday affairs. Surely *she* understood the value in doing things for one's self, not relying upon others.

Watching George scuffle around to create a comfortable resting space for the company of tired sojourners, she casually remarked, "Lady June, we'd have done a better job, wouldn't we have?" Expecting full agreement with her confident perspective, her face fell when the former asserted that, "No, it is better that it be done this exact way."

"But Lady June," Emilie said, "how am I to become *something* or *someone* if I just sit by and watch? Is it not more dignified to partake in the everyday workings of the people whom I will encounter? To learn from them as I live with them?"

"So many questions, my dearest Emilie. Save your energy for the bigger battles." And without much more than that (and a gentle tap on the nose), June happily turned her attention to the cold meats, cheeses, and breakfast pastries prepared by Miss Fist earlier that same day and being handed to her by George, who couldn't help but grin at the conversation being had between the two. He and June understood English society and knew full well that Emilie's naivety would soon be readily challenged; her innocent vehemence, however, was so refreshing that they dared not scare it away. "My my, it does seem like we've been on the road for an entire century. I'm outright starving!" she said gaily to Emilie, who was at this time not in the mood to reciprocate. It turned out, though, that both George and June lauded her conviction to stay true to what was good.

Emilie, however, misinterpreted June's optimistic position as reckless betrayal and sulked off to eat alone.

She had not expected this from her respectable old friend in the least bit. How could she be so careless in regard to these matters? With her back to the group, she sat down against an aging willow standing humbly by the satin ribbon of sparkling water. The tree was fortunate to have for a constant companion this life-giver, which tugged and pulled at its velvety parts. But no matter how hard the pulling of the water, or the tossing of the wind for that matter, the tree stood.

Emilie once again determined in her heart to be as immovable as this old willow. She would not change or be changed for anyone or by anyone if the change meant abandoning her convictions. Having convinced herself one more time, she chewed slowly and pondered about the days, weeks, and months ahead.

June's laughter cut through the sounds of the willow, wind, and water. It rang loud and clear. Her voice contained zero remorse or guilt, which perplexed the young Emilie. She had thought her reticence would bring about a change in the older woman's mental posture and result in her own justification, but it had not.

In fact, Lady June was thoroughly enjoying her time of rest with her company. They exchanged opinions and laughed outright raucously, being concerned with nothing but their leisurely lunch. Emilie realized that her mood served no other purpose than to bring herself back into a state of depression, which at this time had nothing to do with even her parents' passing, but more so with being personally misunderstood or perhaps even offended.

Undone—vulnerable, she longed for a private place where she could hide and sort through it all. Never had she in her nineteen years of life experienced the very many emotions that she had experienced in the past couple of weeks. And this was only the beginning!

She did not hear Lady June come up behind her, and was startled as a hand descended onto her shoulder. The woman steadied herself and, in her usual fashion, allowed herself the permission to speak to Emilie's visibly distraught condition. "Do you know why we laugh?" she prodded gently as her gaze followed the vigorous, winding river.

"Lady June, *no*, I do not know why you laugh or why I hate being told what to do and how to do it," Emilie said frankly. "I don't understand why one person sits and does nothing while another works tirelessly to get something done for the idle one. Oh, I don't know Lady June! Am I thinking too hard? Perhaps Kent...London... all of this was a bad idea. Quite honestly, I expected *you* to expect *me* to just be *me*, but then I was told to sit down and be quiet, and—And, well, I don't know what to make of it. Where to place myself. Where do I belong? I feel like everything I've known is just so terribly different. Will it even apply to this new life you've been telling me about?"

June winced as she prepared to disclose the truth about the Foxes, especially considering Emilie's fragile state. Again steadying herself, now against the willow, she knew that the time had come. "Emilie, what do you know of the Foxes?" she began, determined to prepare Emilie for the worst, yet praying for the best.

"Very little, ma'am. I know that they live on an estate in Kent, and that their three children—my cousins—have done well for themselves. Carleighla and Violette are known to be quite accomplished in literature, music, and the arts, whilst Albert takes up his time with his studies, having just completed his Grand Tour. Aside from this, I know not much else... Oh, I do believe they attend the local parish and are frequent guests at large parties."

June hastily nodded her head in agreement with every word, determined to press on. "Do you know anything else about them?"

"Not much else, Lady June," Emilie insisted, apprehensively curious. "Why, what must I know?"

With her statuesque figure towering over Emilie, who was now earnestly listening, Lady June began to tell of the family's well-known charitable deeds, affluent ways, and somewhat elitist ideologies. Emilie learned that they were easily the wealthiest family in Kent, with ties to the economy of sugarcane and tobacco, and that their high standing in society had won them great respect in London, Liverpool, and even the northern cities of England. Emilie listened and learned about the family that would be taking her in this very evening; she could not, however, help but notice the edge with which June spoke.

Being a close friend of Emilie's grandparents, June had known Clarence since childhood. Even so, she spared no detail in describing the woman's nature, which included her stern disposition and elevated expectations. Emilie could tell that Lady June's relationship with Aunt Clarence was very different than with her own mother. But *why*, she wondered. It was as if her voice carried an underlying warning for Emilie.

Then, as if in response to the unexpressed questioning, June spoke words that made all things clear. "Emilie, darling, are you listening?"

"Yes, ma'am, I am. I'm just thinking about what you're saying, that's all."

"Alright, very good. They are good people, Emilie," she continued—actually, insisted. "Your aunt Clarence, not unlike the other women in your family line, is a strong woman. She expects agreeable behavior and disposition at all times. She does not tolerate frivolity. Her expectation is that one acts perfectly reasonable at all times. She will not appreciate, or shall I say, will not *tolerate* the challenging of her life's ideals. Believe me, this I know. You too will soon see. Which brings me to my final point." She paused at this moment to bring herself to face Emilie.

Emilie swallowed. Actually, she braced herself.

"The Foxes play a role in the English slave trade. In fact, it is certainly in *their* best interest that the slave trade go on as long as they are around. They actively gain wealth with every slave ship that docks in Liverpool. What's more, they own African servants and field slaves that work in various capacities around the estate and its properties. They see this as a symbol of prestige or class. Emilie, they do not share your convictions. You must be wise in your way with them," she finished, assessing the now alarmed girl.

"Lady June," Emilie said with quaking voice, "you mean to tell me that these people... This place... That all these years..." She broke off, lost for words. Her face begged the woman to tell her otherwise, that they were different than other English slave owners, that she would not be living in the midst of these hellish

31

ways. "That all these years, my own relatives have been living in this unthinkable manner? Lady June, why did we not know?"

"Oh my child, you did, or should I say, your parents certainly knew. They sorely disagreed on this one issue, which is why the Forthyns and Foxes have never kept a close relationship. Your momma and father moved to Suffolk after Oliver's birth for this very reason. And after all these years, very little has changed. Emilie," she said with a small smile, *"this is why we laugh,* my darling, and have passionate conversations and don't let offenses settle in, because in the end, we hope that happiness and love win."

"Oh Lady June, but I won't be able to..."

"Hush, Emilie. Yes, you *will* be able to. *I know it.* You are principled and you are passionate, which will keep you strong. You have been raised well. You love well. You see beyond what most see, and this may make things hard on you. This is why it's important to not take things too seriously sometimes. Live and enjoy your days in the high company of London. Make friends and lead by example. Be wise. Guard your heart. And child," June said, enclosing Emilie's right hand with warm, aged fingers, "if you ever find yourself in a situation that's hard and lonely, please find me. I'll only be a carriage ride away."

And with that, the two women embraced, Emilie holding onto possibly the last bit of home on this side of London, June gently soothing, stroking, willing her shaking body to be at peace.

The truth was that neither one had the slightest idea of what lay ahead. In this moment, even June doubted whether this was the right decision for Emilie. Earlier in the week, the plan had seemed flawless. It just made sense. Today, holding this fragile young woman in her arms, mere hours from their destination, even her vision had faded.

Emilie finally sat upright, however, dried her eyes, smoothed her dress, and said, "Lady June, we must go on. I'm ready."

They packed, settled back into the carriage, and off they went. Kent was waiting.

Chapter 6

The afternoon had come and gone. With the setting of the sun, Emilie held her blanket tighter and thought back to earlier that morning. It was as if home was a foreign land, a distant memory. She remembered the kitchen sounds of breakfast, the cold floor of her room, and hidden tears that ebbed and flowed upon her soul. She remembered the way her brothers insisted on knowing her whereabouts and doings and smiled. How she would miss those men. Phineas, too, crossed her mind. She had to admit that she would miss him as well, though beyond that she insisted there was nothing.

Peering out the window, she noted a changing landscape—rather, not so much that the landscape was changing as the stateliness of the estates was ever increasing. *Kent,* she guessed. She wondered what the Foxes home was like and shuddered at the thought of going to sleep there alone tonight. There was one thought, however, that she refused to entertain. *Not now,* she willed herself. She was not yet ready to explore her relationship to the news she had received from Lady June. Fear was already strong inside. She could not afford to break now. She clutched her blanket and looked straight ahead.

"Emilie, look—" June excitedly exclaimed, pointing into the darkened distance ahead. "We are here."

Quickly turning, she looked. Unwittingly, her mouth gaped open and eyes widened. Her heart began to pound. Never had she seen such astounding beauty. The estate was vast with fields, gardens, fountains, and a manor so beautiful that she feared being unable to describe it in her letters home. Oh, that Mick and Oliver could see! In these evening hours, lights had been lit throughout the property, casting shadows here and there, but beautifying the place with deep elegance. Emilie smoothed her skirts, feeling rather humble in comparison to this kingly giant.

June smiled, happy to have arrived safely, knowing that they were certainly in capable hands now. As they approached the large driveway, she squeezed Emilie's hand. "Here we are, Emilie. Welcome to your new home."

Smiling nervously, she nodded her head in agreement. She could not speak at the moment, feeling fretful, overwhelmed, and wondering what to expect tonight. As the carriage slowed to a trot, she began hearing men's voices outside steadying the horses to a full stop in front of the mansion. She did not see anyone she recognized, and wondered if anyone would be home this evening. How small she felt! Then, while the men continued to fuss about the carriage and horses, the massive front door swung wide open, putting on display a marvelously lit entryway with multiple people congregating therein. Emilie's palms began to sweat and her heart refused to slow its pace. She realized that other than hearing stories about these people, she didn't really know them. Had they heard about her? Were they pleased that she would be staying there? And having learned about the family dispute, she wondered if they would welcome her as one of their own.

Someone waved at her from the lit doorway as suddenly the carriage door swung wide open. Lady June went first, accepting George's hand to step down. She felt right at home, as this was not too different from her own luxurious lifestyle in London. Emilie, too, emerged from the carriage and, carefully following after Lady June's example, took Herbert's hand and allowed him to help her down. She inhaled the sweet evening air of autumn, straightened her shoulders, and headed with June toward the front, where a group of people had congregated. They were all watching.

"Emilie! Can it be? Oh, my, my-y-y, what a beautiful young woman you have become! June, she is the full semblance of Elisa. Oh, dear!" The woman, who resembled Momma greatly, continued to fuss and kerfuffle from the doorway all the way to the place where Emilie stood, studying her every inch intently.

Two young ladies followed politely after the woman, boring into her with their gaze, hands clasped courteously before them. Their faces were pleasant, but unreadable. They had sent flowers to the funeral, but themselves did not come, stating that illness had taken the household. It seemed they were better.

"Aunt Clarence," Emilie said with a curtsy, "It is I..." She tried to force a smile. "I'm forever indebted to you and to your family for opening your home to me under these circumstances..." And try as she might, she could not finish the sentence. She could not even look the woman in the face. Aunt Clarence reminded her of Momma—they were sisters, after all. She was here because her parents were not. The circumstance was too painful to speak lightly of. Tired and nauseated with emotion, Emilie bolted into the shadows of the carriage, which was presently being unloaded. Her face burned after such a display, but even more than that she was mortified that she broke and in front of them all. She heard June quietly answering their questions, speaking kind words on Emilie's behalf and advising them to allow her to her room to rest. Then she heard the approach of decided footsteps.

Aunt Clarence.

"Emilie, darling, we *do share* the same pain. I'm sorry to have put you through so much just now. Come, we'll take you to your quarters where you can rest until the morning." She extended her hand and gently instructed Emilie to, "Come, come" again, stating that Violette and Carleighla would show her where to go.

And Emilie went as she was led.

The two girls made light conversation as they walked through the colossal corridors and prestigious rooms of the Fox estate.

Through here, and *just a little past there*, and *almost there* were repeated over and over again as they made their way to the room set aside for Emilie. Was this a cruel trick? Would they ever get there? Emilie prayed that they would sooner rather than later. She tried to speak coherent words, but failed miserably. They intimidated her. She could not help but compare herself to them both. Her faltering display outside was irredeemable, at least in her own mind.

Finally arriving, they entered a suite so large that Emilie's entire family could room here comfortably. Emilie followed after them as they explained where the water was, how to pull the curtains closed, where they had gotten the silk bed linens from, and other such details. Emilie answered affirmatively as needed and refrained from asking a single question so as not to prolong their stay. Finally they asked if there was anything else she needed, to which she hurriedly replied that *no*, she did not need anything else and *thank you for your kindness.*

They looked at each other, smiled politely, and expressed an eager desire to get to know her more in the morning. To which she replied the same. "Good night," they stated together, and left. *Finally.*

She took out the notebook from Phineas, laid it by her head, laid her head down, and hoped for sleep. The scent of the roses brought on a rush of bittersweet emotion, where she longed both for her own bed and family. She remembered Phineas saying that she may need help remembering home, and he turned out to be right; in the busyness, she had quite forgotten. Grateful once again for his thoughtfulness, she turned onto her side, wondering what the world was like outside. What were Mick and Oliver doing? Were they alright living alone, without Momma and Father? What was home like without her?

Hearing muffled voices and varied movements outside her bedroom, she made herself small in the bed, hoping to God that no one would dart in, not wanting to be seen or heard. But it seemed to have only been the servants preparing various bedrooms for the night. The commotion was not unwelcome, she later decided, as it helped her feel less lonely and this place feel somewhat normal. Every home has a familiar hum. The gentle rhythm of activity throughout the place became a soothing symphony that brought her quickly to sleep.

Chapter 7

She awakened the following morning to soft footsteps scurrying about her room. The sun was fighting heavy curtains to get into her room to tell her of the time of day. The place was completely quiet, so much so that Emilie wondered if she were alone on the estate. She lay there, skin relishing the cool silk sheets, feeling a bit lazy and permitting herself to be. Suddenly a young servant girl peeked out from behind the wash stand, shyly standing by, Emilie assumed expecting her to initiate the interaction. Emilie surmised she was there to help her prepare for the day and wondered if this were to be a daily event.

To Emilie's surprise, the young girl stepped carefully out from behind the chiffonier, curtsied, and introduced herself. "Hello, Miss, I'm Mim," she said automatically. "I'll be gettin' you dressed this morning."

Her expression was impersonal, posture humble, and intent fully business-like. She was here to do as she was told. She was dressed neatly, hair tucked under a crisp cap, eyes sharp as a panther. She appeared to be about the same age as Emilie, which gave Emilie the secret hope that they might become friends.

"Hi there, I'm Emilie. What a pleasure to meet you," she said, and curtsied. Emilie did not consider that Englishwomen never curtsied to their servant girls, and her total lack of such

39

proprietary understandings and behaviors caused Mim to suppress a cock-eyed grin.

"Miss, you ain't supposed to curtsy to your maid servant," she said, bemused. And for a moment the two young women stood facing each other, feeling the tension of their dichotomous existence, thinking the same forbidden thoughts.

Emilie looked at her and finally said, "Mim, more than anything I'm looking for a friend. Where I come from, we did not have but four helping hands, and so I did many things on my own. I don't know much about this type of life, which is why they sent me here, to learn how to be an Englishwoman. My parents have died and now—well, here I am. Perhaps you'd help me get to know my way around?"

Mim, standing as still as water on a windless day, studying her new lady, simply smiled. "Miss, it's hard to believe a person you've only just met, but you must be a different sort of Englishwoman for sure, 'cause I've never met one like you before. If we be 'friends,' as you say, we be friends only in here. Lady Fox won't have it no other way."

Although Emilie was frustrated at the thought of Aunt Clarence interfering in any part of her life, she did understand what Mim was saying. Grinning from ear to ear, she nodded and said, "Agreed. Now, what am I to wear today?"

Mim happily helped her wash up, arranged her hair in a very pretty manner, prepared her blush-pink tulle dress, and escorted her through the endless corridors to the breakfast area.

The estate had much to admire in the daylight. As she followed Mim down the many hallways and through the many doors, she began to hear more sounds coming from various parts of the home. She surveyed the massive windows with their views, classic paintings, and various relics tastefully placed throughout the rooms. She so deeply appreciated the handiwork inherent in the pieces and vowed to soon study the arts. This was why she had come, after all. Nearing the dining room, she began to hear the hum of actively conversing voices, and her stomach, quite against her better judgment, twisted into a knot, straining her nerves and freezing her tongue.

Mim quietly led her into the large room, curtsied, and with a nod of her head rushed away.

There she stood, taking in the scene before her. Emilie faced a small crowd of young people seated around a luxurious table, sharing morning delicacies, and leaning in to partake in the discussion of various salacious pieces of information and controversial events. Servants stood by to meet their every whim and fancy. In the high light of late morning, the scene was in the likeness of a still life depicting the richness of England's opulence and charm. Emilie was stunned. Sharp self-consciousness began to heighten as she fought the urge to back out before anyone spotted her. But this was what she had come for. Leaving now would only mean having to come back again tomorrow. She had to break through now. Through tense jaw and tight teeth, she stepped forward. She was staying.

"Ah, good morning cousins," she chimed gaily, making her way toward the table, at which point the crowd suddenly jerked from their intimate conversation to face her.

Albert and the other young gentleman present stood so quickly from the table that tea almost toppled over onto the floor. The presence of a new beauty had startled them in a most pleasant way.

Violette and Carleighla rose from the table and hurried over to greet her, taking both of her hands in theirs and spinning her around cheerfully.

"Welcome, Emilie. Are you quite better?" one said. "I so hope that you are!"

The other, "Did you sleep well? Are you rested? You were so unwell last night."

And also, "Are you hungry? We've been waiting for you, cousin. There's so much food here, we hope you will help us to eat it." They giggled easily.

Then, recognizing the need for formal introductions, Carleighla, the elder Fox sister (but younger than Albert), began by introducing Emilie first to Albert (who had not had the honor of a formal introduction the night before due to Emilie's state of being and that he had never met her prior) and then to John Learson and Fiona, his sister.

John, immediately impressed by Emilie's stunning beauty, walked directly over to her and taking her right hand, kissed it, reassuring her that the pleasure was all his. Fiona simply curtsied with a measured nod of her head.

Albert made the biggest raucous of all, causing Emilie to blush a crimson red from her toes to her forehead. He crossed the room and lifted her up like even her own brothers had not done in years and declared that she was the prettiest cousin he ever did see. The hard ice of formal introductions was officially cracked.

Emilie relaxed into an unassuming posture as she was welcomed to the table. The servant, an elder negro dressed in exquisitely elegant attire, poured her tea and brought over a platter of breakfast items. Emilie took a piece of pastry and, expressing her gratitude to the man known as Lincoln, intended to sit quietly by with a listening ear only.

But as the conversation resumed about what Emilie quickly learned to be ships carrying sugarcane from the islands to Liverpool, she was inevitably pulled in. She wondered if her cousins knew about their families' discordant relationship, which would, she assumed, alter their perception of any response she would give.

"What do you think, Emilie? If the storm hits the ship as predicted, should they throw the slaves overboard, or the sugar?" Violette asked as they snickered and jeered gaily one with another.

Emilie's eyes widened. It was as if someone had punched her in the gut. Silence. *So this is what Lady June was talking about*, she thought. "They should keep that which is more valuable," she said quietly, looking at their faces, searching for signs of life.

"She's right!" roared Albert as he slammed his fist on the table, laughing so hard that his face was now red. "Throw 'em overboard, then!" They sorely misunderstood her words. Even Fiona, who seemed too reticent to laugh, was giggling.

They don't know, Emilie thought. The humor was gravely misplaced.

At this moment Lady June entered the room, pleasantly surprised to find Emilie amongst the laughter and glee of the younger generation. "What's this we have here?" she asked with a twinkle in her eye. "A lively bunch of young ladies and gentlemen, I see? Hello Albert, girls, John, Fiona."

"Ah, Lady June, how grand of you to join us this morning," said Carleighla. "We were sharing a bit of splendid laughter before the day's laborious work begins. Mother wants me to study more on Aristotelian philosophy today but it's such a bore, Lady June. How can I study when we have a new person in our midst? She is getting quite comfortable here in her new home, as you can see," she asserted, extending her hand toward the still Emilie seated next to Albert.

"Hello, my darling," said June gently as she made her way toward her beloved girl. "Did you sleep well? Have you eaten?"

"Yes, Lady June. I am quite well, thank you," she said in response, forcing a smile.

"Lady June, how long will you be staying in Kent?" asked Violette. "Will you be staying for the holidays?"

"Oh no no, Violette. I'll be returning home in a few days, once I see that Emilie is settled. I do plan to return for the winter ball, though, but before that I'm not so sure. These old bones are getting harder and harder to carry around, you know," she said matter-of-factly.

Emilie grieved over the words she had heard. She was not yet prepared to do this alone.

After a few more minutes at the table, the ladies convinced the gentlemen to go outside for a walk in the brisk autumn air. Emilie resisted every which way the going; more than anything in the world she wanted instead to speak with June, but the old woman was quickly pulled away by Sir and Lady Fox after breakfast. Emilie had no choice but to go. They persuaded her so. She began to notice how difficult it was becoming to make her own decisions. It was like a magnetic pull to take her where she did not wish to go. Just like yesterday, when she wanted to help prepare the luncheon but was told not to. She felt trapped, figuring all things out, deeply ruminating about who she was and who she did not wish to become.

As they left the estate and stepped onto the walkway to take them into the garden, she allowed herself to take in the ravishing beauty of this place. Again, this *place* was beautiful. *But how could such a beautiful place believe, say, and practice such* ugly *things?* she thought, reflecting back to the jokes from the table. Similar feelings to those felt on the road yesterday arose within. *What utter confusion*, she thought as her new acquaintances began their long trek toward the garden and away from the estate.

Marveling at the new structures and landscape along the way and fully enraptured by autumn's tranquility, she steadily fell back from the group. The girls did not notice as they chattered endlessly about the latest fashion and gossip; they were more self-absorbed than not, thus losing the inconvenience of a new person requiring their undivided attention was clearly not a loss for them. Emilie thought she noticed Carleighla looking over at John. Then Fiona would try to speak loud enough for Albert to notice. And Violette was just Violette, the third wheel so to speak. *No suitor for her*, Emilie easily concluded. John and Albert acknowledged them accordingly and kept walking.

Lost in the wonder of the quiet beginnings of noon, hearing geese squawking and gardeners working, she did not notice John niftily falling back to where she was walking. Emilie was far too immersed in thought. But suddenly there he was.

"Would it be alright if I joined you on our expedition here? You seem so deep in thought, I'd not want to intrude," he asked, and very much hoped that Emilie would not mind.

"No, it's alright, I don't mind... I think too much nowadays..." she said with a tense brow, looking away. He had heard from the Foxes what had happened to her family and somewhat understood her emotional state. He had lost his grandfather three years ago and had a difficult time coming back around; he couldn't fathom losing both parents as she had.

"I'm sorry to hear about what happened to you and your family. I cannot fathom the grief you must have felt and continue to feel with such loss," he conveyed. "But I do hope that in time you heal and realize that you've much to gain here, in Kent," he finished.

She looked at him and smiled. She appreciated his gentle attention, though she was not sure what he meant by her having much to gain in Kent. It was like...no, *unlike* Phineas's manner, actually. Different, authoritative. *Not altogether unpleasant*, she thought.

She recognized him to be approximately thirty years of age. He was handsome, substantial with his words, and prospectively secure. Phineas crossed her mind. Carleighla kept looking back at John who, immersed in Emilie's fresh presence, did not look back. And that was that.

Emilie felt the waves of an unknown ocean sucking her under. The endless gossip and giggling, heartless humor, and unfamiliar way of life left her numb. She missed home. She could never fully give herself to this place, and this realization left her feeling more isolated and lonely. She would just keep walking, go through the motions, and be on guard.

Eventually the group coalesced into a single unit, walking, mingling, and chatting the entire way back to the manor. Although John split his time amongst Albert and the other girls, he kept coming back to Emilie's side. Her exquisite nature drew him like a bee to honey; she was not like the other girls.

As they walked under the shadows of the south wing of the manor toward the front door, Emilie did not notice Lady June spectating from an upstairs window. The woman saw what she knew she would see. *Hmph*, she reacted. Lips tight, she considered the inevitable.

More than anything she wanted to warn this wonder of a woman of how men would fall in love with her upon first glance— just like this one did—and how important it was not to open her heart too wide, too fast. But being a wise woman of vast experience, she knew better. She would have to bite her tongue and support Emilie through her time of maturation. Deep down she somehow *knew* that this remarkable woman would choose well when the time came. Her passionate soul necessitated full reciprocity and equality. Nothing less and no one else could do. So Lady June braced herself for the stormy waters ahead, not really knowing how to nurture Emilie's strength, but trusting that every single deposit of wisdom made during her younger years would guide her along.

As the group made its entrance known, servants came rushing in, taking their coats and hats away. Lady Fox also came to the entrance, informing her children that she expected their studies to be worked on and completed shortly. John and Fiona briefly albeit reluctantly excused themselves from the day's affairs to be taken home while Albert and his sisters went their separate ways to study. Lady Fox looked at Emilie and informed her that she expected her to study with her daughters as much as possible, as wasted time could not be returned. Hands clasped at the sternum and nose up in the air, she appeared rather snobbish.

Emilie amenably nodded agreement, respectfully requested to be excused, and then escaped faster than the stern woman could utter a disapproving *no*.

There was so much to tell Lady June! Aunt Clarence would not interfere this time.

Chapter 8

*A*nd so Emilie's life began and continued on at Kent. Lady June left shortly after Emilie's first week of settling in— much too soon, in Emilie's opinion. But the energetic pace of Derbyshire prevented her from feeling anything other than a quickened sense of self-enlightenment. This was their way of life, now quickly becoming hers as well. Read history after breakfast, play the pianoforte after that, practice classical painting before noon, take a break for lunch, then proceed to entertain visitors in the afternoon.

They certainly approved of their socializing. On any given day visitors would arrive from all over England, stay for tea, and sometimes linger all the way until dinner. Many were incredibly cultured and learned individuals who had seen more of the world than Emilie could ever dream of, and so she would stand tall amidst that crowd, listen with a keen ear, and speak her mind. Just like she would with her father and brothers in their living room so many months ago.

She found herself developing impassioned opinions on topics such as the role of a woman in culture, education for servants, and fair-trade practices. She was drawn with such an intensity that the others began to notice. She craved true learning. Her relevant insightfulness and hunger for the deeper truths made some uncomfortable, while the more open-minded among them readily appreciated her depth.

One thing was certain: they were not used to such ladies.

Violette and Carleighla certainly did not appreciate being side-lined, as many of the more esteemed guests would find themselves in Emilie's company rather than in theirs. They had grown up in such a restricted environment that stepping outside of their norm was unthinkable, and as a result resentment began to trickle in. Curiously, though, Albert and John genuinely enjoyed her company and ability to carry an interesting conversation beyond the usual giddiness of most of their female contemporaries. She displayed a refreshing quickness of wit and sharpness of thought which attracted their young minds; she was also exceedingly easy on the eyes which was, of course, a most advantageous bonus.

Having watched this go on for two consecutive months now, one evening, after the Williamsons and the Shaws had gone for the night, Lady Fox (who had at this point developed a certain reflexive disapproval of Emilie for reasons not yet clear) decided to address her flamboyant disposition.

"Emilie," she began once the hall was empty, "may I have a word with you in the library?" She clearly did not intend this to be an optional request, as she was already striding toward the library's doorway, fully expecting Emilie to follow. Not wishing to cross her aunt, Emilie walked over to the entrance of the library. "Please shut the door," she ordered sternly.

Emilie had been sensing her aunt's displeasure right along, but could not as of yet ascertain its reason. If her memory served her well, she had not done anything to displease her, and had, in fact, effortfully tried to function with great appropriateness in this home. She was kind, helpful, and respectful to everyone. Sir Fox seemed to enjoy her company.

She failed to understand that such generous goodness toward all was actually a part of the problem.

"Emilie, I would like to speak with you about what it means to be a lady of propriety," she began, posture unyielding, tone cold. "Over the past months I have noticed your lack of restraint, loose character, and garrulous personality."

Huh, Emilie thought. *And without warning.* This was entirely unexpected.

Emilie, who *had* noticed her ability to draw a crowd on frequent occasions and who *had* seen that she often spoke more freely than the other ladies, had not at all foreseen this. Entirely unprepared and feeling strangely misunderstood, she stood as silent as the statue in the corner of the room. She felt stained by the woman's displeasure and judgment, and, realizing that any attempt at self-justification would be utterly scorned, did not know what to say or do. Aunt Clarence was in her own way statuesque, hard and unflinching, feeling that any disturbance to her order ought to be punished. Emilie thought of Momma then, and large tears flooded her eyes. Momma was so different. Lady June was different. *This is what she was preparing me for,* she thought as she remembered their final conversation on the road before reaching Derbyshire.

The combination of grief and utter confusion resulted in the flow of heavy tears down Emilie's face. She was a stranger in this marbled world, standing alone behind heavy doors, restricted in feeling, thought, and action by rules and expectations that tyrannically ruled the way life was to be lived. She felt like a young lioness behind closed doors, finally beginning to taste the beauty of the vast world for herself, but caged. She was meant to be wild and free, a rose amongst thorns, chasing fireflies with those she loved. But what was this? Just when she was beginning to fall into the rhythm of this place and to experience its free-flowing wines of cultured people, worldly knowledge, and wisdom gleaned from life lived beyond four walls—things she had sensed to be true all along—this happened. As silent tears fell in the presence of an unfeeling Aunt Clarence, she wept over her shocking misperception of her presence at Derbyshire.

Over the past months, she was bourgeoning in the varied company presiding at Derbyshire. At least she thought so. She noted Albert's enjoyment of their mutually spent time, and John certainly made every effort possible to share in conversations where she spoke. Sir Fox, too, would often sit back after dinner and unabashedly discuss current events with her, going as far as discussing sugarcane, tobacco, and other shipments from which he benefited, asking what she thought about *this* or *that* and clearly placing a certain value on her insight.

She had forced herself to embrace this place as home, however temporary it might be, quickly becoming known amongst the Foxes' friends as an *exceedingly bright young lady.*

Some, however, were not impressed. Aunt Clarence certainly was not.

"You regard everyone as an equal," she continued scornfully, "but do not show regard for the ways of the estate. Emilie, a lady of propriety *must* know her place over the servants. She maintains a gracefully collected posture at *all* times. She is in *no way* to overly consume any conversation, especially in the presence of gentlemen, and certainly does *not* engage in trivial conversations with servants. *No gentleman wants to hear what you have to say*, and no servant should *ever* become such a privileged recipient. What I speak is true, though you may not agree with me, and it is for your own good." She tried the final part with a softer tone.

For the first time Emilie spotted remorse in her features, it ever so slightly slipping across her face and through her voice. She realized that Aunt Clarence regretted her neglected relationship with Momma, and with her being gone was in a way redeeming a personal sense of loss. Try as she might, however, her rigid ways prevented change, ultimately costing her very dearly. Emilie's features and nature reminded Clarence so much of her sister and of the severe loss, though, that they triggered a guttural sense of resentment toward the young woman.

Running her fingers through the books neatly lining the nearest bookshelf, she continued, "Years ago I told your mother that if anything ever happened to her, I would take you in. I meant it. With all the disagreements we have had in life—and we've had many—I felt it was my duty to raise you if any evil befell Elisa. And here we are today," she said coarsely, looking away. "Emilie, I did not agree with your mother's ways then, and I do not agree with them now. If you live in this house, I expect you to live according to my expectations. Study the ways of an English lady, practice the ways of an English lady, control yourself the way an English lady must, and most certainly know your place here," she finished, head high. "This is not a chatty ladies' club but the residence of the Fox family. Please do accordingly."

Tears spilling over like silent rain in the black night, Emilie could not bring herself to look into the woman's eyes, but instead looked straight ahead at the darkening window at the end of the room. Her aunt had said so much in the span of a few minutes, resulting in a windfall of memories, emotions, and impossible longings. The truth was out. Emilie was not prepared. How she wished Lady June was there to hold her. She had not seen her friend in two months now and severely missed the woman. It dawned on her that she could write a letter to arrange a visit. That's what she would do.

Deep in thought, Aunt Clarence's words came knife-like. "I have nothing further to say at this time, Emilie. You are free to go," she finished, and walked past Emilie into the hallway, leaving the door ajar.

Emilie was broken. She hurt all over. Turning around in the dark room, she ran through the corridor toward the front door. With no overcoat and tears flowing, she burst out of the front door as if gasping for air, running down the entryway stairs and toward the garden. She wanted to get as far away from this place as possible.

The commotion got the attention of Albert and John, who were at this moment discussing business in the late evening hours right outside the door, out of sight to Emilie. They looked at one another quizzically, determining that John would find out. He had grown very much attached to her over the past months and felt that it was his responsibility to be there for her in time of need—which this clearly was.

Her fierce heart was a force to be reckoned with, he could already see, and if he were fully honest with himself he would say that her untainted vision and pure perspective intimidated him. Her decisions were not determined by monetary ambition. Apparently that made all the difference, as she differed greatly from the other ladies.

Stepping cautiously through the dark garden, he listened for her. "Emilie," he whispered loudly, "it's me, John…" He heard her then by the fountain, and saw her lone figure leaning against a cold statue. She was so still. Yet the nearer he came, the more he noticed the trembling, not knowing if it was from the cold or from whatever had caused her to run from home.

"Emilie, are you alright? Albert and I were talking outside the door and saw you come out as you did, and we—rather I—became worried. What is it? Whatever happened?" he asked, coming to face her with a look of concern on his face. He permitted himself to lay his broad hands on her shoulders to calm her, and feeling how cold she was, quickly took off his overcoat and draped it over her downcast shoulders. She had been crying, he could see. His heart yearned to hold her close, but she gave no indication that she would welcome it. She was such a puzzle. She barely flinched as he gave her his coat.

"I'm alright now," she said with a husky voice, body jerking with every sniffle. "I just needed a moment." She had been crying hard, but was completely unwilling to open up to him.

Hurt that she still would not allow him into her heart, especially after all their time together over the past weeks, he received a glimmer of hope when she expressed gratitude for his concern.

"Thank you for your kindness, John," she said. "I truly appreciate it. It would be worse if I were alone." And then, "Shall we go back now?"

She saw his disappointment over her terse words and reserved behavior, but somehow she just could not unveil her heart's deepest places to him. She could deliberate about all sorts of things with him and for extended periods of time, too, but not about this, and not tonight.

As they walked back to the main house together, he began to talk about his plans for the future, and it seemed to her that there was the slightest whisper of desire in his words. He talked about how he planned to purchase this manor in such and such a place and how wonderful it would be to fill the home with children, friends, and family, often trailing off into silence when she would not reciprocate the same desires.

Couldn't he see how broken she was? She wanted silence, not conversation. John was a kind man. In fact, he was a very rare type of man, with all his dreams and desires. She had heard plenty about those. Any young woman would instantly say yes to a future with him. Carleighla certainly would. Then what was it about him that kept her at bay?

As they approached the giant doorway, John led her to the entrance, and as she began to take his coat off, *there it was*, the reason for her distance. In an instant she saw Phineas walking her back to her house from the rose garden on the day of the funeral. She saw his wide, feeling eyes and strong, vulnerable posture. She remembered how quiet and gentle he was in the garden, standing by without a single word, allowing her to grieve. They got through that night *together*, she realized. She also remembered their en-counter on her final day at home, when he gave her the notebook. Something inside her stirred, and as if on cue, her heart began to beat a little faster.

She missed him.

The two men were so very different. They brought out different aspects of her character. Again she looked at John, who was now forlornly standing by the doorway in expectation of something more from her. But what could she give him? She laid her hand on his arm with a gentle touch, said a delicate *thank you*, curtsied in the most graceful way, and turned into the cold entryway to make her way up the stairs. She could not give him more than that.

He tried to understand and to rationalize away his frustration, but struggled to do so. After tonight he wanted her more than ever, but she kept falling through his fingers, like sand to the ground.

Next time, he resolved. *Next time I will tell her the truth.*

Emilie avoided everyone that crossed her path as she made her way to her room, a way that she knew so well by now. Mim had turned down her sheets and prepared water for washing. She left the rose-scented notebook on the side table by her bed. Emilie noticed fresh rose petals and lavender sprigs in the water basin as well, and savored the luxurious experience her life had become. She wished Mim was still around, because she desperately wanted to talk with someone about the evening's events. Just as Emilie had wished the two would become friends, sharing life together in secret. Mim was as much a free bird as Emilie, though her cage was even smaller than Emilie's. This was their bond.

But now, washed up and alone, she found herself daydreaming about two very different men. One pursued her openly, a valiant knight on a mission to present to her a whole new world with the hope of winning her hand by nightfall. The other had turned into the pleasantest sort of memory, living far away and having likely forgotten her by now. What was she to do? She picked up the notebook, placed it on the empty pillow next to her, and closed her eyes. *Time will tell*, she thought. She could not think clearly at the moment. Aunt Clarence's murderous words kept running through her mind.

No gentleman wants to hear what you have to say.

She wasn't so sure of that, for many gentlemen had loved to hear her speak, insisting on hearing the entirety of her thoughts during conversations. What was she to do now? How could she show her face? And could she still participate in the entertainment hours that were so much a part of her life now? She knew the answer to that question, and it brought her great sorrow; she was as good as exiled in the name of propriety.

Exhausted, she lay on her side, turned off the side lamp, and fell into a deep sleep.

Chapter 9

Over the next few weeks, she had managed to avoid Aunt Clarence's disapproving gaze and the unpleasant verbosity so common to her cousins. The stark irony was too much sometimes. They chatted endlessly when not in their mother's presence, and it seemed to Emilie that the only reason they acted so "properly" amongst their guests during visits was because they had so little to contribute. Thus, they fulfilled their responsibility of exchanging vague and giggly pleasantries with the various gentlemen present— always potential suitors, of course—and would afterward direct themselves to calmer discussions with the women, or should it be said, the proper English ladies who were inevitably seated in a corner by a window somewhere. From such a corner they would all proceed to attract attention to themselves with strategically spoken words or deftly dropped handkerchiefs.

Emilie most certainly was not drawn to gossipy English ladies. She detested the mindless talk and wanted nothing to do with the latest news. She neither shared her opinions nor cared about theirs when it came to the ways of the world. Momma would never have behaved in such a manner, for she had far too much self-respect.

She would always be her mother's daughter.

Lady June, during visits, would sit off to the side on her own, hands perched atop her silver-plated cane, eyes and ears scanning the room but rarely speaking up unless directly asked. She was greatly respected by their majority and in this advantageous position learned much about everything.

These days Emilie hid in various corners of rooms where few people spent their time—reading, pondering, and dreaming. She learned to time her aunt's daily routine and would sneak out of hiding just in time to avoid crossing the woman's path. She felt both excitedly roguish and slightly ashamed of her current state. Lady June would likely be by shortly, as she had written the woman a letter requesting a meeting to share what she was going through. Sharing her aches would lighten the burden.

The rediscovered freedom of having personal time and space reminded her of younger, less complicated days. She loved the thrill of being anywhere she wanted and doing anything she pleased, recognizing in the process how truly enslaved she had become. She was a butterfly shedding its cocoon, stretching her mind and testing the strength of her thoughts.

Mim was the only one who understood what she was up to. She would sneak food up to her bedroom, and the two would enjoy tea time together whenever it was possible, discussing with great fervency topics that were ordinarily reserved for the House of Commons. Mim's lived experiences coupled with Emilie's passionate learnedness created an explosive force to be reckoned with, and as they were prevented from attending the parliamentary meetinghouse for reasons defined by English culture, their combustible energy was left to ferment between the walls of her bedroom.

Mim was not the only servant to love Emilie. The others did, too. They recognized how respectful and kind she was toward each one of them, and having never received such warmth from any of the Foxes or their friends, they ensured that she was well cared for. The older ones would often wink at her or sneak a smile behind Lady Fox's back, while the younger ones would offer all sorts of humorous doings. The acting was at times outrageous, and Emilie savored every bit of happiness that found her throughout the day.

In her open confinement, she was beginning to find a newfound sense of self. She crossed boundary lines set in place by Lady Fox. The rules and expectations that were so rigid and unforgiving, she often wholly neglected. Not to her own or to any other's detriment, of course, but solely in the name of freedom. Rules such as the requirement to read nonfictional literature for one hour every morning and fictional novels for only thirty minutes, because nonfiction had more to be learned; or if at dinner you sat next to a gentleman with whom you had not yet been properly acquainted, you had to relocate to a different seat so as to not appear despairing for a gentleman's company; or finally that as a lady you could not stay in a men's conversation longer than fifteen minutes, as this may potentially cause the lady to appear intrusive and would lessen the chances of the man speaking with her ever again.

Such rules deserved the severest disregard.

One morning while Emilie was dressing for the day, she heard a commotion outside. Mim had mentioned a certain dinner that was being planned, but aside from that she had not heard of any special guests to be expected. Peering over the windowsill, she noticed a familiar carriage pulling up to the front, and then another shortly after. The estate's structure prevented her from seeing much more than their arrival. She wondered who would be here so early. She also had not heard of any plans for visitors other than that same dinner to be planned in the next few days for distinguished friends of the family. Eager to find out more, she hurried to dress.

This morning she wore a lavender dress with purple stones in her earrings and a matching necklace. Her hair was adorned with a few fresh flowers that Mim always managed to bring for her from the servants' quarters. She looked refreshed and more like herself today than ever before since her arrival at Derbyshire.

She planned to see who had arrived at the risk of being reprimanded again. She had heard the arrival of John and Fiona earlier this morning and knew they would be down in the dining room as per their usual (being close friends since childhood, this was like their second home). She had not seen John since the evening when he met her in the garden.

Emilie did not know what to expect from any of them. But she would go down there and act as if nothing had happened. She would face them all, and in this way face her fears. She still felt like a stranger amongst them, and try as she did to open their minds about certain practices their culture possessed, they simply could not conceive of life any other way. Today she would come and be unapologetically herself. Her confidence had grown over the past days of being alone; she was able to clear her mind, process the questions life had given, and steady her heart. She again determined that goodness was always going to be good. That could not change.

Mim walked her to the dining room again more for support than for anything else, curtsied as was the practice, gave her an encouraging nod of the head, and left to complete other morning chores.

Emilie lingered for a moment, again before a choice. So much had changed within her since their last breakfast together. She was not as frightened this time around, and most certainly not as depressed. But just as she was about to speak up to make her presence known, the door burst open with laughter and activity.

Those voices! Emilie could not believe her eyes. There stood before her Oliver, Mick, and Lady June, who had at this time the largest grin on her face. Her excited joy had permeated the space to overflowing, and theirs only magnified it. Emilie, overcome with pent-up emotion that now found permission to be released in the faces of her siblings, ran to her brothers in front of the entire group and hugged and kissed each one. Oliver picked her up with such strength that she felt giddy in his strong arms. She felt so safe.

"Lady June, did you arrange this?" asked Emilie, breathless.

"I won't say I didn't, and I won't say I did," she replied with an even bigger grin.

Emilie smiled radiantly and gave her beloved friend a tight squeeze. How she loved her.

"I thought you needed some family and friends to cheer you up, my beloved," she said in that mischievous way, eyes ablaze, holding her gaze.

Then suddenly and without warning, Phineas strode through that same door, hands in pockets, fixing his sleek dark hair back into place. He walked over to the boisterous group and tried to fit right in, but the moment at hand was different than what he had imagined it would be, and so he could no more than nod his head toward Emilie and shift his attention to her brothers. At which point the brothers proceeded to introduce themselves to the individuals at the table whose attention had been arrested by their rowdy entrance.

Aunt Clarence arrived to see what the ruckus was about, and seeing Lady June with a bunch of men whom she guessed to be the Forthyn boys, groaned inwardly. She was neither expecting them nor prepared for them. "Ah, gentlemen, how long has it been since I've last seen you?" she questioned with a superficial smile as Sir Fox also came strolling into the dining room in response to the noise.

"Can it be? Are these the renowned Forthyn boys?" Sir Fox asked. "Which one of you is Oliver? Ah, young man, I remember the day you were born—clear as day! How long it's been. What a happy occasion to have you all here. Now do tell, who's who in this bunch?" It was clear to Emilie that Sir Fox never really had anything against her family, but was merely a follower of his wife's directives. This made her smile, as he was truly a good man who always made her feel welcome.

Thus the formal introductions began. Oliver and Mick introduced themselves to Sir and Lady Fox and conveyed the greatest respects from their now forlorn family, which had undergone the most horrific of circumstances. They again turned to the ladies and gentlemen at the table who were now standing in anticipation of further formalities and shook hands and bowed as was proper.

Sir Fox then noticed Phineas and said rather loudly, "And who is this handsome young fellow who does not seem to be one of the Forthyns as far as I know them?"

"I'm Phineas, a friend of the family's, sir. It's a pleasure to meet you." And with that he reached out his hand and shook Sir Fox's so impressively that the man gave him a good-natured pat on the back. "That was a good shake, son." He clearly approved.

Emilie, planning on calm collectedness, was intensely flushed. She felt multiple sets of eyes boring into her all at once. Lady June watched kindly, assessing her state as she often did. Aunt Clarence watched sternly, wondering where she'd been these past couple of weeks and feeling mildly remorseful that she'd spoken so harshly with her that evening. Sir Fox observed her changed nature and thought he knew why. John, standing since the moment he laid eyes on her, was once again ravished by her beautiful nature. And lastly Phineas, standing quietly by, was noted to be taking quick glances in her general direction, but more than anything asserting himself in that room. He was not family, this was true. He had come for reasons of his own. He needed to play the part for now.

Once formal introductions were completed, the newcomers were invited to the table where more food was brought in by servants rotating in and out of the room. It was a sight to behold. And Emilie's heart was once again full.

"Dear cousins," said Mick, "what are you up to nowadays?"

Thank goodness for men who were not afraid to exchange decent conversation, thought Emilie; she appreciated not being the center of attention. At least, she wasn't the center of attention yet. She sat by Lady June. Actually, more like she hid behind the older woman's broadness. Emilie felt rather shy at the moment. She was overjoyed for this most pleasant interruption of her daily existence at Derbyshire, but she was also caught off guard seeing the man whom she had thought so much about since leaving home. It was difficult to discern what these emotions represented: was it silly nervousness to see an old friend all grown up? Or was it a mixture of fear, sadness, and pain as he reminded her so much of her parents' burial? Phineas was more like a brother to her, so what could it be?

And then it happened.

"So, darling sis," boomed Oliver from across the busy table, "what have *you* been up to here in Derbyshire? You're sorely missed at home." All eyes turned on Emilie. Phineas, John, Lady June and the rest, all looking intently at her.

Emilie sat upright, straightened her dress, and clasped her hands in her lap, knuckles white. With as much confidence as she could find within, voice steady, she retorted, "Oh brother, you know, young lady-ish things." This received some good-natured chuckles and an insistence that she continue. "On Monday mornings I find myself reading old English literature for precisely one hour, then poetry for a half of an hour. If I'm overly enthused, I may sneak in some studying on Roman architecture and Latin. Then, oh then, what do I do... Ah yes, then I play the pianoforte for forty-five minutes, followed by water-color paintings in the parlor. Then lunch. Some days of the week I stitch and embroider in the family room. Yes, I've even embraced my inner poet, though I did not even know it," she chimed with a smile, a twinkle in her eye.

"Bravo!" her brothers cheered. "We are mighty proud of our sister, now a proper English lady! Father and Momma would swell with joy!" And with that there was much laughter and activity. Violette, Carleighla, and Fiona were thrilled to have more men in the house, even if they did drop in unannounced. Sir Fox was happily satisfied with the liveliness brought in by the Forthyns, and even extended a formal invitation to attend the big dinner party they were planning for the end of the week.

"Oh, sir, we couldn't intrude," responded Oliver. "We thought to stay for only a couple of nights, planning to leave early Thursday morning."

"Nonsense, son. You'll be joining us for dinner if I have anything to do with it! Your father and mother will have known that you were well cared for at the Fox residence." It was settled. They'd stay for the dinner and leave during the weekend, and mostly all were satisfied with this decision.

As breakfast came to an end, it was suggested that they all go for a walk past the gardens into the countryside. Having been constrained in a carriage for so long, the Forthyn men heartily agreed. They were always up for adventure. Phineas seemed quietly excited as well.

Now it came time to change into something more comfortable, with the plan to reconvene at the front of the house in one half hour. The girls, once again giddy with excitement, ran off to pamper and prepare. The servants were called in with the request to pack some light foods for the walk.

Emilie stayed by Lady June's side, savoring the safety and happiness this morning had brought. She was curious about the woman's decision to arrange this meeting so unexpectedly, and asked many questions about this very thing, which Lady June answered, but generally. She had reasons of her own that Emilie need not know about.

As they spoke privately in a sitting area under a renowned Rembrandt painting, romanticizing a profound woman reading a mysterious letter from her lover, the men stood around the table learning of one another's occupational endeavors, business prospects, and economic productivity. It was amazing how uncomplicated the male sex could be; their talk was straightforward and air unassuming. Emilie would casually gaze at the group, trying to read the makeup of the ongoing conversation, wondering what her brothers thought about John. She would also glance over at Phineas, who kept himself occupied with the conversation.

He had grown taller, she thought, and his shoulders had broadened a bit. He wasn't vulnerable like last time when they had been together, but instead seemed comfortable and confident. He had relaxed quite a bit since the initial point of entry, and she could see an unpretentious smile frequenting his features as the conversation touched on more interesting points. Hands in pockets, as per his usual, he listened just as much as he spoke. Then Emilie turned back to Lady June to continue sharing about her life these past couple of weeks.

Hmm, June would voice, shaking her head and emphasizing accordingly, but doing nothing more than that. She knew that Emilie needed to talk.

As the time had come to meet out in front for their walk, Emilie, preparing to help Lady June rise from the couch to go up to her room for an afternoon break, glanced over at the young men who were similarly preparing to leave. Her heart sank when she did not see Phineas standing there with them. Then suddenly, a strong arm took Lady June and raised her easily from the couch, saying in a most familiar voice, "If I may, my lady."

It was Phineas.

Lady June thanked him warmly. "Ah Phin, you are so timely. Thank you. I'm about to go up for an afternoon break. I do hope you enjoy your walk." And with that, she turned toward the door and walked gracefully away. Then there were two.

They stood in silence for a moment, staring at one another, asking themselves why this was different than before.

Then Phineas, more handsome than she had remembered him, took her right hand and kissed it, saying how wonderful it was to see her. "I am happy to hear of your accomplishments, Emilie. I'd love to hear more about your life here, if time permits."

"Phin, why yes, of course. I would like that very much. There is much to be said for this new life I live. But I would equally enjoy hearing about your studies. Are you almost finished?" she asked, looking into his eyes. Yes, she remembered them well, so deep and distinct. As they spoke, she fiddled with a flower that had fallen from her hair when Oliver picked her up and twirled her. Its fragrance accentuated the moment's delicateness, lingering in the mystery of scarcely perceivable longing.

"Well, I have one more apprenticeship to go through, and that may take up to two years. So no, not quite finished. I am very much enjoying it, however tedious some of the studies may be. My parents have been able to free me up with their new helping hands, so I'm a free man pursuing his career," he said with a sweep of his hands and a smile. His genuineness warmed her. He did not work at concealing pieces about his life, but instead spoke normally about these very natural things. He also did not puff himself up about things of the future, speaking realistically about the present. She was comfortable conversing with him. He was steady and grounded. As they spoke about home, she remembered the notebook.

"Phin, before we go on, and please accept my apology that I had not brought this up earlier, I'd like to thank you for the note-book—your gift—the rose petals, your thoughtfulness. It all means so much to me. I cannot explain to you," she said, laying clasped hands over her heart and looking intently at him, "how it spoke to me on the road here. I opened it, a-and I heard my momma through it. This may sound rather daft, but it was life-changing for me. I needed it so much to get through letting go of home."

She looked at him then, wondering if she had said too much, or perhaps he didn't want to hear about how emotional she had been? But in his face she saw contented satisfaction and a sweetly boyish smile. He was pleased. She did not go on to tell him that she slept with it every night because it reminded her of home, however, feel-ing that it was not appropriate to do so.

It seemed to Emilie that neither one of them wanted the con-versation to end. They stood there, face to face, switching positions nervously for reasons not yet known, but holding onto these mo-ments alone. The group, however, was already convening at the front as planned, compelling them to stop. Emilie's brothers rushed past them, Oliver winking at his little sister, and then John strode in their direction. He was ready to take her away.

"Emilie, may I have the honor of walking with you this fine afternoon?" he interjected, offering her his arm, splitting the two up. Whether done intentionally or not, Phineas surely felt the hit. Before Emilie could say a thing, her arm was intertwined with his, and she was surrounded by the ladies asking her questions, such as why she had not changed her attire for the outing and did she know at all about her brothers coming. There was so much happening around her that she, too, started feeling giddy.

Deep down, she now knew why.

Phineas was here. That was why. She could no longer deny that she had feelings for him. The extent of these feelings she did not yet know; they were real, though. But did he feel the same way about her? This she also did not know. Time would have to tell. They had until the weekend.

Putting her coat and walking shoes on, she smiled as she thought of the week in store. With her family here, she could let her guard down. She would not have to stay away from meetings with friends or gatherings with visitors as she had been doing. She hoped to spend more time with Phineas, though she did not know how to make that happen proprietarily. For now, she was satisfied in knowing that her loved ones were near, her soul was well, and her heart was beating to a new song.

Stepping outdoors, she inhaled the sweet air of late autumn. It was colder than expected, but she was glad for the cool air quieting her hot cheeks. At this moment she did not mind the ladies' chatter and the men's rowdy laughter. In fact, she realized that they were all more similar than different. Each desired to be happy, free, and loved.

John joined her side shortly into the walk, asking questions about where she had been since that evening, clearly concerned about her well-being. She answered casually, carefully, not wishing to disclose information unnecessary to his ears. He was very much a man of the world, and she could see how inherently grandiose all his plans were—she felt that he often misunderstood her more simple words and ways. Though she did enjoy his company and spoke quite sincerely with him on all topics of interest.

"I can see how happy you are that your family is here, Emilie," he stated, "and I'm so glad of it. Your brothers are brilliant in how they manage the business. I can see there is much to be learned from them. Perhaps this will develop into a thriving friendship..." he finished, looking straight ahead at the back of Phineas's head who currently walked with Oliver and Mick, then glancing at the lovely Emilie out of the corner of his eye.

"Yes, good friendships are hard to come by, this is true," she returned. "But a few good-willed people who can relate on similarities and tolerate differences is likely the best approach," she said. "I think what matters most are their priorities in life. If those are vastly different, then is there any hope? What do you think?"

"Yes, priorities are certainly important. Perhaps there should be more discussion about what these are nowadays..." he said dryly.

Then, as if on cue as they strolled unhurriedly through the countryside, watching the people work in the fields, the slave trade was brought up. Oliver and the others wanted to know what Albert and John had thought about it. There was no ill will or malicious intent here, just a desire to see where these men stood on such matters. The ladies, of course, were quick to join the conversation.

Mick began, "Seeing so many so called 'slaves' working your fields befuddles me, Albert. Are you not concerned about the growing discontent amongst some in England over the trade? How do you see it? I hear their numbers are growing."

"It's complete nonsense, man. What these people *don't* understand is that it's this exact force that stabilizes our economy. These negros are well cared for, anyway, and generally don't have any complaints." He was about to start on how many of them lived better here than in their countries of origin, but was prevented by Emilie, who almost choked on her own spit. Her cousin's condescending attitude, heavy with willful ignorance, collided with the image from the road that continued to haunt her.

"Albert!" she exclaimed with a dead stop. "Have you any idea how these people are treated? You think they're treated better here in this foreign land to which they were dragged against their will to be *slaves*, than home? Sir, I beg to differ," she finished with a glare so intense that Albert's spine began to sweat. He did know better. He had seen and heard about the ugliness more than he'd care to admit.

The crowd stood awkwardly by. No one really wanted their pleasant afternoon promenade to turn into a bicameral political discussion. But the injured nerve created a painful reaction.

John, who had been suspecting this difference in opinion from Emilie for a while now, did not know how to soften this whiplashing blow. Since Emilie's arrival he had been doing much soul-searching, seeing how to justify his own involvement with the African slave trade, for he and his family had gained great wealth shipping slaves to Barbados and the Americas. The money bought them an exceedingly wealthy lifestyle. The sounds of unrest of which Mick spoke had already been bothering him to the point of considering an eventual exit strategy from the triangular trade of human lives across the sea. But was it all so bad, he kept wondering? It had been done for so long, why must *they* be the ones to end the game? His hunger for affluence resisted the truth, but his desire for Emilie forced him to face it. *Not now*, he groaned, *not yet. This can still work…*

The crowd offered various approvals and objections until Phineas spoke up. "I know of a man who was beaten so horribly that his innards spilt out and he died. Pardon the grotesqueness, ladies. His so-called 'owner' thought that he had stolen a knife from him, reacting in such a murderous rage that he killed the man. I know because my family hired his now widowed wife to work for our estate. Ladies and gentlemen, as much as we would wish to justify it, the practice is in no way defensible. Once the majority of the English recognize this—and it's only a matter of time—the slave trade will be abolished."

The voice of reason stood tall and proud. Emilie burned within in a way she had not before. Not only was she wholeheartedly in agreement with Phineas, she was entirely falling for him.

Her change was twofold: passionate for justice and desperately in love.

The rest of the walk was full of attempts to rekindle normalcy. They were all a bit shaken after the sharp discussion just a few minutes back. The men partnered up with the ladies in an attempt to enjoy the remainder of their time together. Phineas chose to walk with Fiona. And Emilie felt rather awkward. She had, after all, in a moment's span of time spoken without forethought or filter, and as a result had shattered the genteel balance. She felt both foolish and brave all at once. Had she not thought things through? Wasn't her wrath justifiable? Was she wrong to address Albert so fiercely? She wished she could speak with Lady June this very moment. Her cheeks burned as she held trembling hands in her coat pockets. Even John walked at a distance.

Desperate for affirmation, she could no longer walk on with the crowd. The tumult had gotten to her head. Non-affirming voices crowded her thoughts. Being at the tail end of the group, she slowed her pace to a complete stop. She turned and began walking in the opposite direction. No one would see her leave anyway, as they were too busy having basic conversations about nicer things. Drifting away, she fought the urge to weep. Her eyes burned until finally heavy tears prevailed, rolling down dry, pale cheeks. The world had crushed her. In the stories of her past, the just voice of the heroine cut through darkness to set the world aright. She became that voice today. The sting of the backslap hurt. She longed to be alone.

Seeing a large tree just up ahead, she walked over and sat against the cold, raggedy trunk. She had shown herself, and not one of them was impressed.

Then out of the gray she heard, "Em, are you alright?"

Phin. She let out a sigh of relief.

"I saw you leave the group and came to make sure you were alright… May I sit with you?" When she did not object, he sat down against the same trunk and pursed his lips. "Thinking about what happened, are you?"

Was he mocking her? Awareness of the importance of his opinion shot through her. He had spoken up on the topic, but briefly and only once, staying quiet the rest of the time. Did he think that her outburst was excessive—infantile? Was he frustrated that she ruined the walk? Feeling utterly humiliated, she dared not look his way. Instead, she looked down at the dying grass. Her breaths were shallow. If she breathed deeper, she'd draw attention to herself. And that was the last thing she wanted. *Small*, she thought. *Please, I want to be small.*

Watching her carefully, Phineas tried to understand what was going through her mind. Why did this hit her so hard? It was just conversation. Unless…it was John's opinion she feared losing. He leaned his head against the trunk. Was Emilie afraid that John would think less of her because of her strong opinions? He felt a twinge of pain inside. It mattered to him.

He had been watching the two of them since he first arrived. John was certainly confident toward Emilie… Did she give him reason? How his mind ached from the tension of the unknown.

Small, he thought. *I never felt deserving of her, too insignificant to gain her attention.* Sitting there with her, he thought back to the many summer nights spent running throughout the countryside together, catching bugs, eating berries, and skipping rocks. He had often felt the need to prove himself, but because she was so young, she never noticed. On the day of the funeral, however, he faced those fears dead on as he went after her into the rose garden. He somehow knew that just standing by her side would be enough.

Sitting here now, he yearned to become the man that she needed. He longed for openness and trust. But he had no idea where her heart was. He could not be direct until he knew.

"Don't overthink it, Em," he offered. "I think we just have to be alright with standing alone sometimes." She heard his words—they fell like water on parched ground—but resisted facing him. "Some people don't want to hear truth," he finished.

She faced him then. "Do you think what I said was alright? Was I wrong to say it?" she said, eyes pleading, brow tense.

Phineas could see her internal war. He could see the struggle of a lone truther amidst a sea of clones. He could also see clarity of vision and the birth pangs of purpose. If he could do anything for her today, it would be to encourage her to stay the course, not allowing fear and doubt to get the best of her. He also longed to see her smile.

With those goals in mind, he said, "Well, if your Momma was here, she would be proud. And Lady June? She thrives on adversity; they're her bread and butter. Em, does it really matter what anyone else thinks?" He nudged her gently with his elbow to loosen her up and to turn off the torrent of despair. He was also hoping for a flagrant 'no' in response.

"Yes, I know, Phin. Momma always told me that standing alone is sometimes the only way. She always managed to inspire me to make these hard choices well when the time came. It's come, Phin, and I feel *most terrible*. And as much as I tell myself that I don't care about their opinions…I do," she finished quietly. A world of a difference stood between what Emilie meant with those two small words and what Phineas *heard*.

John's opinion matters, he told himself. Face drawn, he looked bleakly away, seeing birds scattered in flight across an empty blue sky. He was frustrated that he had come. Was he too late? Ultimately he was here on business that he was not at leisure to disclose. He came to further his work on a highly-classified project. His heart, however, begged to have a glimpse of her face and moments of her time. But was it ending before it had even begun? Now *he* fought despair.

Emilie, in contrast, was relieved by his words; they reassured her. He had changed since she last saw him that morning at the Forthyn estate. He was bolder, speaking more decidedly. The fact that the two of them agreed on the topic of the slave trade exhilarated her for reasons she held gently inside for now. She glimpsed at him again and was startled at the expression on his face. Then, as if annoyed by her presence, he quickly rose and, mentioning that it was time to return, gave her a hasty hand of assistance. She took it, and arising, searched his face for understanding. Neither spoke. He looked away.

"Phineas," she spoke his name, "thank you for coming. Once again, you've shown me only kindness."

"Think nothing of it, Emilie," he replied brusquely. "Anything for an old friend. Shall we head back before the others worry?"

As often as she had daydreamed about this very moment, when Phineas McGray would walk her home again, this was not what she expected. Their conversation was dismally formal. He spoke of his parents, university life, and the books on his shelf. She, still recovering from the feeling of being deemed an *old friend*, returned talk on her favorite authors, the lavish dinners at Derbyshire, and her favorite rooms at the estate. Back and forth they went, carrying on as if the locksmith and baker on a busy summer morning when the marketplace was abuzz with business. The talk was shallow, any connection gone.

Approaching Derbyshire, Phineas did something that stunned Emilie even more. He stopped her mid-tracks, before they would be visible by curious members of the house, turned her to face him, and rattled off, "Emilie, I am so very happy for your success here at Derbyshire. I wish you only the best in the years to come." And with that he roughly kissed her hand, turned decidedly away, and strode hastily toward the back entrance of the house. He did not want to see anyone or be seen. He wanted time away from the noise.

Emilie, standing alone at the corner of the driveway, knew not what had just happened. Had she said something to insult him? Had she not spoken enough? She had never seen Phineas so terribly insensitive before, and what did he mean by wishing her the best in the years to come?

What had happened?

Heart heavy, she lifted her head, let out an anguished breath, and headed toward the front doorway. She did not know what she would say to the hordes of questioners, curious about where she had been with Phineas. He surely wasn't there to help. Walking in, she gave her coat and shoes to Lincoln, one of the oldest servants of the manor. He was a kind old man who had developed a sweet friendship with Emilie, and she had found him to be a wise confidante with whom she could share some of her struggles.

"Miss, they all be in the east wing drawing room, waitin' on dinner. Go on ahead, before you miss it. It's pot roast tonight," he said with a brilliant smile.

"Thank you, Lincoln. How kind of you, though I'm really not in any mood for dinner right now," she said, shoulders sagging.

Looking down the hallways to ensure the coast was clear, he slowly lowered himself onto a marble bench and patted the seat beside him. "Come now, tell ol' Lincoln what be botherin' my lady today."

Emilie sat and offered him a brief exposé on how she had spoken out rather harshly today and ruined the walk. She didn't know who was worse off: Albert and the crew of Derbyshire, her family, or she.

"You know what, Miss Emilie?" he said with that brilliant toothy smile and a refined sense of knowing. "There ain't enough people like you around nowadays, and I don't say that lightly. You don't worry about no one. Mm-hm. Keep on doing whatchu know to be right."

She lowered her head, studying her hands. What were these hands made for? Could they accomplish great feats, like the heroines in the stories of childhood? Could she—a seeming misfit in this bodacious culture—say anything to bring change?

Silent when her voice was needed, then loud and brash when it wasn't. What good was she when she couldn't discern the difference?

"Lincoln," she retorted, "based on today, I'm not so good with my words. No one even listens…"

"Who said anything 'bout words, my lady?" he exclaimed. "Just be you'self, and that's enough. You'll see…" He gave her hand a gentle squeeze and chuckled. He strongly believed that one day, this particular one would change the world. In fact, most of the household servants believed this.

At that very moment and quite unexpectedly, Aunt Clarence burst through a door in the darkened hallway on her way to ascertain who had come in through the front door. Seeing Emilie's intimate moment with the household servant, her eyes widened and head shot backward.

"*Emilie Forthyn,*" she spat repugnantly, "and what, pray tell, are we doing?" She was livid.

Lincoln, horrified that they had been spotted, began to pro-fusely apologize to the lady of the house for his lapse of judgment. "Silence, Lincoln. I would highly advise that you tighten the reins of your personal freedoms. You are excused," she warned, to which he bowed penitently and hurried off toward the ser-vants' quarters.

Emilie wanted to say many things. For instance, she wanted to understand why her aunt treated this most kind elderly man as if he were a child. Next, she wanted to shake some sense into this woman's high-horse ideologies. But instead of speaking, which would inevitably lead to a worse outcome than the one she had found herself in earlier today, she looked straight ahead and waited.

"Emilie, what would possess you to treat Lincoln as if he were some nobleman of England? Didn't your parents teach you any-thing? This is *precisely* why your mother and I never spoke. We live by certain laws here. You cannot keep doing what you're doing and expect everything to remain alright. Don't think I haven't seen you engaging in various carousals with the servants—this is simply not acceptable. It needs to stop. It must. Do you understand? There are boundaries for a reason. It's for the best of everyone involved," she finished with an aggravated wave of her hand in Lincoln's direc-tion. "I'd like you to think about this very seriously. Now, please wash up and join us in the drawing room for dinner. We have a full table tonight."

The words, which at this point she was not unprepared for, still hit like nails on a coffin. Cold and final. *Don't bring Momma into it*, she thought. *Don't mar her image with your misperceptions.* And as much as she would have loved to excuse herself from tonight's din-ner, she knew she could not. Her brothers were here. Then, vacantly verbalizing that she had heard the aforementioned requirements set forth by Lady Fox, she excused herself.

The sun had already set, casting deleterious shadows like prison bars across the long hallway. Step by step she went, pondering her present condition. The Derbyshire crew was likely relieved to be rid of her and her brothers, well, perhaps they would stick up for her tonight. The memory of her nonconformist response toward Albert still had bite. Even more, she was certain that by this time their gossip had christened her as scandalous at best.

And Phin. Would he come? Could she face him? She ached from the painfully disappointing experience she had just lived through. He had changed so quickly and without the slightest indication as to why.

In her room she found a humming Mim preparing her evening attire. She had laid out a satin dress, ribbon to weave into her hair, white gloves, and pearls.

"With your family here, I thought to make you look extra special, miss," she said eagerly.

Emilie acknowledged her absentmindedly, walking over to the notebook given her by Phineas. The fragrance had mostly subsided by now, though a remnant remained. Perhaps this was a reflection of his feelings toward her—fading and lifeless. She couldn't bear it any longer.

"Oh, Mim," she cried, "what a miserable day today has been!" She didn't feel like she could share everything right now, but she did describe the perplexing nature of her situation with Phineas.

Mim listened, asking questions about what had been said and whether this was said or that, concluding that *there must be more to it, miss.* And because Mim did personally feel that Phineas needed to pay more attention to Emilie—though she wouldn't say this to her—she took particular care in preparing her tonight.

For Emilie, it was time to face the aftermath of the day's disaster. She was going to have to face it sooner or later, and it may as well be tonight.

Chapter 10

*S*he could hear someone playing the pianoforte as she walked toward the light of the drawing room. There was gusty talk. Some laughed in response to the jesting of others. As per usual, Oliver's booming voice was heard above the din, whilst Sir Fox engaged himself with Lady June regarding matters of England's changing landscape. Lady Fox was seen speaking to a servant about dinner preparations, ensuring that all was divinely orchestrated. As Emilie stood in the doorway taking it all in, she felt hopeful that all would be well.

"Ah, Emilie! How lovely you're here," beamed Sir Fox, breaking with Lady June to escort the young lady into the room. Emilie thanked him with an elegant curtsy. Violette and Carleighla whispered something to one another. Mick and Oliver came right over, giving her a tight squeeze on the shoulder. They were most interested in ensuring that their sister was alright. John stood by, unsure of the appropriate move. But he quickly decided that he'd rather spend an evening in her brilliance than outside of it. Their current opinions may be different, but things could change. Even Albert, who was most impacted by her fierce tirade, gave in. He walked over and informed her that she looked wonderful and that he hoped they could continue on as before, to which she wholeheartedly agreed.

Lincoln, who was serving in the room, was delighted that Emilie was once again smiling and, when able, snuck a wink in her direction.

Beaming, Emilie nodded acknowledgment. This particular evening brought relief, showing that good people were often simply misguided and misled. That the Foxes—the said good people—were so deeply entrenched in this business of the trade that perhaps they needed someone to help them to see truth.

The spark of purpose was toying ever so gently with the fragile embers of pain, which continually reminded her of its constant presence, though she felt clearer than ever. She could not yet see how the past—losing Father and Momma, coming here, discovering Phineas—could impact the future.

People of the past could not change. They turned into memories. It dawned on her then that what one did today would define how they would be remembered forever. She thought of Sir Fox, Albert, and John, and her heart sank. She longed to ask how possible it was for a slave trader to walk away from his trade. Was it possible to change identity? But other than Lady June, no one was really wanting to be asked.

Enmeshed in her thoughts, she lightly accepted John's arm to walk into the dining room with Oliver and Carleighla right behind. As they were walking past the pianoforte, Phineas unexpectedly strode through the nearby doorway, caught totally off guard by John's smug acknowledgement, as evidenced by a lofty nod of the head. Emilie caught Phineas's gaze for a matter of a second, then was turned away toward the dining room. What could she do? After the encounter earlier today, she did not feel at liberty to speak with him.

Seeing Violette, Fiona, and Mick nearby with Sir Fox, Phineas walked over and offered Fiona an arm. His head was spinning. He didn't care whose arm it was. John's proprietary behavior toward Emilie perturbed him so greatly that he nearly toppled a large antique vase standing by the pianoforte. Fiona's arm stabilized him.

Lady June, however, was not perturbed. She duly noted the scenario. Phineas's undoing was only a matter of time, she knew. How long could he stand by watching the woman he loved be led about by another man? Sitting calmly by, she knew one of two things was true: one, Emilie was not yet entirely aware of her feelings toward Phineas, in which case he needed to act quickly to help her see, or two, he loved her but was prevented from speaking by reasons not yet known. Lady June let out an impatient puff, eyeing Phineas as he made conversation with a delighted young lady, raised herself up, and slowly made her way to the table.

"Mother, did you put in a request for Brussels sprouts for dinner, the roasted ones with the balsamic dressing?" asked Violette, scanning the table voraciously.

"Ah yes, Lincoln?" Lady Clarence charged petulantly. "Might you please bring it? I do not see them, either. The side seems to be missing."

"Certainly, my lady," said the man, head bowed, immediately turning toward the kitchen.

"Mick, Oliver, how is business faring?" asked Sir Fox from across the table over the silvery clamber of forks and knives. The young ladies seated across from Emilie giggled quietly in their usual huddle of secrecy. Phineas conversed calmly with Fiona.

While Oliver chewed heartily, Mick replied, "It is going well, Uncle, though more is required of us now with Father being gone, God rest his soul." He looked over at Emilie, who acknowledged his words softly.

"We manage quite well, Uncle," asserted Oliver.

"Ah yes, it appears that you do. I've heard of the success of your newspaper. I understand it's gone as far out as Yorkshire and Cumberland. How many work for you? Are they all paid?" he asked, genuinely astounded. He knew that the Forthyns disdained slave ownership in all of its forms, and so wondered how so small a company could be as successful.

Oliver sat back in his chair. "Yes, it's gone even farther north, actually. And we do have a sizable paid staff. We've found that over the past years, people's interest in the news has grown."

"Indeed, it's like we've caught some wave with the type of news people are wanting to hear," added Mick, "and our writers travel as far up as the northern counties to build connections and find stories. I think that's been it. Our motto is, 'Your news is our news,' which seems to resonate with all of England."

"It is a wonder, though," Lady Fox chimed in, "that you do so much with so few workers. Don't you think, darling," she addressed Sir Fox, "that they'd do so much more with a larger staff?"

"Yes, it would seem so, darling," he replied. "But where would they get the people down in the country?"

The side conversations around the table began to dwindle down and hone in on the central one. Emilie, who sat with Lady June on one side and John on the other, could sense where the conversation was going. Her belly began to burn. She noted Sir Fox's innocent curiosity and paired that with Aunt Clarence's noxious perspective. They struggled to see that business could succeed with willing hands being paid a fair wage. This intrigued him and bothered her.

"I suppose they could advertise, but then, one would hope that the addition of more workers would bring in more gains than losses. You would have to pay more," said Albert. "If you hire more but don't achieve parallel growth, that's money lost."

For him, this was always the bottom line.

"Yes," exclaimed Emilie with an intentional evenness, "but the satisfaction of people gainfully employed is immense. There is reward in it. They work by their own accord, get paid to feed their families, more newspaper is made and sold, thus more money comes in. It's a win-win for all," she finished, pleased to see some nodding approval. This felt more controlled than earlier. She maintained her composure, emotions tethered tightly within. She would not show weakness this time. She remembered Phineas's words spoken hours ago under the old oak, that standing alone is sometimes the only way, and decided that tonight she would practice. The thought and sight of him seated across from her, though, engaged in pleasantries with Fiona, tore at the raw chord broken earlier today. Sulfuric anguish flooded her face as she recognized how perfect the two looked. She tore her gaze away, reprimanded her heart, and forcibly resurfaced to hear the following fragment of words.

"But eradicating the trade would be like national suicide! And what about France? Don't think for a moment that they would do the same," finished Albert, fist clenched on the table. He was so repulsed by the thought of slavery-free labor that beads of sweat and crumbs of bread lingered on his face without attention.

"Albert, yes, yes, I know," she assured. "So much depends on the business, it's all a vast cobweb. But think of it, isn't there another way? Has England so forgotten her conscience that she can continue prospering like this? Is it not repulsive that men and women are dying overseas for bags of sugar? Or that children are forced to work under hellish circumstances for a drop of molasses? Look, our family has been able to create income without funding from the trade," she said, looking over at her brothers. "We've created a sustainable enterprise run by common decency." Shaking her head affirmatively, she looked at Sir Fox and Lady Clarence. Gentle conviction had softened his features. Her face was stone.

"Emilie, child," Aunt Clarence rushed feverishly, "at nineteen years of age, you speak as if you know all things. If the slave trade were to—as you say—end, this nation's institutions of finance, law, and commerce would all fall to rubbish. Now how would you like that? Is that suitable to your conscience? One—as you say—'evil' ends for another to begin. What do you say to that? What about our children, who know a good life and who would end up in the slums? Hmm?" The challenger had spoken, hatred seeping through every word.

"Now Clarence," Lady June asserted, "ease your nerves. Let her learn her way in life. Please." And with that word, Lady June silenced the contender. Under the table, she squeezed Emilie's tightly clenched hand. *It's ok*, she seemed to be saying. *Just listen and learn.*

John cleared his throat. "Well yes, it seems most of us are done with dinner. How about we take a turn with some dancing?" He looked at Sir Fox, who lit up with the idea, eager to escape the hot seat he felt he was in, and at Emilie, who had just looked at Phineas. "Emilie? Shall we?" More a declaration than a question as he stood from the table, offering her his arm.

Uncomfortable to be put on the spot again, she briefly excused herself from the table. The rest of the table began to shimmy and shuffle after them. Small words were exchanged throughout the room about the excellence of the dinner and the kindness of the hostess.

They weren't used to raw truth. Lady June, who was like a mother to Aunt Clarence, was heard speaking with her regarding the appropriateness of her sharp tone with Emilie. And Phineas was at this time distancing himself from Fiona, recognizing that he was spending far too much time with her. Being an honorable man, he did not wish to encourage her in unintended ways. He had his heart set elsewhere.

Coffee and dessert were called into the candlelit drawing room as Carleighla assumed her position at the pianoforte, beginning a playful tune to lift the atmosphere. She had called out to John to come over to the piano to show off her abilities, and out of respect, he let Emilie go and went over. She passingly commented on how drab some people left the atmosphere, insinuating Emilie and her persistence against the slave trade, aiming to gain some approval.

He merely nodded his head and commented on how passionate of a young lady she was, eyes keenly attuned to her whereabouts.

Left alone, Emilie floated about the room with a cup of coffee and an otherworldly elegance. To her surprise, it was Oliver who had invited Fiona to dance, and Phineas was talking with her uncle. Albert, still fired up over the massive challenge once again given by Emilie, offered to take Lady June up for a dance. He needed to calm himself, and the elder woman's timeless steadfastness would certainly help.

Standing off to the side, looking out a massive window over the darkened contours of the hillside, Emilie was suddenly swept off her feet by Mick, who was clearly in a much merrier mood, intent on having evening fun. "Let's dance, sis," he insisted, pulling her to the center of the opulent room. "It's been far too long."

As they danced, she remembered home and dancing with Father as Momma laughed, enjoying their whimsy. Her brother's energy and mutual understanding liberated Emilie. She laughed and twirled. What they had was magical. The love they shared as brother and sister pleased everyone watching. And a certain couple of gentlemen were envious of Mick's freedom with the woman they knew they loved.

As the song ended, Emilie, delightfully self-aware, now insisted that her brother go dance with Violette, who stood by without a partner. "Go on Mick, our lonely cousin could use your excellent footwork," she chided breathlessly after him.

He winked at her and agreed, making his way toward Violette. Tonight, dancing was a must.

She walked back to where her cup of coffee waited and caught her reflection in the window. Hair wild, cheeks rosy, a different woman looked back. A younger but mature version of Emilie stood before her. Whatever happened earlier this afternoon was fading into the background of memory; new thoughts occupied her mind.

During dinner she did not speak out of anger, she realized, but out of compassion for both slave and owner. The realization was striking. Earlier today her words so struck at Albert that he was forced to react. This evening, though, she spoke confidently with the belief that truth would fight its own battles. She need not stir up fights. She needed wisdom to know what to say and how to say it.

She felt as if she had been given a key to a mysterious doorway, beyond which was that magical land of princesses and valiant knights of honor. Now she longed to know precisely what was on the other side, what lay ahead for her. As she stood there reveling in the freedom that came from gradual understanding of her identity, suddenly and without warning, a man appeared beside her. She looked, and there stood Phineas.

"Emilie, I'm sorry to have left you so suddenly earlier today. My behavior is sorely inexcusable. Please, accept my apology," he said, eager to say more but prevented by doubt and uncertainty.

"It's alright, Phin," she said, studying his features, striving to understand. "I'm quite alright. No need for apologizing." He need not know the effect he'd been having on her.

Music playing in the background and conversation flowing throughout the room, Phineas and Emilie resumed where they had left off in Suffolk so long ago. She again wondered why he'd chosen to place himself here with her—the same thoughts she had had the day of her departure when he surprised her in the doorway of home. The maturing woman inside silenced whispers of hope. There was no certainty in this. Yet here they were, getting lost in their history.

"Do you remember that day when your horses got loose?" he asked with bated breath. Emilie, eyes wide and mouth agape with the horribleness of that experience, smiled and said that *yes, she did*. "I don't know who was more cross, my parents or yours," he said with the widest smile she had yet seen on his face. It was delightful. Memory after memory, they uncovered a wellspring of life from which they did not wish to stop drinking. Being refreshed, they held onto this moment in time. Elbows clasped in her hands, arms across her body, she stood unmoving so as to prolong the encounter. These moments with him always seemed so fragile.

"I remember almost dying the night you and Oliver decided to stir a den of snakes. That is likely my worst memory. We never even told our parents. They'd have never let us outside again," she said, feigning astonishment. She knew it wasn't true.

Phineas chuckled in agreement. Then, on a serious note, "And I'd never get to see you again." His words were tender, intentional, measured like stones on quiet waters, causing a rippling of questions. His gaze lingered on hers. "Emilie," he said, taking a step toward her, "that would be the worst thing ever for me."

Head spinning, heart racing, she was rendered speechless. His words were salve to her wounded soul. But did he mean them? How much could he mean them? Could she trust the man who had so strangely abandoned her earlier that day? And what about Fiona?

Caught up in the cosmic shift of two expanding hearts, she looked at the starlit sky and thought of Momma. Her mother loved him, she knew. She always spoke so highly of his character, strength, and sacrifice. Emilie wondered how pleased her parents would be if…if their hearts surrendered to the greatest joy one could experience. Was this why he had come?

He had spoken plainly that she meant something to him. Words, these words spoken by this man, were not empty. He was not one to mishandle words. She looked back at the man who had occupied her mind countless days and nights and couldn't help but smile. "Phineas McGray," she began, "here we are, so far from home, yet still being our unchanged selves, still friends. Your friendship is so dear to me. However, the worst thing ever would be if you took me dancing with two left shoes," she giggled lightly. Then, "Will you be here tomorrow…with Mick and Oliver, of course?"

He lit up, sensing the delicateness of reciprocal desire.

The piano player changed, and as such, so did the music. Violette, unlike her sister, played more elegant compositions which lent themselves greatly to slower dance.

Tonight he would make his intentions known.

"Yes, we should be here tomorrow before the dinner. The following day I am occupied in London. I have work that needs to be done. This evening, though—what should we do this evening?" He attempted to subdue his boyish elatedness, but couldn't help himself. He felt like a boy who had just won the most coveted prize at the fair. "Ah, yes," he continued with a restrained grin. "May I?" And with a sweeping bow, he offered his hand and led her to the dance floor. Little did either know, all eyes followed.

Phineas and Emilie took not only the spotlight, but the starlight and moonlight. Bathed in iridescent rays of subdued lighting, they bedazzled the room into a dreamlike standstill.

Mick and Oliver exchanged a look of disbelief as understanding dawned on both at once. How could they have been so blind? Lady June almost wept at the sight. Was it really happening? Was it all going to work out with her beloved Emilie? She dared not breathe a word to a soul. Sir Fox, too, seemed pleased with the pair taking center stage. He had been suspecting all along that Phineas's reasons for coming were far more personal than he had led on.

Others, however, watched in agony.

John hated him. He detested his coming—his intrusion on this family gathering. He felt he had no right to be here. How could this country boy steal his prized possession right out of his grasp? He couldn't let this happen. He wouldn't. Something had to be done.

But reality was just so obvious tonight. As the pair danced, the world was lost to them. Her hand in his, Emilie felt safer than she had in months. If she could stay here in this moment forever, she would. Wrapped up in light, the end of the song too quickly approaching, Phineas considered how to finally share his heart. He didn't want to rush. Perhaps he would take her aside at the end of the evening, before they parted for the night. Yes, that would be perfect.

Then suddenly, as if a cold draft across a dancing candle, John appeared.

"May I?" he directed at Phineas. "You can't have her all evening," he challenged. He was not playing games. He intended to do or say whatever was necessary to sway Emilie back. He had worlds more to offer her, he knew. He offered his hand to Emilie, who all of a sudden felt chilled, though no doors had been opened. Then, another shot at Phineas. "Don't you have some personal business to attend to? What sort of business is it, anyway?"

Phineas straightened, jaw tight. "That's something I'm not at liberty to discuss, John." His eyes gripped John's.

"Secrets? Hm, fascinating," he taunted. A challenge. The words cast a shadow not only over Phineas's demeanor, but also upon his integrity. They shattered his sacred moment with Emilie.

Intent on Phineas's undoing, John proceeded. "Emilie, might I interest you in a tour of the Foxes' gallery? My father helped them acquire many of those pieces, so I know a great deal about them. Shall we? Perhaps the other ladies would like to join us? What do you think?" he asked with cold confidence.

Emilie sensed bitter resentment between the two and wanted no part in it. She was about to voice her regrets when suddenly there came a murderous knock on the front door.

All eyes fell on Sir Fox to attend to the matter. He wasted no time in getting to the door with the other men right behind to ascertain the reason for the disheartening intrusion. It was half past eight. Lady Fox swore that no others were to be expected this evening. The younger ladies huddled behind the gentlemen, waiting to hear the news. Servants trickled in as well, watching from a distance.

It was the courier, a long-time friend of the Foxes. Fretfulness shrouded his face as Sir Fox ushered him into the entryway, briefly scanning the outdoors to ensure all was safe before shutting the door. Lady Clarence had made her way to where the action was and ordered that a glass of wine be brought immediately for the gentleman to ease his nerves.

He, gulping the contents down in a second, raised a forefinger to the crowd, signifying that he needed a minute to catch his breath. He had run his horse nonstop from London to Kent with what seemed like grave news.

The crowd waited nervously, eyes darting anxiously from one to another, shoulders shrugging.

Lady Clarence was known for many things; imperturbability was not one of them.

"Well?" she insisted impatiently. "What is it, Simon? What in God's name happened?"

Chapter 11

"*I*t's the abolitionists, Clarence," he let out. "They have filed a public suit against Bartholomew Forester, claiming that the Bank of England has been illegitimately withholding their money." His eyes were wide with disbelief. "They're accusing him of stealing large sums of money. I came to tell you immediately, knowing of your connections to the man."

"How dare they?" Lady Clarence spat. "Mar the reputation of the man who was funded countless charities all over England and beyond! Who upholds the very backbone of this nation. They've done nothing but stir up trouble all these years with their saintly agenda. As if their perpetual discontent is not enough. I suspect it's Wilberforce spearheading the whole of it. What else is being said, Simon?"

"And has Bartholomew had the opportunity to speak on it?" appended Sir Fox. "How far along is this thing? What's being said in the House? And what about evidence?" His questions sidestepped his wife's emotional outburst, seeking to clarify the facts. If there was anything to be known, Sir Fox wanted to know it. "Simon, I'm going to London first thing in the morning. I must find out more. This is indeed severe."

"I'm going with you, Father," added Albert. "This doesn't feel right. I've not once heard of any complaints about Sir Forester, and then to hear this. Phineas, you've been to London recently, have you heard anything at all? Have you any acquaintances privy to the matter?" Albert directed his gaze at Phineas, who stood a shadowy figure, seemingly hiding from sight.

"No," he stated firmly. "I have not heard anything at all about the matter, but I will be in London in two days' time. Perhaps I'll learn something then."

"Why don't you come tomorrow, instead? We may benefit from your expertise. I have friends with whom we can stay. What do you say? I promise, you'll not be bored with us," Albert queried, genuinely interested in making use of Phineas's training. He personally had never taken his law studies seriously, and having been impressed by Phin's sharp mind and perceptive disposition, felt that he would be an effective addition on their trip to London.

"Thanks Albert, but I'll be staying here tomorrow," he said, stealing a brief look at Emilie, who stood a few feet away, consumed by awareness of what this news could mean for the movement and the people that were becoming so dear to her heart. Privately planning to spend tomorrow with Emilie, he firmly reiterated that he would join them the day after. He was not going to budge. Their opinions did not concern him.

Then, in an amateuresque display of propriety, John began preaching on the merits of applying oneself to every opportunity provided to improve one's ability to impact the world for good. Ensuring that Emilie was within listening distance, he began with his usual air of self-importance and continued with the hope of putting Phineas to shame.

"I, personally," he began after clearing his throat, "feel like I owe it to our society to go and search this matter out and to get to the bottom of it. If I were a law student, I wouldn't want to miss a single opportunity to apply myself. One never knows what difference can be made. As one also does not know what important information might be availed tomorrow that may not be availed the following day. Every moment is valuable. Albert, I'm coming. Let's see where the truth lies," he finished as the ladies (all excepting Emilie) bobbed their heads in wholehearted agreement.

"Ah yes." Phineas shook his head in disbelief at the man's puerility. "One does not know what one does not know." And with that, he turned to tune him out.

Lady June was more pensive than usual. She had heard the others give their take on the situation, that Wilberforce and his cohorts were planning to further their abolitionist agenda by discrediting the premier handler of England's money (which they insisted was stained with African blood), but could not come to terms with what she was hearing.

She had known Wilberforce to be a man of the utmost integrity. And although he associated with individuals from all walks of life, he was known to stay deeply committed to his faith in God. So, was this an attempt at character assassination to slow his momentum, or did Forester really steal from them? Or, were the others right? Had Wilberforce turned into a reprehensible outlaw overnight? She chortled under her breath. *There is more to this,* she once again concluded. She was still under the pleasantest impression from this evening's soiree. Not even a nefarious Wilberforce could take that away.

Ten past ten. The conversation was so gripping, no one wanted to leave. There were so many ostensible questions and base assumptions being made that the Forthyns felt like they—the anti-slavery few—were being attacked. They insisted that until the evidence was examined, not one of them could make such claims. They did not know whether to believe that a good man had gone bad, or that a rich man was wronged. And Phineas, the one with the most to offer, surprisingly offered very little to the discourse. He maintained an open ear to the noise with a distance adequate enough to feign disinterest. Lady June noticed that his insipid deliberations were shaky, however, and wondered whether he knew more than he was letting on. He had certainly displayed interest in abolition the past several days, so his current posture was a bit of a mystery.

But knowing that Phineas was an honest man, she deduced that whatever he may have known he was not at liberty to speak about.

Understanding that perhaps he needed a partner to facilitate the façade of concealment, she walked over to him and began asking unrelated questions about his parents and their estate in Suffolk. He relaxed in the covering of the conversation, and she guessed she was right—he knew more. As they spoke, she observed how often his eyes found their way in Emilie's direction, where she stood toward the back with Mim, talking about Sir Wilberforce, whom she had not yet met but about whom she had heard many exceptional things and whom she had hoped to one day meet.

"Emilie is radiant tonight, is she not?" she risked, catching him entirely off guard. She levelled with him then. Face to face, he could not hide his feelings from the woman under whose gaze he had grown into a man. "Phin," she continued tenderly, "she is, is she not?" Her eyes piercing, she wanted to ensure that he was sincere in his intentions toward Emilie.

He colored in surrender. "Yes, Lady June, she is indeed."

She tilted her wrinkled countenance slightly so as to study his face, and clicking her tongue, said, "Yes, I think you've got it, Phin." Her eyes beamed. "Now," she continued, "can you help this old lady to that door there? I think it's past my bedtime."

Phineas readily obliged. Still caught up in the fact that he had been discovered by this gutsy force of a woman, he was now pondering how he would tell Emilie what he had just told Lady June.

Once every single detail had been drenched in curious conjectures several times over and the clock had struck eleven, the harried elder Foxes excused themselves to their quarters, but the younger generation insisted on continuing on with the possibilities of either a conviction or an acquittal. Did Forester have reason to withhold money from the men? Was there actual proof of such a thing taking place? If so, how much? And what would this mean for England's slave trade, which was so indelibly tied to Forester's bank?

The heated discussion continued on as Kent's crowd insisted on the man's admirable character, but the others insisted on there being no reason for the abolitionists to pull such a stunt unless it were true. What would be the gain of such a ruse, they posited. Forester had greater pull than they, and as such could obliterate their movement with the strike of a clock unless there was truth to the suit. Having no way to determine what was actually true at this hour of the night, however, and no longer opposing the idea of sleep, they all agreed to pick up the conversation tomorrow at breakfast.

"Let's sleep on it, ladies and gentlemen," offered a yawning Albert, "and see what we can learn tomorrow. I bid thee all a good night," he finished, and turned toward his chamber. Violette and Carleighla followed sleepily after, wishing the same. Then John and Fiona bade the remnant a farewell and turned to the front door, where a carriage was waiting. Before walking away, however, John took one last look at Emilie and informed her that he would make it his mission to ensure that righteousness prevailed. Kissing her hand, he bowed low, then made his way after Fiona, who had just stated her farewell to Phineas.

"Well," yawned Mick, "it is high time we went to bed. Isn't that right, Oliver?" He caught his exhausted brother off guard and had to plant an elbow in his rib to get him on the same proverbial page.

"Oh—yes. Totally agree, Mick. I'm dwindled. Good night Phin...Emilie... See you tomorrow!" And, in their usual manner, the brothers escaped toward the hallway where their bedroom was, leaving the two singletons alone.

The foyer went quiet. All save Phineas's beating heart, which he was sure she could hear.

He had not yet been alone with Emilie under such circumstances as this evening had provided—dancing, laughing, and reminiscing. Undeniable progress had been made. He believed that if he spoke openly about his love for her in this very moment, she would not resist. Her frame had melted into his as they danced, something that would not have happened if she did not allow it. Even John no longer appeared threatening.

Here was his chance to tell her how incredible he thought she was and how much he loved to be with her. How much he loved her.

As the final door resounded somewhere down the hallway, he stepped before her. "Em," he began, "there is something I need to tell you."

Emilie's sense of awareness was immensely heightened as she stood with him. She knew something was coming, though she could not fathom the extent of it.

He reached out and took both of her hands in his, holding them tenderly, hoping that she could feel in them security and strength.

She began to shake. This *was* happening.

"When your mother and father passed, I watched you grieve. I watched you close in on yourself. The thought of losing you struck me so hard that I made a commitment to help you live past your loss. Then," he continued hoarsely, "as I focused in on you, as I watched you rise from the depths of pain, I saw who you truly were, who you are. I-I made you that notebook to ensure you would remember me. That's the honest truth. I wanted to come with you. I wanted to walk through the changing world with you, to be there for you. Emilie, I want to be there for you every second of every day." He stopped then, looking intently down into her shimmering eyes, searching for that hint of mutual desire.

Spring came in his words. She felt icy clouds part as buds of relief lifted their powerful heads toward the sun. She gripped his hands and steadied herself. "Phin, I…" She looked eagerly, stammering, "*Yes*, I-I would like that very much. After all that's happened these past days, I dared not hope…"—she smiled, thinking back to those nights when she had no answer regarding his feelings for her—"that this could one day happen. I could find no reason for you to feel this way about me, and thought that you would find someone far away from home, during your studies…" She thought of Fiona, and more relief cascaded over her soul.

"Emilie, you're the only one I've ever loved." He had thought these words a thousand times over every day, wondering how he would one day open his mouth to say them. When they finally came out, he wondered why he hadn't said them earlier. They were so right. He loved her more with every passing day. And seeing her light up at their sound gave him such an exhilarating rush that he picked her up and spun so fast that she had no choice but to wrap her arms around him. His wild heart, intoxicated by young love, would move mountains for her.

As he set her down, she pressed her cheek against his chest, embracing his unspoken promise.

Yes, he loves me, he will protect me.

We will stand strong together.

I will no longer have to fight alone.

As they embraced in the fading candle light of the marble entryway, Phineas holding onto her delicate frame with love's possessiveness, an intruder entered—fear tapped on his shoulder, sending a bitter chill down his spine.

It was a matter of time, he knew. He only held tighter. Thoughts of the future taunted him. As the candles died one by one and darkness prevailed, Phineas knew he had to let go.

Come hell or high water, love would prevail. He willed it with every fiber of his being. He vowed it. And he prayed to God for this to be true.

A certain change had come across his face, and Emilie could not even pretend to know what it meant. But the blissful evening hours easily overcame any fleeting perturbations of this singular moment. Saying their goodbyes, she smiled the entire way to her room. She had not yet told him that she loved him, but she would. Tomorrow was another day.

Chapter 12

*S*he wished to linger in her dreams when morning came. Falling asleep in the security of Phineas's love did elicit the pleasantest sort of dream there was. They were together in her sleep world, running through the sunlit fields of summer toward a river where both Father and Momma awaited, beaming with happiness over their coming. The light cast down all shadows and the breeze played with things airy and light. An otherworldly peace permeated the air as perfect rest covered her parents' features. Emilie strained to hear the words they mouthed, but could not due to the limitations of this particular dream. She thought she saw Father instructing her to stay strong, but could not be sure.

As if happening in real life, she awakened with the sense of straining her ears to hear. The dream was brief, but the impression lasting.

Emilie refused to open her eyes, clinging to the dematerializing vision of her parents wading in the sparkling waters of the river. Happiness of a supernatural sort defined them. She wished she could touch them, look into their eyes. And what were they saying? She couldn't shake the significance of it all.

A dream is but a veiled picture from another realm. She had heard it said that some have had miraculous encounters in their dreams that changed their lives, and had they not dreamed such a dream their life would continue unchanged. Whether this one was for Emilie's comfort for a coming time, she did not know. But the all-encompassing bliss of the four was unmistakable. And Phineas loved her. This was as true today as it was last night. Then, as if in a final impulse to commemorate the significance of this experience, she took her notebook and began to write. If she waited any longer, the invisible ink of the dream would be all but gone.

Mim, expecting Emilie to be asleep, had just quietly crept into the room to begin her morning workings in preparation for the day. But seeing that Emilie was propped up on pillows writing something in her notebook, she crossed the room as was her custom and swung open the heavy curtains. "Mornin', Miss Emilie." She smiled. "What you doin'?" Standing tall with arms across her chest, hair tucked under a crisp white cap, Mim was glorious. Emilie often thought how remarkable she was, considering the abuses of a past owner.

Owner. She spat the word out. It was an eternally repugnant word. There were a billion other words to use.

"I had a dream, Mim, and my parents were in it, and..." She froze as crimson red colored her cheeks.

"And, miss?" she pried mischievously. "I think I know who else, miss," she grinned as she worked through Emilie's closet, looking for the perfect dress. "Will that someone else be here today? What dress shall we surprise him with today?" She giggled into the lacy belongings of Emilie's wardrobe.

"Oh Mim, what do you know?" Emilie teased back. The two young ladies appreciated their private times. They confided in one another their lived experiences and learned about the world in this way. Mim reveled in Emilie's stories about the life of an English noblewoman and dreamed of one day living just as well. Emilie absorbed every word about Mim's past—her life in Africa as a young girl, the day when she was relegated north, her first experience as a slave girl (which was too painful to speak of lightly), and now her experience on the Fox estate. Every opportunity they had to speak convinced Emilie over and over again that she utterly despised one man owning another. Phineas crossed her mind. She knew he felt the same. Butterflies unreservedly swept through her, inspiring a shy smile.

"So tell me then, miss, why you smilin' nonstop as you are? Is it because he could not stop staring your way last night? Or because he didn't want to stop dancin' with you?"

"Oh Mim, yes, all of these things are true. He told me he loved me last night. Mim, he said that I'm the only one he's ever loved and that he wants to live life together with me. Can you believe it?" she finished as Mim sat on the side of her bed, took her hand, and said that she could easily believe it.

"Miss, you two were made for each other, so yes, I believe it. He is a good man, better than those that I've seen in and out of this house. They all so self-important in their eyes. Phineas be different. He shows strength and goodness. Emilie, in my culture man carry himself with dignity and honor. Honor for their brother. And every man is a brother. I see this in Phineas. I am happy for you, miss," she finished as a tear alighted on an emotionally overwhelmed face. Talking like this often brought tears to her eyes.

"Mim, I'm sorry..."

"Don't be, miss," she interjected. "Here I have learned much about the world. Nothing is wasted. I shall be free one day, miss. I feel it inside," she said, pointing to her heart. "But for now..."—she got up from the bed and turned to the wardrobe—"what shall we wear today?" Wiping stubborn tears away with her starched maid's apron, she smoothed out her dress, fixed her cap, and began to busy herself with the wash basin.

"Mim, I am so glad that we're friends," said Emilie. "I hope we always stay this way." And the two young women embraced to solidify a lifelong friendship. Mutual passion strengthened their bond, and the struggles of such passion unfulfilled interlocked their hearts.

They spoke of dresses and perfumes and where they thought she and Phineas would go today. Mim casually questioned if Lady Fox had given her approval, knowing full well that the woman detested a man without a large fortune. And although Emilie had trifled with these same thoughts before, she did no more than that. Now she recalled the day her aunt had read the requirements set forth in her inheritance bequeathed by Grandfather, emphatically underscoring that the man she would marry had to have both stateliness and good standing in all of England. Or, as Aunt Clarence generously interpreted during a later discussion, "an opportune man of good fortune."

Emilie's state of being the only daughter of Sir and Lady Forthyn necessitated the specifics of whom she was to wed and whom to avoid, as dishonest men often went after young ladies with large fortunes. And as her aunt was by personal request of Momma given guardianship over the inheritance until the time appropriated (her twenty-first birthday), she purposed to exercise this power radically.

Emilie brushed Mim's words—a recalcitrant stressor—aside and determined to extricate out of the bond of the inheritance in some way or other. She even considered joining the women who followed the abolitionist movement or writing for a living. If she chose a man of wealth, what joy would there be in a life where her passions and principles were ceaselessly scorned? If it were up to Aunt Clarence, Emilie would consign to marrying John Learson tomorrow, host a lavish dinner party the following week, and entertain England's parliamentary heads the week after, all while practicing the pianoforte, perfecting her Latin, and providing visual enjoyment to John's guests.

As safe as this was, she wanted more. *Much more.*

Voices outside her bedroom urged her up from the chair. Her blue dress flowed river-like across the floor as she crossed to the door. Violette, Carleighla, and Fiona stood in a huddle not far from her door, whether waiting for Emilie or hiding something from her, Emilie could not tell.

"Hello," Emilie began. "Are you waiting to go down to breakfast? I'll walk with you, if that's what you'd like."

Eyes wide, they nearly toppled over with their words. They couldn't speak fast enough.

"An unknown gentleman has brought a letter for Phineas this morning, and we were wondering what was in it, Emilie," reported Carleighla, willing Emilie to speak to it. They, as Emilie understood it, were hoping she knew something of this mysterious letter. Walking toward the dining room, they proposed idea after idea, every one of which Emilie dismissed as either too unlikely or plain ridiculous.

"He does not have a secret lover at the university, girls," she laughed. "That's going too far. How about we see what's going on downstairs?"

On arrival, Albert was heard planning the itinerary, still trying to entice Mick and Oliver to join. John was half-seated on the arm of an armchair, arms crossed, involving himself in discussion with Sir Fox, who was rubbing his stressed forehead. Phineas was seated a distance away in an armchair by a small table upon which lay a folded letter, rubbing his eyes, a crisp sheet of paper also in his lap.

Emilie separated from the girls quickly, briefly greeted the gentlemen, and inconspicuously made her way in Phineas's direction. This was not inconspicuous, of course, as curious eyes followed.

"Good morning, Phin," she began with a light curtsy. "How do you do?" Picking at nervous fingers, she was waiting for his sweet acknowledgement to assuage the concerns raised by the ladies. She hoped to pick up right where they had left off.

His face was distressed. "Emilie, good morning. I-I just received a summons to meet with my university staff today over in London. I can't say much or stay long, I'm afraid," he said, running a shaky hand through dark hair. "I'd rather hoped to have spent the day with you," he finished hoarsely. With furrowed brow, he rose from his chair and handed her the letter from the table. He held her hand longer than a man would proprietarily hold a young woman's hand, but he didn't care. Changes were coming quickly. He had hoped for one more day with her.

One more day to convince her of the man he was, and at least a full day's hours more to solidify her trust in him. But this was unexpectedly cut short by the urgency of the letter in his lap. Now his letter, penned quickly in desperation, was all he had.

"Emilie, please read this when I am gone. It seems this is not the first time I make such a request of you." He half-smiled with a pained expression. "I hope to be back the night of the dinner." At this, he kissed her hand and released it.

Emilie stood unfeeling, drowning in rapidly encroaching fear. "Phineas," she tried, voice tight, "is everything alright? Are you safe?" She tried to slow him down with a hand on his forearm, grasping for anything that would have him stay. His eyes were so disturbed.

Yes, this was unexpected. It was miserable. What made it all even worse was that she had no idea what was going on with him.

He stood with her for a moment longer as if ensconcing her image in his mind, tenderly closed her hands over the letter, bade a final farewell, and strode briskly across the room, stopping only to briefly address the rest of the room, which was busy with preparation for their imminent departure. The faster he left, the faster the business would end, and the faster he would be able to tell Emilie the truth.

"Everyone, I bid thee farewell. I must be off. Urgent business calls. See you likely in two days' time. I wish you well on your trip," he finished, and tipped his head briefly.

As he was turning to go, "Phineas, what's so urgent that you can't travel with the rest of us? What can possibly be so important?" started John deprecatingly. "We hope your secrets don't bring any of us harm," he finished, glancing protectively over at Emilie.

Phineas felt the blow, and having had enough of the man's insults over the past few days, was about to turn around to address the incendiary challenge, but seeing Emilie out of the corner of his eye, he could not. He could not bear to hurt her. Gritting his teeth, and for her sake alone, he responded in the manner of a respectable nobleman, gave a nod of his head, and left through the same doorway by which he first came days ago.

Outside in the crisp air of early winter, he thought of nothing and no one else but of Emilie as visions replayed in his mind. He remembered her slight figure standing there during their first encounter the day he had arrived with Mick and Oliver, fiddling with a flower that had fallen out of her hair. He thought of the evening they danced, when her innocence radiated like a gemstone and her beauty reached angelic heights. He heard her morning voice asking him how he was doing this day or that day. And he couldn't forget the look of dread in her eyes this very morning when he told her he had to leave. Leaning against a column as he waited for the carriage he requested, his jaw clenched. He hated himself for leaving her again. *How will she ever trust me?*

The enormity of the responsibility before him assailed his mind, as if the weight of earth's seas and oceans descended mercilessly upon him. Alone in the cold, he despaired. He wanted to explode. As if her pale face wasn't enough to bury him, every doubt and fear imaginable began to stifle his sense of purpose and direction. He wanted to give up. To not go.

But there was *no other way*. It had to be done. The lives of innumerable individuals depended on him. What was one man's loss if countless others gained?

The heart continued to beat in his chest and bleed. *What will I do if I lose her?*

And now that the carriage had pulled up to the front, he had no choice but to move forward. He picked up a small bag of necessities that had quickly been thrown together when the letter arrived and entered the carriage. His breath clouded the frosty windows so that he could not see the outside world. *How fitting*, he thought, *I cannot see.*

Phineas's journey to London began on a bitter winter day. The love of his life remained in a glowing, warm place, surrounded by people, of which some wanted her to succeed, others to fail, and one wanted her as his own. He winced.

He would go on.

Chapter 13

*L*ike vicious mosquitos on a miserable summer night, the ladies swarmed around Emilie with sharp questions that further perpetuated her own despair. They asked not because they cared for her well-being, but because they wanted to know what Phineas had said to her this morning. Searching for information with which to satisfy their need to know, they relentlessly trampled over her.

"What was the letter about? Who sent it? Emilie, did he say?" Like entitled school children, they pried.

John also approached with his own concerns, concealed by attention to her general well-being. "You look awfully pale, Emilie," he remarked as he guided her to an armchair. At this point Mick and Oliver, who had been convinced to travel with Albert and John to London, albeit for reasons of their own (for pleasure, of course), were gone packing.

And because John (being a man with a wealth of experience) in his mind believed that a young woman's heart could be easily guided to change course, he continued to pursue her. Now that the prime obstacle was out of his way, he determined to woo Emilie's heart all the way to the altar. He planned to capitalize on Phineas's secrecy and to play it against him. Being competitive by nature (whether at a game of cards, for instance, or at horse racing), he was not accustomed to losing; he fully expected to prevail in her heart.

Emilie, the beautiful and strong Emilie, mesmerized him to no end. He had never met anyone like her before. Whereas many of his contemporaries felt uneasy in the company of a woman who managed herself as effectively as she did in conversations as convoluted as theirs sometimes were, he was intrigued. And so he continued to build momentum with the severest intention to win her. Now with Phineas as good as gone, he did not think it would be so hard.

"Please, get this young woman a glass of water, you over there." He pointed to a young servant who was clearing the breakfast table. "Yes, you. She's feeling faint." As soon as he said those words, she did begin to swim around a mental black hole, willing with every fiber of her being to not go under. But the more she struggled, the smaller she felt, and then, as if letting go was the only thing left to do, she did.

Hearing hushed voices around her, she surveyed the surroundings through slitted eyes. She was in bed with Mim at her side and the three ladies sitting by her window talking in low voices. They thought she was sleeping.

Aunt Clarence entered the room with a servant girl carrying a glass of wine. "Is she awake yet?"

"She's rustlin around, my lady," replied Mim, who had jumped from the bed with hands clasped before her as soon as the lady of the house stepped into the room.

"Alright, I'm glad of it. Please have her drink this fully when she comes to herself," she ordered, and Mim willingly obliged.

Then suddenly, as if startled by gunshot, Emilie jerked to consciousness.

The letter.

Eyes shot wide open, she frantically scanned the bed and side table with as little commotion as possible so as not to attract attention to herself. Mim noticed her movements and was about to speak when Emilie signaled with wide eyes not to. The ladies were busy by the window, talking about new developments in the case against Forester and who they had hoped to run into at the winter ball, not minding Emilie in the bed.

"Have you seen a letter, Mim?" she mouthed quietly to Mim, who shook her head *no*. Then, by a stroke of genius, Mim boldly requested that the ladies leave the room so that Emilie could be changed into more appropriate attire now that she was awakening. Admittedly, it did bother at least two of them that a slave girl working as their servant would dare speak to them as Mim had just done, but they did not want to get caught up in having to help Emilie out of bed or into her clothing, so they left without another word. They owed her nothing.

Alone at last, Emilie asked Mim about the letter. She remembered the smooth sheet of paper in her hands as she stood before the large dining room window, watching Phineas's carriage leaving the property. She could not possibly know who had it or where it was. She needed to find it. When Mim answered that she had not seen any letter, she began to scramble out of bed.

"Miss Emilie, please slow down. We will find your letter, I promise. You had a faintin' spell where you fell down to the ground. Please take care so you don't fall again," pleaded Mim.

At these words, Emilie froze. The last thing she remembered was John's face from this morning. Had she really fainted? Her throbbing backside indicated that this was true. Rubbing her lower back, she accepted the wine Mim handed to her. "I had no idea that I actually fell," she retorted as the last bit of red wine went down. "How did I get to bed, Mim?"

"John brought you, miss. He carried you all the way here. And there was no letter with him or with the servants who helped," she claimed. "Perhaps it remains on the floor of the dining room? Miss, I'll head down there as soon as you're feeling better."

Emilie could only envision John's arms carrying her body here through the house. What was this emotion she felt? Was it a thrill over this man's desire to protect her from harm, constantly aiming to land within her heart with the things he said and did? He was faithful. His presence and pursuit tangible.

But wait, this was far less thrilling than it was terrifying. She was mortified that her heart could betray her and fall quite easily for the man who was constantly before her. Sorrow overwhelmed her. Would weakness overpower to choose the easier route? The intricacies of her current state were as inconvenient as the downpour of rain on a wedding day, or Christmas without snow. How she wished that Phin's arms had carried her, instead. She felt treacherously cheated. The more she rejected John, the more he stole into her heart. And the more Phineas revealed his heart, the farther he became. Was it just the inevitable happening, or did she have a choice?

It then dawned on her that John, too, had gone to London, and she was glad of it. She fretted meeting him after such an intimate experience, knowing quite well his hopes for her heart. Resoluteness was so evasive these days that she could only pray for strength when such moments of vulnerability came. Strength that she would choose well those things that mattered—such as how she would wait for Phineas.

Perhaps his letter would bring clarity. She had to find it.

Having used up several wet washcloths on Emilie's face and body when she was first brought to bed, Mim informed Emilie that she would shortly be back with more.

Not wishing to dispute with her stubborn caretaker, she waited for her to leave, then quickly climbed out of bed and crept out the door. She had one thing on her mind—to read his words penned hastily prior to leaving.

Down the hallway, past several bedchambers, through the library, past the south-wing piano room, and down two stairwells, she arrived at the dining room, which was at this time deserted save Lincoln arranging flowers on the table and Lady Clarence standing at the main window with her back to the door. Emilie did not wish to be seen by her aunt especially. She crept over to the armchair and table where she'd found Phineas this morning and began looking around the furniture. She would have gotten on all fours if the risk of discovery was not there. The place was tidied and back in order, his memory wiped away.

Then, as harshly as ten crystal vases crashing onto the marble floor, she heard, "Looking for this?"

In riveted horror, Emilie faced the spiteful visage of the woman chosen by her momma to be her guardian. Thoughts of tender Momma rushed through her mind as the stark contrast once again stood before her. *Oh Momma, this can't be what you wanted.* She was about to open her mouth to request the letter, but was sidelined.

"I see I've been blind to things, Emilie," Lady Clarence stated, running trembling fingers along the edge of the mishandled letter. "Have I not? Did I not swear an oath to your mother to care for you as I would for my own children? Yes, I did. Perhaps with this knowledge you will better understand what I am about to say to you." With these words, she transitioned smoothly to the next piece of furniture to her left, as if encircling her prey before the pounce. Also closer to the fireplace.

"Emilie, Phineas is not the man for you. He is a nobody from nowhere. He has nothing. He has accomplished nothing. Savonne Manor—our family name—will suffer greatly with the stain of such a man. Neither I nor Sir Fox approve. This must end. As soon as he leaves after the dinner, I forbid any further relationship with him. Do you understand? If you do not, I will personally ensure the forfeiture of your inheritance, for which your grandfather gave so much of his life. Your mother could not keep it due to her frivolous convictions. I wonder if you, too, will mishandle it. Please appropriate your convictions and behaviors."

The lifelessly still Emilie ran her eyes to and fro, searching in her memory what Momma had said about the inheritance. It all made sense now: Momma had left Savonne due to its intricate connection to the slave trade and her own father's proud involvement in selling slaves. This was how the family gained affluence. Momma, unlike Lady Clarence, could not continue living in support of the savage ways. Emilie remembered Lady June's words on that first day's journey to Kent. This was the sore point of contention between the sisters, why Momma ran north with Father and Lady Clarence stayed behind at Derbyshire, managing both estates until Emilie was of age to take over.

Savonne Manor was specifically intended for Emilie.

Although Momma did not openly speak of this piece of her history, she did pass on to her children the ability to love and respect all people atop the face of the earth. And as the pieces of this family story—now Emilie's story—were falling into place, a righteous indignation began to arise within her.

"Lady Clarence," she began, "I am my own person and will choose what I deem appropriate for myself. Thank you for your concern. You have with great success described your contempt for both myself and those dear to me. I shall no longer allow you to please yourself at my expense. May I please have what is rightfully mine and be on my way?" she finished, having met her aunt's gaze, and truth be told, leaving the woman uncomfortable in such a position. Arm outstretched, Emilie willed Lady Clarence to give the letter, but instead, the woman walked over to the fireplace and dropped it into the flames.

"No!" Emilie cried, fists clenched. "How *dare* you?" *This wasn't supposed to happen!*

"Don't trifle with me, young lady, or else you will see worse than that," she released in a low growl. Then, as if nothing had been done, shoulders straight and chin up, she clasped her hands in her usual manner and finalized the encounter. "I'd better see you at the dinner party. Lady June, your brothers, and—" She paused, refraining from mentioning Phineas. "And others will be there. I don't want any questions asked on your account, do you understand me?" she stated, eyeing Emilie, who stood silently, face turned away. "Very well, then. Let your silence speak for you." And she left the room.

The more Emilie gained understanding about the people and the ways of her current world, the smaller she felt.

If her heart began to feel, it was beat down.

Her voice, the one piece she felt was gaining in strength, was silenced.

Giggling voices and piano songs reverberated around her from a not-too-distant room in the house, taunting her with memories of yesterday.

Picking up her long blue dress and running to her room, she had made up her mind.

If the resplendent place of Derbyshire with its luxuries had so quickly become a prison cell for her, what did a true prisoner feel like? It took one to imprison another. England was rife with conceited overlords and owners who gloated at their human stock and played cruel games for their personal gain. What would it take to open their eyes to see?

She would run to the fields to find out.

Chapter 14

*I*n her room, she tried to explain her plan to Mim. She talked of how she needed to see how they lived, wanted to listen to their stories, and play with their children. Her speech was so flighty and pressured that Mim had to stop her in her tracks to ascertain whether she was ill after her fall.

"Miss Emilie, what you talkin' about?" she insisted with concern. "Did you find the letter? Did it make a request of you, is that what's happenin'? Why and where you runnin' to?"

"Mim, you'll find the chaff of the letter in the dining room fireplace," she said dismally, her body finally stilling. "My aunt threw it there." Speaking the words for the first time as she did caused a rumbling effect throughout her body; she began to weep convulsively about the hardness of this place, the loss of Phineas, and the burial of his final words that were now gone forever. She wept at the implacable injustice of one human being spitefully mistreating another, thinking at first of her own loss, and then, as often happens when pain meets passion, of the loss of countless others who had it far worse than she did.

She had lost the final words of the man whom she loved more and more with every passing day.

They daily lost their rights to humanity, freedom, dignity, and peace.

All the more reason to go, she affirmed.

"Mim, I'm going to the fields. I want to find them as they live. To speak with them and to listen to their stories. Oh..." She stopped as Mim's confused facial expression conveyed she had no idea who *they* were. "Mim, I'm going to visit *your people*."

Mim was dumbfounded. Her proprietress certainly did not have a single feminine fiber in common with other English noblewomen, but *this* different was in a realm of its own. Hands on her hips and feet apart, Mim began to shake her head as her eyes measured the greatness of the English lady before her. Horrid scenarios of what could happen to Emilie alone beyond the estate's property played out in her mind, causing shuddering down the spine. She kept shaking her head, staring at Emilie, thinking.

Finally decidedly, as if an older, wiser sister, she spoke, "Emilie, I can't have you going out there by yourself. You can get hurt. There are evil ones out there who would do bad things to a young woman alone. You must listen to me," she began, about to continue if only Emilie had let her.

"Mim, today showed me something. I live in this house, fighting for something I know very little about. It's quizzical, but my entire life feels like a journey to this—this *neverland*, a place where people are kind and where love truly does prevail. Perhaps I am foolish or perhaps I've heard too many fairytales where the heroine risks everything for the greater good. I am drawn to go *out there*, Mim, to meet the people whose fight I seem to have taken on. My momma fought for them in her own way. Even Lady June has done things like this before. You can't stop me, Mim, no you won't. I'm going whether you like it or not. Now, please stop gaping and do help me pack," Emilie finished, and was just about to turn to continue gathering a few certain items when Mim placed a strong hand on her shoulder and spoke words that forever solidified Emilie's resolve to one day facilitate her freedom.

"Emilie, what I meant to say is...I'm going wit' you," she said regally, as if a queen from a distant land across the sea.

Emilie dropped the bag in her hand and hugged the girl as if the two had just committed to freeing the slaves at the risk of personal demise. Wiping twofold tears of fear and relief, the two in hushed voices discussed the details of their journey. Emilie had planned to go tonight, but Mim reported that the only way she could leave and be covered for is if they went early the next day, as she was needed to help prepare for a dinner the Foxes usually hosted this night of the week. Mim knew that Emilie would need her if she actually wanted to speak with the people working the land, and reminded her of the same.

Mim was to make arrangements with Lincoln and a couple of her trustworthy co-laborers so that if the Foxes asked, she would be protected. The risk was great, Mim knew. Lady Fox could throw her out to the wolves with the flick of a finger. But the potential of furthering the cause of her people—through Emilie, Wilberforce, and the others—fueled within her bones a fire greater than fear.

This night, as opulent dinners were served throughout the land and lofty conversations were had about the state of the nation's affairs (including prognosticative dabbling on the case of Forester—a friend to many, a business partner of most), Emilie and Mim pondered in their hearts about tomorrow's fate.

If vision was something to be gained through years of lived experience, Emilie was beginning to see more clearly. Her experiences thus far had been limited to discussions with sons and daughters of wealthy nobles, observations during afternoon tea time when guests who had traveled all over the known world would visit Derbyshire with their exhilarating tales, and interactions with people like her aunt, whose statuesque facade contorted at the slightest mention of change.

Momma fled the lifestyle a half a day's journey north. She married Sir William Forthyn, a simple man of adequate fortune begot by his own two hands (the newspaper business where a man worked as a man, never a slave), and time showed a wonderful father and husband. Against her sister's wishes, she left the comfortable existence offered by her own father's bequeathal. But, Emilie now saw, her family name today demanded more than just fleeing north. Her mother's decision so many years ago planted seeds that gave way for the unrest to develop purpose in her own children. Tomorrow she, an Englishwoman, would extend a hand of peace to the African man. She too would run, but instead of north and away from it, she would run to embrace the truth of it. She couldn't shut off the images dancing in her head.

Thinking about how her past was influencing her future, Emilie smiled. *Momma, you were so brave to be first.* Emilie realized how much she had missed her parents and the home of her childhood. She missed the purity of an uncomplicated life.

Tomorrow was her day of discovery, when she would once and for all experience for herself the fate of her African contemporaries slaving on the land of England. She braced herself for a long day and anticipated the many stories she would share with Phineas on his return to Derbyshire for the big dinner.

Phineas, she knew, shared just as passionately the same convictions as did she; this was why the Forthyns and McGrays held such a lasting friendship. Despite Lady Clarence's threats, Emilie promised herself time with him. She wanted to hear about his business in London and to tell him about her exploration of the fields of Kent's laborers. More than anything, she longed to be with him.

But thoughts of current complications stifled the excitement within. Concern crept onto her brow, and suddenly things weren't as clear anymore. Her aunt's words left no room for the possibility of change. Perhaps Lady June could help. She had done so before.

Her final thoughts before sleep were about how she and Mim would manage to escape Derbyshire without getting caught, what would Lady June think, and how Phineas was doing tonight...

Chapter 15

"Shhh." A rough hand covered her mouth as two bright eyes implored she be quiet. Mim. "Lady Clarence is up," she whispered fiercely.

Emilie, still recovering from the harsh awakening, could not figure out the hour of night it was. Everything was pitch black. "What time is it?" she mouthed.

"Early, Miss Emilie," was the response. "Early enough that we not be found out. We must go soon, before the herders and land-workers awaken. If they be up, their dogs will be on our backs quick." She spoke as one with experience.

Emilie forced herself out of bed, understanding that time was at their back, too. Quietly slipping into the plain dress laid out the night before, she washed her face and allowed Mim to wrap her hair so as to not get in her way. Putting on her overcoat and taking a long, raggedy shawl for concealment and warmth, they slipped out the door of the bed chamber and tiptoed down the long, dark hallway and through a hidden door reserved for the servants. From within the darkened inner hallway, they suddenly heard footsteps coming toward them in the outer one.

Leaning against an inlet in the wall, they died to a silence. It was Lady Fox walking with Lincoln, asking him why she was hearing noises so deep into the night.

"Are you sure one of the servants isn't out and about somewhere, Lincoln?" she snapped. "I swear, I heard someone scurrying down this hallway."

"Yes, Lady Clarence, they all be sleepin'," he replied dutifully. "Last I checked they was."

She lifted her candle to his face, scouring his face with piercing eyes, showing neither pity for his age nor concern for his wariness.

"Very well, then, if you say so. If I hear another sound, I will personally count them all myself to be sure we're all truthful here," she informed him, storming hastily away toward the hallway where her bedchamber was located.

Lincoln, knowing how close they had come to being discovered, slowly exhaled and muttered, "Praise ye, Lord," as he turned into the same door the other two had just entered. As his eyes met theirs in the dark corridor, he grinned and whispered, "Come on now, and God be with you."

And in order to cover for their footsteps, they walked slowly in his shadow until they got to the ground floor, where the floor absorbed sound better than upstairs. Mim knew exactly which door was quietest and so led the way to the outdoors which, when they arrived, hit them with sobering cold.

They tiptoed along the shadowed parts of the house, under every portico, then bolted toward the garden, where long, moon-drawn shadows served as protectors. Lady Fox's bedroom was on the opposite side of the estate, which gave the ladies some degree of comfort.

The two walked briskly in the dark along the tree-lined road that Emilie knew well at this point. She remembered her talks with John as they enjoyed the serene autumn scenery of Kent. She was so new at Kent then, enjoying its immense beauty. This was an entirely different experience.

They would stop if they heard any questionable sounds, hiding in the bush until they were certain the source of the sound had passed them by. Generally it was an old merchant on his way toward the city's marketplace to get the best lot that comes to the early risers, or a younger coach driver driving his drunk master back home. They could not risk any exposure.

The longer they walked, the gladder Emilie was for Mim's company. Her so-called servant girl knew more about these parts than she did. What's more, Mim had been preparing her for the specific houses they would visit, as she knew the people living there. The first one, Emilie soon learned, was the home of Sam and his sister, Judica, who had been tilling this land for five years now. The hut was but a few yards ahead when Emilie asked Mim how appropriate it was to awaken them.

"Emilie, they up, trust me," retorted Mim with a knowing face. It dawned on Emilie then that this was their normal rising time. With shadows and stars as their guides, the ladies stepped up to the door, with Mim knocking with the tip of her forefinger. After a few seconds of scuffling feet upon a creaking floor, the door opened a razor-thin amount with a man's voice asking what was wanted. "It's me, Mim. Open up, Sam," she whispered.

And he did. The next moment Emilie stood in a dark, cold hut with scarcity written all over everything. A ragged blanket lay on the floor in one corner, and a couple of rough, dirty towels lay on a chair in another. Next to the chair were two cracked bowls, broken but clean. A faint candle was lit near the door, and the windows were covered with a tarp-like material. Emilie felt rather irrelevant standing here in this hut with Mim and two other African slaves; the disconnect seemed irreparable. She could not comprehend how to reconcile the vastly different realms of her world. Yet here she was.

Memories of Momma's stories of brave noblewomen bringing good to the earth, of Lady June's adventures with leaders of state who could give no answer for the practices their own souls secretly detested, and of Sir Wilberforce's pursuits for a freer humanity coupled with her experiences at Derbyshire reminded her of why she had come here in the first place.

Daylight was on the rise. Every moment counted.

Extending her hand to the young man with deep voice, she began, "Hello, I'm Emilie Forthyn. I've come to Kent from Suffolk to learn a thing or two about being an English noblewoman. I've come here to start. What are your names?" she asked, lowering her hand when he made no effort to accept it.

The young woman with him picked up the candle and looked closer at Emilie, then at Mim. She could not fathom why an English noblewoman would be standing in her hut at this hour of night; she was wondering whether this was a deep dream and whether Emilie was an angel.

"Judica, this is my noblewoman who is now my friend. I've told you 'bout her, 'member? Sam, Emilie wish to see for herself what the slave trade is. I brought her here first. Please, give us a moment of time, we will not stay long," she requested, looking him directly in the eyes.

Emilie could tell Sam was hardened against the Englishman. He barely looked at her.

"Sam, I've not come here to spy or to bring harm. I wish to understand what your life has been like since leaving your home country. I believe I can carry your story and the stories of others like you to places where it can count. My mother left behind a lavish estate called Savonne located but a few kilometers from here, and an inheritance that could easily supply for one's needs for ages to come because she detested the slave trade that England—that her father—had embraced. I did not know her full story until I came here this past fall. Since my parents have passed, I am learning of the horrors of your people and wish to bring about some good. I wish to meet with Sir Wilberforce one day. Have you—"

"My sister and I come from Senegal on the west coast of Africa," he let out so sharply that the atmosphere split. He had heard enough from Emilie, willing himself to believe her, sensing the innocence with which she came. "My mother and father and two other sisters were taken to the West Indies to work on a sugar plantation, but Judica and I were taken here. I know not what has happened to them now. In Africa, I was the nephew of Kalith, our tribal leader. Here, young English boys spit at me, use a whip against me for nothing I've done, and yell at me to work faster. My sister"—at this he paused, brow furrowed, seeing visions that only his eyes could see—"she has been hurt more times than I can say by the older men." He looked her in the eyes then, a deeply rooted helplessness encircling them.

He was likely Albert's or Oliver's age, a young man with a strong build. Fear stole the youthfulness his face should have exuded, an inexorable expression of pain having settled in its place. As a man he cared not so much for himself, but for his sister, whom he could not protect. His manhood had been stripped away by incessant and unexplainable torment; his compass for what was normal had been destroyed. He lived to survive. As did his sister.

After a few more moments of talk and as rays of sunlight began to pierce into the dusty hut, Emilie and Mim had to move on so as to not be seen. After quick hugs between Mim and—Emilie quickly learned—her dear friends, Sam extended his hand to her. His shake was firm and trusting, as if he had transmitted to her the undying force of life bound deep within him and his entire family. In her presence he felt like a man again, for she assessed him with the eyes of a fellow being created in the image of God, not a man denigrated to nothing.

"Godspeed," he said with a quick bow of the head, and quietly shut the door.

It was around six in the morning, based on the sun's position in the sky. Having reached the main road Emilie walked in silence, keeping close to the unforgiving sharp shrubbery to the left of the road. Mim led the way briskly as Emilie followed, lost in thought. Her breath came in soft plumes as her nose fought the biting cold.

They briefly stopped by another hut, where a woman and her son lived. Rosa and Thomeus had been taken from Sierra Leone twelve years ago. They shared a hut with an even older woman named Persy, who had lost her husband and children ten years ago when the English invaded her home by the Niger River, taking her north and shipping them to the Americas.

They all seemed to exist by the hour.

Still, as broken as they were, they never gave up on hope, and sounds of unrest that had been reaching their ears stoked the lowliest embers of hope's fire.

Can an entire country change? Emilie kept asking herself. *If Sam's story is heard, will it change their hearts? Will Rosa's open their eyes?* She continued to deliberate, lost in thought.

"Careful, miss," warned Mim just as Emilie was about to walk into a low-hanging tree branch. "You'll have explainin' to do if your face be all scratched up. You can say 'I fought a dog' if you wish," she finished, chuckling at Emilie. She allowed the freshness of the morning light to flood her face. "Let's see, where is the ol' general's place?" she trailed, thought half-finished, searching the land on the other side of the road. She leaned against a large tree trunk, scanning the sparsely scattered huts out in the open field beyond the line of trees.

Emilie felt nervous at the prospect of running across the field with no trees or shadows to cover for them. "Mim, are you sure? We'll be right out in the open. Anyone can see us…"

"I know it, miss, but you've got to meet him. If anyone does, he's got the story for you," she alleged, looking to her left and right before running across the road to the other line of trees.

Emilie did the same. It was bright enough to see clusters of workers out in the fields with men on horses surveilling them. Emilie heard the occasional crack of a whip. She was so grateful that the Fox estate did not employ such measures; they were to be praised at least for this.

Looking back toward Derbyshire, she wondered what would happen if Mim was found out. *No*, she could not afford such thoughts right now. She needed to hear these stories. She planned to document them in her notebook and to offer them to Wilberforce as her part in the abolitionist movement.

The two young ladies appeared unsightly in old gray dresses with worn shawls covering their heads and backs. They may as well have been servants sent on errands by their masters. Emilie felt exhilaration building as she and Mim took their first step toward this "old general's" cabin. Instead of running, they chose to step slowly up to his doorstep so as to convince all that they were merely dropping in for work purposes or bringing clean water for the old man. He was in his nineties.

Again knocking gently, Mim prayed that he was home, alive, and well. She had not heard otherwise.

A moment later, the termite-ridden door opened to present an old, crippled man hiding his face from the light. It took a moment for Emilie's eyes to adjust to the darkened interior.

"General?" asked Mim, hopeful he still remembered her.

He squinted his eyes, craned his neck to adjust his sight, and then half-cried, half-wept, "Mima! My dearest Mima. Beloved."

She came over to him and allowed him to fall on her neck, holding him up with every bit of strength she could muster. "Yes, it is I, General. And I brought a friend." She waved for Emilie to enter and to shut the door behind her. Before proceeding with the conversation, Mim peeked out through a crack in the wall to ensure no one had been attracted by their coming. Coast clear. "General—" she began, but was unexpectedly interrupted by the old man's silent albeit emotional weeping.

Then, to her surprise, he said the following, "I know why you's here, my child, and I know why she here. Work has to be done, thas why. Things are shakin' because change comes nearer. I feel it in my bones. I will not be here much longer, Mima, so you must do the work." Then, to Emilie's astonishment, he turned to her and took both her soft pale hands in his cruelly overused ones and spoke every word with calculated measure. "It will take you and those like you to bring this change. Do you hear, child? God don't hate color. He made it so. He see the heart. He love color. You... Tell me the name again?" He paused with the question, leaning closer to Emilie's face, intently studying its features.

"Emilie Forthyn," she responded as emotion welled up within her. His eyes, now so near to hers, spoke volumes and tomes on behalf of the suffering of his people.

"Emilie...*hmmm.*" He closed his eyes as he spoke it. "Emilie *Forthyn*... Yes, yes, I see it now. You are not too different from your mother." He let the words drop softly, recognizing the immense power they carried.

"Y-you knew *my mother?*" Emilie stammered with even greater astonishment now.

"I have been living here at the foot of the Fox estate since your mother was a young woman, dear one. We all hear the tale of two sisters. One who loved a life of luxury, and one who hated what it cost. When your mother left north, your aunt's behavior cast a shadow upon us all. And now, it seems," he said as a smile spread upon his face like the light of dawn spreads across the becoming sky, "it seems that it is your turn."

With trembling hands, he continued to hold hers as he retold his beginnings. He spoke of his father training him to one day become his successor as the general of one of Africa's armies to protect their way of life. That was who he became. His wife, he said with a distant look of longing in his eyes, was of royal lineage. Their sons and daughters were important members of the tribe, bringing about change for the good of the people. His grandchildren were many in strength and number; they were his pride and joy.

One calamitous day the sun stood still as death came to their land, for, he acknowledged, a spear cannot resist a rifle. His people were either brutally murdered or wrapped in chains to be taken across the sea as soulless bodies for labor. He never saw his family again.

As Emilie watched and listened, she heard everything. Beyond his spoken words, she noted the effects of years of questioning *why* this would happen to his people, after that more years of resoluteness to keep going *in spite of* the happening, and lastly she saw a hint of hope as he spoke directly to her about the purpose found in her passion. He would say things like, "You are your mother's daughter" and, "Listen to your heart"—the precise things she had heard her entire life.

She loved this wise old man. He knew her mother, or at least knew of her. The connection was so enigmatic that she could not help but feel the hands of destiny working out her path. His life, now shared with Emilie, engaged her heart and soul so deeply that, like a womb of nine months, something new labored to awaken. He was getting tired, she could see, but he continued to pour life-giving encouragement upon the seedlings of purpose, knowing full well this may be his only opportunity.

Then suddenly, out of nowhere came a hard knocking on the side of the hut. A horse brayed. The three went still.

"DeLeone, it's high time you've started your work. What's the delay? And who's in there with you?" the stone-cold voice demanded.

Emilie was about to move forward, but was forced by the two of them to hide behind a blanket hanging over a metal rod. Mim sharply put her finger to her lips and shook her head, indicating that she should stay hidden.

"Forgive me, sir," answered General DeLeone humbly as he emerged from his hut, hands up in request of mercy.

The man on the horse waited for Mim to come out. He knew he had heard another. "Who's this?" he demanded. There was not an ounce of mercy in his voice.

"My name is Mim, sir," she began with downcast face and voice. "I work on the estate. I come to fetch ol' General some supplies. Please forgive my not askin' to come." Finishing, she clasped her hands before her as she usually did, standing as still as a deer before the kill.

The next thing Emilie heard caused her to weep louder than she ever had, though no louder than silence allowed. Others had joined the first-comer by this time.

She heard endless thuds and cracks of a whip, with groans and whimpers that reminded her of the man they encountered on the first day of her journey to Kent, the one beaten by an enraged owner. The one she couldn't forget.

She curled up as small as possible and rocked back and forth on the floor of the empty dirt hut, trying to drown out the sounds. Then, to her horror, "Toss him in the back of the barn," the original voice said. "Take *her* back to the estate. I'd like to see what Lady Fox would say to this."

Straining her ears, she could not hear anything that would indicate Mim was alive. And her new friend, the sweet old man whose furrowed brow and trembling touch carried more history than she could ever read of in her books—he was gone.

Curling up into the drafty corner of the empty hut, darkness began to swallow every last bit of hope. *This is all my fault*, she anguished. *Old General is gone. And Mim...what about Mim?*

She lay as still as possible for what seemed like hours, not wanting to move for fear of someone standing and watching over the hut. She felt like a caged animal going mad as the dirty walls continued to close in. Fear encroached upon what sliver of light was visible through the tattered drapes covering the windows. Old General had spent countless days in this exact space, dreaming, hoping, believing. Now he was gone! She sobbed then, every bodily fiber trembling. As she feared being heard, the sobs came out silent, violent shaking compensating for the missing sounds. She ached all over. She longed to be held.

She questioned every single one of her motives until a delirious emptiness set in; fatigue and hunger had stopped her from thinking anymore.

She knew she had to get back, but the idea of leaving this cold, lifeless corner was so insurmountable that surely she would just lay here and die.

But how would she explain her absence? Lady Clarence would instantly implicate her in Mim's incident, which may potentially cause Mim more harm, as she would likely be blamed for the idea.

Fears surrounded her like crazy wolves, but she knew she had to go back. There was no other choice.

Then, against her will, an even greater darkness came.

She awakened to the sound of footsteps walking past the hut where she lay hidden. Laying still as a rock, she strained to hear what the voices were saying. She couldn't determine the hour of day, or whether it was even the same day, but it was dark.

"Poor bastards," a rough voice said semi-compassionately, "they think Forester's case is their saving grace. They sure are acting up nowadays." She heard him spit like laboring men often do.

Then the other, "Don't I know it. Too bad for them he's covered, fully insulated against the lot. I feel bad for 'em, Will. Why can't they just get along and go along? They got what they need, don't they?" he said sneeringly. Then, "It's late, let's clear the hut out tomorrow. Arnold said he'll settle in another lot soon as the newest shipment arrives." And like that they were off toward the main house adjacent to the field, talking profits, women, and Irish beer.

She had heard it from their mouths. Forester was insulated from a conviction. The pangs of hunger, thirst, and exhaustion tore at her, making her normal daily movements unforgivingly unbearable. Hoisting herself up with the help of the metal rod above, she gripped the wall for stability. Stiff as a board, she began to stretch her spine and extremities to mobilize again. Her head spun. *No*, she instructed herself, *not this time*. Breathing deeply in and out, she braced herself until equilibrium set in. Half her body had fallen asleep being curled up in one position almost an entire day. She limped over to the window facing the house, inspecting the grounds. Fully lit up, the house was full of life. Then she saw the barn and her heart sank.

She thought of the man, the *true* general, who lived for others and died by the hand of an oppressor. At that moment, as images of Persy, Sam, Judica, and the others filled her mind, she vowed to embrace the destiny that was so horrifically birthed today. She felt like a new woman—a bolder, wiser, stronger one than yesterday, or even this morning.

She could not yet ascribe words to this day, and until she returned to the safety of her room she could not allow herself to even feel the fullness of her emotions—rationalization would have to wait. It was time to focus on one thing: getting back.

Tilting her right ear to the house to listen, she slowly pushed the door open and stepped out. The moon was high in the sky, casting a long shadow off the lonely little hut. The shadow wasn't falling in the direction she needed, however, causing nervousness to arise. *What if they see me?* she pondered as panic restrained her legs. Standing there against the doorpost, before setting off in the direction of the main road, she touched ol' General's cabin, promising to play her part in the destiny of his people, praying to glean strength from the man who once lived there. Then, with the sound of laughter to her right and shadows of demons to her left, she bolted forward in the fastest sprint her legs had ever undertaken, trailing a dust storm from behind. Whether any one saw her or not, she could not tell. She had to touch those trees.

Seizing the crude bark, she swiftly slid behind the trunk, catching her breath while listening for followers. Aside from a scurrying night creature, though, all she heard was the musical rustling of glossy gray leaves and an occasional, almost imperceptible sound of human life coming from the huts on the field. She surmised that the tired laborers were preparing for bed. Thinking that they would soon discover ol' General's missing body, she began to retch violently. The irreversible damage was too much to bear.

Suddenly she recognized the bright tinkling of bells from a horse's reins, and quickly turning saw a fast-paced carriage bolting in her direction. There was nowhere to hide. Eyes wrought with fear, vomit on her chin, she felt like a squirming, wild thing searching frantically for an escape from imminent demise. The trees along this side of the road were naked, standing sparsely side by side, and running to the other, more protected side was impossible, as they would easily see her.

With nowhere to go, she looked up. Then, with no more than a minute until the carriage accosted her, she jumped for the lowest branch and swung herself upward toward the next. With feet steady on a solid branch, she climbed higher, moving her body behind the trunk where she was less visible. With the passage of the unsus-pecting carriage full of rowdy men and women beneath her (most likely leaving dinner at the Foxes), she slid her body back around the trunk away from their line of vision, and figured two things. One, it was likely around ten o'clock in the evening, as that was when such dinner parties typically ended, and two, she had better make a run for it, as more carriages would likely follow suit.

Descending the tree proved harder than ascending, as every part of her clothing became entangled and torn by the tetchy branches. Cold, weak, and achy, she dropped to the ground like a sack of potatoes. It hurt to fall from a tree. Crossing to the other side, she walked in the shadows of the thicker trees and shrubs. When she would see a carriage coming, she would lie prostrate under the shrubbery with the shawl as her cover. The gray shawl fit right in against the early winter shrubs. Once the carriage passed, she'd immediately resume her pursuit of the estate.

She knew that going through the garden was the safest, most discreet way. The Foxes at this time were likely sending their guests homeward, saying their farewells as carriages arrived at the front entrance.

Yes, she was exactly right. She spotted a cluster of sparkling gaiety at the entrance with guests shaking hands and exchang-ing expressions of gratitude. Off she went toward the lowliest back entrance.

Fumbling with numb fingers for the knob, she leaned her head against the cold door, too exhausted to turn the heavy handle up as they usually did. Then, she heaved upward. Locked. Hot tears began to roll down her cheeks. She was so close. Stuck behind the servants' door, she began to guess what they would say to her, about her. Didn't they know that *she* involved Mim in the outrageous scheme? Would they despise her for Mim's suffering? Her restless mind began to paint all sorts of scenes where she was utterly scorned by the servants, despised for her foolish ideas, and blamed for the loss of their friend.

Leaning forward, she tapped the door like Mim did on the field. *Tup-tup-tup.* Again. *Tup-tup-tup-tup.*

Please, she pleaded. *Someone please help me.*

Exhaustion had brought her to her knees by now, head leaned up against the door. All she wanted was her bed with her sweet friend brushing her hair and sharing her stories.

Ahh yes, she thought, *stories. I have stories now.* Her eyes became heavier as her body began to find comfort as a heap of flesh upon the ground.

As she was beginning to give in to the urge to shut the world out, the door opened. A hurried Lincoln, whose bright eyes were rapidly scanning his left and his right, lifted her by the arm with the strength of a man in his prime and began to hurriedly walk her toward one of the secret hallways. "Wait here," he insisted in a firm but gentle tone. "I be back, miss."

And with that, he left.

A few brief moments later, he did return with a cloth with what appeared to be food and drink. "Let's go, miss, get you to your room as quick as we can. You need to eat and rest."

The thrill of finally being safe was so overwhelming that Emilie sobbed quiet tears while following Lincoln's footsteps through the dark corridors. She didn't care how she looked. The inner turmoil was so great that it drowned out all reason and practicality. If only the others had seen her now. Would they deem her worthy of the title of an English lady? A lady of propriety?

The same questions of purpose and motives followed her through the winding hallway.

Did she have to do what she had done? Could good come out of the day's experiences? And could she ever redeem the indescribable loss of ol' General, the man who encouraged her to follow her passionate heart as they sat atop a cold floor in a hut on the field where he labored not as a man, but as a slave? How perfectly unexplainable certain experiences could be. Then, hit with the startling realization that she might have had to spend the entire night outside, she asked with strained voice, "Lincoln, were you waiting for me? How did you know to come to the door?"

"When Mim come back without you, I knew somethin' had happened. Something bad. So I've been running to this door all day hoping to find you as I did. God kept you, sweet one. We prayed for you to come back to us." This hit a bleeding wound.

"Lincoln... Mim...?" Her voiced broke as pain and sorrow surfaced. "It's all my..." A beastly sob arose from within, preventing her from finishing the self-indicting statement.

Lincoln stopped and turned. Her brokenness didn't need empty assurances, it needed unconditional safety to just be as she was. He held her for some time, like a father holds his little daughter after the loss of an only friend or after a bleeding, scraped knee, except here the wounds were far deeper than in childhood. These would likely leave scars.

When Lincoln did finally speak, his timeless wisdom was like soothing balm to the pain she had been unable to escape. She had carried the heavy burden all the way here. "Little one, this world is steeped in darkness. So much so that one act of goodness might need to be tried many times over before it breaks through that darkness. Do you see? What you did today, you and Mim, you did with hope that one day some'ting good will happen. Not one of us here—Now hear me." He said, and tilted her chin up to face him. "*Not one* will look upon you with anger, because we know that you are playin' your part as you are able to now. Evil does not like to be spoken to or be asked to change. This is why the suffering. But take heart, little one, you will soon see the fruit of this suffering, as will many others." Then, as if speaking to himself, "Not long at all, in fact. I can feel it in my bones."

All Emilie could feel was strain, pain, and exhaustion in her bones. The closer they got to her bedchamber, the more she worried about missing Mim. "Lincoln, where is she?" she finally asked.

"She is recovering, little one. She will live, I know it. But we may not see her for some time." He silenced her next question with a finger to her mouth, stopping to listen to the sounds of the hallway.

Her familiar hallway. When he was assured of its emptiness, he opened the door and let Emilie run to her room. When she was safely behind her own doors, he stepped back into the inner hall and began his descent down the stairs. "We may not see her for a very long time..." he repeated. Walking downstairs, Lincoln wondered how Emilie's heart would change after today. He prayed for her then, asking God for a special touch on her life. "She'll need it, Lord," was all he could give for a reason.

Back in her own room, Emilie did not wait for anyone to come in to help her remove the dirty, odorous rags now stuck to her body. She wished Mim was here and that things were normal again. She tried to undo the back of her dress but couldn't, too tired to fight. She tried to resume the usual evening practices, but fumbled through everything she touched, an ache marking every movement of muscle.

What had she been thinking about prior to today? Dreaming about? She couldn't focus.

Phineas.

She felt so detached from her norm that she could not even picture his perspective on her current situation. Would he call her a murderer? A fool? Or would he understand?

She feverishly searched for his face in her mind, but couldn't find it. His words and ways were so elusive at this moment. She had experienced so much today which she could not even begin to describe to another, anyway. The experiences buried her under a massive mountain of reflections and questions, so much so that she could not feel her normal emotions. Collapsing onto her pristine bed, she dropped her head into dirty hands and wept. She felt like all was lost. Absolutely all.

She feared that she had lost Phineas. That she would crumble in times of weakness. That she would disappoint ol' General, the others...herself.

The door creaked open then, with a servant girl younger than Mim stepping inside. She had to tiptoe over to Emilie and stand right before her before Emilie noticed.

"Oh," said Emilie. "I'm sorry, I didn't hear you come in."

To which the other replied, "My name's Bailey, miss. Lincoln sent me. I'm here to help you prepare for bed." Then, after a moment's hesitation, "I'm sorry you's crying so hard. Would you like me to wash your hairs, miss?"

"Yes," she whispered coarsely, shaking her aching head. "Do you know where Mim is?"

"I'm sorry miss, we ain't 'posed to talk of it," she said, eyes down, hands clasped before her. She was frightened.

"I'm sorry," Emilie recollected herself. "Yes, please do help me wash up."

Bailey washed Emilie thoroughly but gently, scrubbing the dirt off and detangling her wild hair. She rubbed lotion onto her now softened skin and massaged lavender oil into her hair to help her sleep. The bath did help Emilie to relax and to begin sorting the mess within.

She knew what she had to do.

Thanking Bailey for her excellent work, she relieved her for the night. Climbing under her satin covers, Emilie took her notebook to release in writing the stories she had heard and lived through today. The front page held the dream from the night Phineas had told her he loved her. *Perhaps Momma and Father were telling me to hold on for this very reason, preparing me for hard times to come.* She pondered a bit longer on its profound significance and timing, and then began to write.

> The stories of Sam and Judica...Rosa and Thomeus...ol' General DeLeone...
>
> Ol' General comes from Africa a few decades ago. He was a high-ranking general in his region, trained by his own father and mentored by the village leader. This kindly soul lost his wife who was a royal, his two sons and three daughters, who were very esteemed members of their tribe, and several grandchildren whom he loved more than words can

say. He notes that the boys loved to build and to improve on ways to facilitate solutions to agricultural needs, and the girls were often seen occupied with the creation and selling of handmade goods (such as headpieces or baskets). He remembers the day his life changed, when everyone and everything he loved was torn from his grip...

Heavy sleep began pulling her under in a matter of minutes. In the momentary span of time between light and deep sleep, when hand loosened from pen and paper and weary head dipped, profound tears gently caressed her face. She wept for the tumultuous present she had been thrown into. She did not feel ready. Not at all.

This day Emilie Forthyn had for the first time encountered the brutality of cold-hearted humanity, something she had never faced in her life at Suffolk. But as unprepared as she was to handle the weightiness of the experience, she did not die beneath it. She kicked and screamed, wept and sorrowed, but still permitted the beauty of her gains to strengthen her. Those moments with ol' General, Mim's sacrifice, Momma's decisions, and Phineas's steady presence in her life intertwined to form a safety net. Messy as it all was, she was safe.

Chapter 16

After night comes day.
The day of the long-awaited dinner.

*E*milie awakened feeling physically sore and emotionally drained. Taking a deep breath in, she lifted her hands to inspect her fingers and arms. *Clean*, she thought with relief. She couldn't give the slightest indication that she was with Mim yesterday. Getting out of bed, she went to the basin to wash her face. Footsteps outside the door indicated that it was around eight-thirty in the morning, when house activities were in full swing and likely even more so due to tonight's event.

A wilting sprig of lavender floated upon the still cold water.

Not knowing whether Bailey would come, she began to look through her wardrobe for a dress. What could she wear to indicate to watching eyes that all was normal? And to suffering eyes that all would be well?

Yes, this is perfect. She pulled a long gown with flowers embroidered with the finest gold string, catching brilliantly in the light. Mim loved flowers, they all knew. This was for her.

A gentle knock on the door announced Bailey's arrival, for which Emilie was exceedingly glad. She spoke gently to the young girl, giving as much encouragement as she could without appearing insincere. Watching her tension subside told Emilie that this was ok. And under an hour later, Emilie was ready to go down to breakfast.

As she walked her usual route down to the dining room, she recited the ways of normalcy before stepping foot before them, reframing her mental state to what it was two or three days prior. The audience was exclusively female today. The men had not yet returned from London.

Now whether this was actually true or not and she was only imagining things, she did think that there was a heightened sense of kindness and respect from every one of the household servants with whom her path crossed. They bowed their heads a bit lower and longer than before, some placing a hand over their hearts as she passed them. What this meant she was not perfectly sure, but it resulted in an eased, confident posture of mind.

Walking into the dining room, she was herself surprised at the composure that carried her. "Good morning, Carleighla, Violette. How do you do?" she asked, reaching for her usual seat and requesting Lincoln to prepare a cup of tea. *All is as it was*, she repeated to herself over and over again.

"Fine. Glorious as usual, Emilie," responded Carleighla in an unusually edgy voice. "How are you? We were told that you stayed laid up in bed all day yesterday," she pressed. "John mentioned how sorry he was he had to carry you to bed." She seemed to insinuate that Emilie had planned the whole thing. Her eyes glowed with envy.

Then Violette perked up, as if her news was more interesting than her sister's. "Have you heard of what happened to that servant girl? Supposedly she was found out on the south fields, instigating trouble—"

Carleighla interrupted. "Of course she knows her, Vi. My sources tell me they were friends."

"Of course we were," Emilie returned evenly. "What does this have to do with anything? When you get to know someone, friendship is natural, is it not?"

"Under other circumstances it is, but..."

"But not when she is black and I am white?" Emilie emphasized coolly, facing Carleighla with the power of her lived experiences. She emanated an authority she was not yet aware of. But Carleighla noticed.

"Not exactly what I meant to say," she fumbled. "I don't believe we should maintain friendships with our servants, that's all." But inwardly she knew Emilie had hit the nail on the head. Truth be told, Emilie intimidated her, and today more than ever. Squirming under her gaze, she quickly changed topics to something more agreeable. "The men are due back shortly, right Vi? That'll be nice for a change; it'd be a horridly boring existence without them... Oh, what are you ladies wearing to dinner tonight?"

Emilie relaxed into her chair, understanding the change in dynamic. She was not as easily intimidated by Carleighla as she once was; she felt grounded and determined to chip away at this darkness, as Lincoln put it. While they expressed various qualms about their potential dress choices and even entertained wearing matching ones, gauging whether fresh flowers in the hair would be preferable to jewels, Emilie caught the mirthless echo of Lady Clarence's laughter in the nearby corridor.

Involuntarily triggered to attention, she coerced her shoulders and jaw to loosen, coaxing herself to stay coolly above the scrutiny, anxiously affirming that Aunt Clarence had no way of knowing anything at all, when suddenly the woman materialized right before them, poring over her with the razor-sharp skill of a shrewd diamond assessor. On the tip of her tongue was a single question that she ached to ask of Emilie, but quite visibly preventing herself, proceeded instead with a different one.

"Good morning ladies," she addressed the group, to which her daughters replied in upright unison that it was. "Emilie, are you feeling better? They said you needed a day in bed, so we let you be."

That was it! The extent of her aunt's knowledge of yesterday's events totally excluded the possibility of Emilie's involvement. Exhaling discreetly, Emilie let worry drop to the floor. Her approach was also more amiable this morning, due in large part to a realization of how poorly she had been treating Emilie. "Yes, Aunt Clarence, I'm quite well today. I thank you for allowing me the day I needed."

"Good. Now, I presume you have heard from your new servant girl that Mim is no longer with us?"

Emilie choked on a grape. She did not need to act or pretend. This was truly news to her. "Why so, Aunt Clarence?" she asked as indifferently as she could once the coughing subsided.

"This is news to you? I suppose they are all stunned into silence after what's happened," she remarked sensibly. "Mim was found snooping around the southern field, delaying work and causing trouble. The field master brought her here mid-morning yesterday, reporting as such. I'm surprised you did not know. Was she with you in the morning?"

"Yes, yes she was," Emilie responded slowly, distantly. *She was with me all morning*, she repeated to herself.

"Hm, she must have slipped out after you, then. As such, we have traded her back to her former owner, Charles Wimberton, and now have the new young one in her place. I've forgotten her name...?"

"Bailey," Emilie delivered absently. "Her name is Bailey."

Mim was back in the home of the man who had crushed her, stolen her identity. *It's my fault. I should never have gone.*

Lady Clarence mistook horrified shock for sadness. "Emilie, I have heard that she was good to you. You must understand, I cannot condone such intractable behavior on this estate. All must know that punishment for such behavior shall be...*grave*," she stated, emphasizing the word, then continued, "Servants are not meant to be friends, Emilie. You've got to understand this. Please keep this in mind with the new girl."

She arose then, as if the solemn news was nothing to fret about, and surveyed the three of them. "You'd better look your finest this evening, girls. We've got a full array of exquisite guests coming!"

Between Wimberton, who was known to abuse his servant girls, Forester, who was weakening the abolitionist force by stealing their money, and Sir Fox, who was a good man too weak to do anything about it, she floundered at the list of accomplices to be present at the dinner.

At the thought of sitting to dinner with people who determined the course of the country but had not the slightest sense of the value of a human life, she wondered what she could say to them to reach deeper than most would. Could she share her stories gained from the terror of the field, or could she convey Mim's lived experiences including the happenings of yesterday?

She knew she had to be careful, for her own destiny was now intertwined with these stories. How would she explain knowing them? And what if someone recognized ol' General or Rosa and insisted that she had spoken with them? They would know that she, too, was an accomplice in Mim's so-called treachery.

She would have to be more diplomatic than that. Based on her experiences of speaking with Albert, she discovered that men involved in the slave trade to any degree at all often responded defensively, escalating quickly to an angry momentum as their livelihood was being attacked. How could she bypass the defenses?

Hadn't she been told before that truth was on her side? And that, being on its side, she did not have to fight its battles but instead need only speak on its powerful behalf? She understood then that part of her role would consist of acquiring relationships with these so-called 'exquisite people' in sincere kindness and speaking truth when the opportunity would arise. She had already gained trust from many of the tea-time visitors who would likely be present tonight. They were drawn to her ideas, thinking them to represent some sort of platonic society, one as desirable as it was unattainable.

Pure perspective coupled with lived experiences, carried with the *true* dignity of an English lady, would now be her weapon.

As the ladies came to the end of their unhurried breakfast, Emilie excused herself to step outdoors. Fiona had just arrived with the expectation that the men would soon be arriving, and the three of them escaped to indulge their feminine graces. They invited Emilie, but were not at all disappointed when she declined.

Emilie instead went outdoors to sharpen her newfound sword.

For Mim and ol' General. For Momma. For thousands who desperately awaited change.

Sitting on the grand stone steps leading up to the front entrance, she held onto the high hope of seeing Phineas turn into the driveway.

Instead she saw florists, cleaners, bakers, and cooks scurrying about in preparation for the extravagant soiree. She heard plenty of, "Excuse me, miss," and, "Pardon, miss," and, "Good day to you, miss," as she observed the activity. They were often caught off guard to find a lady of the house sitting atop the cold steps. It was December, after all.

Cold and fullness of anticipation defined the morning's passing, and yesterday was beginning to feel like a fading dream from another realm. She could no longer demarcate ol' General's wrinkles as clearly, or feel the disparaging emptiness of each cabin. The more the normal pace of life settled in around her and safety surrounded her, the more surreal the experience became.

After close to two hours in the pure sunlight, covered with a warm overcoat brought kindly by Lincoln, she arose to go inside. To read or to write—she did not care. To do *something* to take her mind off the things grieving her heart.

Turning to go, she was most pleasantly surprised to see a familiar carriage turning into the driveway, now trotting toward the entrance. The elegant vehicle could only mean one person.

Lady June.

As the carriage approached, she quickly descended the stairs to meet the woman with the full respect due her ravishing nature. She missed her so!

"Why, I daresay darling, what a pleasure it is to see you! The cold colors you finely," Lady June claimed, lovingly patting her smooth right cheek. The two embraced as she assessed Emilie's person with great intentness, catching traces of something changed. "I had to return home to pick out my gown for the evening. I couldn't pick just one. Perhaps you can join me in my chamber and help this old lady decide?" The twinkle in her eye betrayed the simple request with something much more.

Emilie knew she was feeling the undercurrents of something different within her, and with immense relief grabbed the opportunity. She would tell her everything.

Lady June listened with utter horror to the things Emilie shared. The range of emotions she experienced could not possibly be fully accounted for: fear for Emilie's very life, pride at her indescribable fearlessness, sorrow at the unjustifiable loss of life, and anger that neither she nor anyone else of significance could be there to help her when she needed it most. She clenched her fists, welled up with deep-rooted tears, and strained her heart at every word. She paced about the room, perching both hands atop her cane when she could no more take it, then would turn and pace the other way, yelping in disbelief phrases such as, "The utter horror," and, "Good Lord help us all," as she went.

The gowns lay forgotten, tossed off to the side.

Lady June, fully aware of the sudden change that had overcome Emilie's face, walked directly to her and, cradling her head in her hands, spoke words that forever remained a pillar of strength within her. "Don't you *dare* think that any of this is your fault. Do you hear me?" She spoke with such intense passion that spittle sparked from her wrinkled mouth. "Look at me, Emilie. It's the fault of the world systems we have given power to. Little by little we allowed this evil neighbor to settle in one, then two houses upon our streets, then three, and soon all save a few could see its ways for what they truly were. You need to know you did no wrong, my love. Your actions were braver, more selfless than the vast majority of the men sitting comfortably in our Parliament. I'd like Wilberforce to hear of this. I will ensure he does, in fact, because it's stories like yours that will give power to the position of full abolition." And with that, she invited Emilie to sit with her in peace, resting upon her bosom.

Just like in days past, Lady June covered Emilie with unconditional love and acceptance.

Weary from its retelling, Emilie suddenly remembered one more piece of her story. "Lady June, I just remembered something that may be of importance. As I hid in the hut, I heard a couple of men jesting about how the slaves were becoming antsy, and I'm sure they said Forester was 'insulated' from them and that they stood no chance."

As she was about to finish with the question of what this meant for him, Lady June's face completely changed.

"I thought as much!" she bellowed. Then, quickly, "What exactly did they say, Em? Can you remember?"

"They said that he's covered—'insulated' is the word they used. It was as if they were confident that the abolitionists stood no chance against him."

"Yes, I'm sure he is. Those men likely have connection to men he has dealings with. Oh, Emilie. How do so few of us fight against this behemoth? I've felt from the beginning that something was not quite right about the case. I wonder what news will be brought back today? I'd like to speak with Phineas about it." At the mention of his name, Emilie leaned in harder and closed her eyes so hard so as to stop the tears. She would not show this weakness. She needed to weep for the weeping…for Mim.

As if in answer to the unspoken question, and based on the sore spot opened by the mention of his name, June comforted Emilie with the promise that Mim would be ok.

Chapter 17

With evening steadily approaching, Emilie continued to look out through various windows and doors for any sign of him.

He did not come.

The arrival of Albert and John's carriage did not improve her state of being. Her brothers, it turned out, decided to come back separately, or at least that was what Albert had said when asked where they were.

"Hello, Emilie," greeted John warmly. "I brought you something from London. May I show you? Are you quite occupied?"

His eagerness was too much. She could not find it in her heart to act in a way so as to stifle it. She had learned what brokenness was, and did not wish to propel anyone into such a place. Treading carefully, minding her words and body language, she maintained a cordial attitude as he led her to a chair for the two of them to sit on.

Carleighla, unexpectedly bumping into the pair, smiled bitterly, commenting on how pleased she was that they had arrived safely. Her disappointment was poorly hidden, however, as she sharply turned and stomped back to where she had come from.

John still aimed to win Emilie, and for this Carleighla hated her. She was the far better match, even if her mother had other plans.

Seated on the chaise by his large frame, Emilie could not help but feel small. John was older. Considerably wealthy. He was stable and in love with her. What more did she need?

As he removed a costly bejeweled brooch from a charming wooden box, he requested tenderly that she would wear it to dinner tonight. "It would please me so to see you wearing it, Emilie," he expressed hopefully. She did not know what to say. He searched her eyes. Looking into his, she searched her heart.

She could not bring herself to love him. He represented the very thing she detested. She had personally seen and now experienced the terror that was a daily norm for men, women, and children powerlessly enslaved under this iron-clad system. One perpetuated by John, Forester, Wimberton, their wives—and their children to varying degrees, yes, but if one even dabbles in darkness to the slightest degree, can they ever truly love the light? Can they carry the light to dark places?

In her mind, these two worlds existed. Could one claim loyalty to the one while at the same time espousing friendship with the other?

A house divided cannot stand.

For this reason, she could not look upon him with love.

Pity. She felt pity. In that respect, she accepted the brooch but made no promise to wear it.

She did not know how else to be with him.

Could he change? she wondered. She had witnessed glimmers of pure insight and understanding here and there, but were they enough to change his life? She could not tell.

She thanked him, curtsied politely, and went away to the library, followed by his lingering gaze.

She would wait for Phineas.

Chapter 18

After ticking and tocking impatiently all day, the clock finally struck seven. The moment of the first guest's arrival opened an enchanting portal that superseded every other lavish dinner that was had here. Soon, highly acclaimed guests poured into the house, each emanating power, excess, and wealth. The atmosphere exuded elegance of the highest kind, with perfectly seamless operations throughout and perfectly untainted manners within. Lights flickered flirtatiously, flowers fragranced ecstatically, and delicate wine glasses sparkled and clinked.

Endless laughter and gaiety had certainly found their resting place this evening. And if Emilie tried hard enough, she too could drink the wine of revelry tonight.

In fact, she did try.

Dressed in a primrose regency dress with elegantly cascading skirts and matching embroidered gloves, Emilie attracted looks and stares from both male and female attendants. She had adorned her hair with jewels, and this time decided to apply blush and lip-coloring. Her pleasing manners and confidence had many questioning who she was and where she was from.

She caught Lady June's eye, who readily walked over to greet her, looking her over with immense pleasure. "Emilie." She leaned forward to kiss her, whispering by her ear, "If you were my daughter,

I would not give you away to less than a hero or a king." The woman had noticed Emilie scanning the room distractedly, knowing full well who it was she was looking for. She squeezed her hand, commented on the beauty of the evening, and fell gently into the background.

Is he here?

Has he returned?

Is he well?

From one room to the next she went, gliding gently about, seeking the one noble face amidst a sea of pampered thousands. If she got caught up in conversation, she exited as unsuspectingly as she had entered—smoothly, softly. She smiled freely and would occasionally laugh at the jests of a few young men, who felt exceptional earning her laughter.

Aunt Clarence accosted Emilie briefly, roughly rearranging one of her hair jewels, claiming it needed adjusting. She was in a daze, though, so anything that happened didn't seem as bad as it may have actually been. By the piano she found Mick dressed handsomely and smiling from ear to ear, enjoying the skillful playing of a blonde beauty he had not yet met. Oliver stood close by, caught up in conversation with young men and women whom he had just met. He, too, looked regal. Then she bumped into Sir Fox, who took her hands into his and, commenting on her remarkable beauty, briefly introduced her to the Earl of Malmesbury, who also approved. She did not wish to linger in their company.

The night was young, and Emilie was restless. She thought she heard some hushed mention of the court case and Forester's fate, though as soon as she looked in the direction of the words, they'd disappear, leaving her wondering.

She avoided John. The brooch remained on her nightstand; she could not give a man hope if none was there for the giving. Every time he caught her out of the corner of his eye he would look again, but she would slip away. His heart pounded possessively every time. She had caught the eye of many bachelors tonight. For this reason, this night he would finally speak with her about his hope of having her hand in marriage. He would tell her everything, acknowledge his flaws, and express his newfound sense of hope that she could help him change. Phineas was not here, and he was relieved.

Seven-thirty.

The dinner bell rang out, calling the various pairs and clusters to meander to the many lavish tables set out in the formal dining room. Wafts of mouthwatering, herbed meats and delicate broths mingled with savory truffle oil pastries and buttery sides. Freely flowing wines and champagnes spilled from glass to glass without a single worry in mind. The biggest worry, actually, was where to sit tonight. Hurried servants poured seamlessly in and out to replenish every delight imaginable.

Emilie, standing in the midst of the frenzy, closed her eyes.

She saw a dirt floor, four dilapidated walls, and a dying old man. She felt the draft. She heard children crying. Men, too.

She opened her eyes.

There stood Phineas.

And if a moment could hold the weight of the world, this one did. She stood lost to the movement around her—which raised an eyebrow or two—fastened to the face of the man she loved. Tears welled up deep within, held back only by her own sense of pride. He stood there, hands straight to his sides, dressed no less importantly than the men known as leaders.

Holding her gaze, he tipped his head gently in acknowledgment, then proceeded across the room toward her.

If given pen and paper at this very moment, she would write books and books on the fullness of beauty and love and all things good and kind. His presence inspired her to see the essence of life clearly. It grounded her. It was the thing unconditional love did— bring the freedom to inspire the very best in humanity. Yes, she could trust him with her stories.

All around was hectic, but in his gaze she knew only peace.

"Hello, my lady," he said softly, kissing her hand and bowing low.

"Hello, good sir," she returned with a delicate curtsy. This game they played, it wasn't to feign self-importance like others did, but was instead to commemorate a fresh beginning to their blossoming relationship.

"How do you do, my lady?" he continued. "You look *radiant* tonight."

"As do you look handsome tonight, Phin," she returned delightedly. He was here, the same Phineas as earlier this week, yet something about him was different. Studying him, she recognized a maturity to the way he carried himself, as if in the past couple of days he'd had the world upon his shoulders. Without asking in-depth questions, she couldn't ascertain the reason for his change. She hoped to have time later tonight to have this conversation and to share her own story. *After dinner, that's when we'll reconnect,* she planned. She longed to share her burden.

"Emilie, I must prepare you," he suddenly said, looking around at several pairs of eyes throwing glances his way. "Tonight, I must ask you to trust me. I *need* you to trust me tonight," he again insisted, running his hand through his hair, slicked back to the side opposite his usual. He held her hands fast in his, tightening his grip as if gaining strength.

She didn't understand. "I'm sorry, Phin, I—I don't understand. What do you mean? Is everything alright?" she asked, once again feeling that things were about to change.

"Everything is alright. I promise," he said, boldly caressing her face with his right hand in the middle of the room. He didn't care who saw or what was said; he had her for this moment. He willed for her to understand, to trust, and to grab hold of his undying love. "It's going to be alright, darling. I *promise*," he repeated again. "Please, you *must* trust me." And at that he let her go, as the final announcement was made for all the respectable guests of the house to find their seats at dinner. As if on cue.

Phineas circled a few times around as if distancing himself from those he knew, then sat near a member of Parliament, a friend of the chancellor, and a friend of a lawyer. Somehow he fit right in. There was neither questioning about his seat choice nor challenging of his propriety.

Lady June had been observing him since his arrival a few minutes back. There was something about him that caught her perceptive eye, and his interaction with Emilie all but infuriated her. She just could not understand. What was it about Phineas that she couldn't quite appropriate? What had changed?

And then it hit her.

He was a man on a mission.

His behavior was so measured and intentional that to an unassuming eye it was beneath scrutiny, but to one who knew him it was all but average.

She understood then that Phineas had a secret. And just like on the night when the news of Forester had first arrived, she determined to trust him and to help in any which way she could.

She had no trouble trusting him, in fact. She had watched him all those years during her visits to Suffolk, never once disturbed or disappointed by the then boy's—and later, the young man's—decisions. Lady June knew goodness and strength when she saw it. And she loved this good man like a son.

To see Emilie's longing unfulfilled once again, however, shook even her resolve to stay strong.

He loved her, this she could see. But his endless delay was perplexing. What did Emilie have to do with his secret in London? Lady June, against her better judgment, worried that any more of a delay could cause Emilie's lovely frame to wither and die. Not physically, but inwardly. And then, weak and lonely, John would come to her rescue.

She continued to keep an eye on both as dinner ensued and continued, keeping eyes and ears open to the flow of conversation around the multiple tables.

At one point Sir Fox had made a toast to the strength of Great Britain and to her fine leaders and friends, to the uproarious applause of all. With the entirely segregated lifestyle they led, they could in no way fathom the despair of those in the cold huts scattered throughout the fields. Or less yet the distant plantations beyond the sea where millions worked their lives away under the brutality of an oppressor. Nothing could mar their blissful existence. They were not bothered by what they did not know. And they chose not to know.

Emilie sat quietly between the verbose wife of Sir Rupert Beckinsdale, the treasurer, and the fiancée of the son of the Duke of Pembroke. They, apparently more than anything, were most interested in talking about other young ladies, the presentation of a true English lady, the qualifications of such a one, and the appropriate attire for such a one. They soared from one topic to the next while Emilie sat quietly by, disinterestedly playing with her meticulously crisp green beans and perfectly saucy potatoes. Cordelia, the young betrothed, spoke highly of her fiancée and of wedding preparations occurring even as they spoke, and Emilie eventually simply tuned her out. Cordelia's propensity to talk prevented her from noticing.

Emilie guardedly lifted her gaze at Phineas, who was lost in conversation, now a man of the world fitting right in with the other highly decorated men. He was an altogether different man, it seemed. His questions, like the tossing waves of an unreasonably perilous storm, reeled around her mind:

Do you trust me? I need you to trust me. Please, will you trust me?

Phineas, I would run to the ends of the world with you, she whispered inside. *But I wish you would let me in, share your burden with me. I can see that you're not you.*

From across the table she searched his face, studied him, all the while maintaining the highly-demanded decorum of the night. Once she thought she saw him turn her way, but he simply turned to respond to a gray-haired man on his right; given the man's mirth and enjoyment, he'd apparently said something of a delightfully witty nature.

After what seemed like hours, as the third course was being brought out, a turn in the conversation led certain individuals to raise the question of Forester's situation. The tables erupted outrageously, as most considered the man to be above reproach and felt personally insulted that the abolitionists would undertake such a scheme. That was what they called it—a *scheme*. Passionate opinions and certain strong words crossed their lips over and over when, suddenly and quite unexpectedly, from across the table came a question directed pointedly at Phineas.

"Young man, what's your name?" came the question from an ogling man of daunting importance and wealth.

"My name is Phineas, sir," came the even, confident response.

Emilie sat upright immediately, grasping that this might be the moment needed to speak against the evils of the slave trade. Together, she and Phineas could do it. Eyeing Phineas, she then measured the threat of the interrogator. Her foot began to tap under the table.

"Well then, Phineas," he said, weightily emphasizing his name. "I've seen you being chummy with the legal assistants in the House of Commons just about a day or two ago. Tell me, what are they saying about Forester? What's the outlook?"

If any one question could command the attention of a billion people, this one certainly did the entire room, free man and servant alike.

Phineas, knowing his moment had come, sat straight up and, enlarging his chest, exhaled. He knew exactly where Emilie sat. He felt her gaze. Lady June, too, watched with bated breath. John, the Foxes, the Forthyns—all watched.

"Sir," he began, knowing exactly what he would say as he had recited the words hundreds of times the past two days, "a good name is easy to defend."

Pause. Anticipation climbed as understanding steadily trickled in, first in one, then in another.

The old, extremely interested man insisted with a hand gesture and head nod for him to continue.

Emilie wondered where he was going with this…

"Forester has little to worry about," he affirmed credulously. "The case will surely prove his innocence." Every word was spoken with surgical precision. Swallowing hard, he knew his words had successfully allayed the questions of complications and frustrations in connection to the potential conviction of Forester, as he managed most of their money. What would his demise mean for them?

The room snapped into a more jovial state of merriment as a flood of affirming words rushed upon their lips in his regard. Some nodded their approval, whilst others exclaimed emphatically how certain they were he was right. Phineas was hailed as a hero by all. Even Lady Fox, who raised an astounded brow to Sir Fox as the words alighted upon Phineas's mouth, was for once pleased with him. All celebrated.

All but one.

Emilie sat silently, shaken to the core.

Praise roared throughout the house. As was appropriate to such celebration, more champagne bottles were brought out with corks popping like fireworks. The festivities heightened. And with their appetites now sated, they reveled in relief. They were safe.

Phineas, who naturally conveyed a sense of trustworthiness, had said enough for them to believe him. Certain men of importance surrounded him and rather unguardedly discussed all things of law, trade, and finance, whilst other more deviant ones joked more specifically about the court case. And in varying degrees of drunkenness, they spoke with varying degrees of openness, saying things that perhaps they should not have.

Emilie sat as a shadow in the rising moonlight—an ever-increasing void within.

She exchanged a dead stare with Lady June, who did not need words to understand.

All was suddenly and profoundly strange.

Seated in the same place and in the exact position as when understanding of Phineas's words first began to dawn on her, surrounded by revolting excess, she knew she could not stay any longer.

As a toast was being given on Phineas's behalf, she arose from her place—cascading skirts gathered in trembling hands and head held high—seeking her route of escape through the busy room.

The end of a very feeble beginning of...of *something* too lofty or hopeful had come.

Some have said that sorrow hits hardest after decades of life have been lived together, and that young hearts are far too immature to experience the same pain. But what if the entirety of one's hopes, dreams, and plans had been placed in the face of one person? What then? Emilie didn't know whether to throw away her heart or her dreams. Why was it all so enmeshed? The more she thought of her passion, the more she envisioned his face, and the more she wept.

Traitor.

Phineas had betrayed them all.

Alone in her room at last, she locked the door and collapsed her body against it. She felt blood rushing to her fingertips and heard its pulsing rhythm in her ears, wondering if one could die from heartbreak.

She could see the smugness on his face as the approval of man surrounded him. She had already lost so much of him through her recent suffering that she wondered if there was ever anything good to begin with. Was Phineas this way all along? She remembered the time he covered for a younger Oliver when circumstances did not turn out as Oliver had planned, and the time he ran miles to get his ill mother help, or the time he stood by her side in the rose garden the day of Momma and Father's burial. More heaviness descended as she remembered his disposition the day she left Suffolk, when he gave her a neatly wrapped package "to remember home," he had said, recently admitting that he desired that she would remember *him*. These memories served no other purpose at this time than to snuff out the bit of life left.

When and where had he become lost to her? And what was she to do now?

Sitting on the floor against the door, face wet with the torrential downpour of tears, her eyes alighted upon the notebook. It contained a dream that promised some sort of happiness, and stories that needed to be told. She had to find the right listener for them. She gave up on finding happiness.

It was time to pack.

Tomorrow she would go to London.

Chapter 19

As December mornings are, this day was particularly cold. The bright morning light, also characteristic of winter mornings, persisted with misleading hints of outdoor warmth. If she would not have glanced out the window, Emilie may have believed that the day she was leaving for London was going to be warm and kind. Snow on the ground and the tossing of bare trees, however, said otherwise.

Expecting Bailey to arrive any minute, Emilie looked at the single suitcase she had hastily thrown together the night before, wondering if she had packed enough for the indefinite period of time she would be gone. Was leaving the answer? She did not know where she would go or stay, yet she knew she had to leave. This place had quickly become an unpleasant sort of stranger that one wishes never again to encounter. It had struck her with biased blows, cruel memories, and shattered dreams. She had not much more to give.

As Bailey was for unknown reasons delayed, Emilie began to prepare for the journey. She felt like her old self again back in Suffolk, tending to her own needs and requiring very little assistance. The freedom of self-reliance was marvelous. How she had forgotten it! Her person from a previous life longed to resurface.

Her plain dress and undecorated overcoat reflected a desire to blend in against the backdrop of London society. She did not wish to attract anyone, instead planning to experience her journey entirely alone. When Bailey did finally arrive, she simply helped prepare Emilie's hair and ensured that she had everything she might need to sustain herself. Assuming her part, Bailey picked up the suitcase and began to head out the door when Emilie suddenly stopped her, informing her that she would carry it herself.

"Bailey, thank you for your kindness, but I shall do this myself. I'll be back at some point…in the future. I do not yet know when or I suppose even *if* I will be back. But I cannot say now for certain what the future will bring. I will think of you often. Thank you *ever* so much for everything, and please, take care of Lincoln for me," she finished, taking the suitcase and turning to go, leaving the young girl speechlessly behind.

As Bailey watched her mistress disappear down the hall, she found herself standing a little taller, realizing how perfectly human she felt in her presence. Emilie was unlike any Englishwoman she had ever met, and she secretly hoped for her quick return to Derbyshire.

But Emilie's mind was determined to put distance between Derbyshire and her future. Thus a quick turn to the servants' kitchen readily supplied a few necessary food items, while a stop at the carriage master's secured the way.

She was leaving.

What started out as a hopeful endeavor to establish Emilie's place in society turned into an endless struggle against a ruthless power that wanted nothing less than to destroy her. The happiness she was assured of and the temptation of stepping into destiny were taunting memories of yesterday, no longer an expectation for today or tomorrow. Pain filled her vision whilst the voice of cynicism enticed her desperate soul with the false promises of bitterness, ensuring her of its full justification and power to make her feel human again. There were no more tears left to be cried, as they had been a never-ending river all along. She was the willow pushed and pulled to be dragged underneath a suffocating current, weeping endlessly into the cold waters beneath.

The temptation of succumbing to human frailty was so strong. Clutching her suitcase in the frigid morning air, awaiting her carriage to pull up to the front, she suddenly understood something about a piece of her life story.

It dawned on her that she stood where she stood this morning precisely because she had *not* changed since arriving at Derbyshire. She was the ancient willow thriving by turbulent waters, determined to stand tall despite the powerful current. The day she had arrived in Kent she swore that she would not change for anyone or anything, and that her convictions would not topple at provocation. Well here she was: a picture of conviction in a harsh world. Broken and alone.

Inside the door, Lady June had been making her way downstairs, having had a restless night where sleep was relentlessly evasive. She was briskly on her way to the dining room, feeling as if something was amiss with Emilie, and since she wasn't in her room, perhaps she'd find her in the dining room, when suddenly she bumped into a ghostly Phineas.

"My sincerest apologies, my lady," he said hoarsely, disoriented, as if he had had a night-long wrestling match with death itself.

"No worries, Phin." She waved his apologies away, then asked, "Might I ask if everything is alright?" She eyed him with the severest concern for his well-being, wondering if he had turned to a drinking habit or if he were ill. He with disheveled hair and stained shirt was certainly not the young man she had known. "Phin, are you well?" she repeated when he did not answer.

"Lady June, in some ways everything is precisely the way it should be," he began with a sigh, shoulders sagging. "But in others, not so much. I… I can't say much, I'm afraid, but please know that everything will hopefully be alright," he finished, and was about to walk away when Lady June stopped him.

"Phin, I'm here should you need anything—anything at all, do you hear? Look at me," she enforced tenderly. "You don't have to… do anything alone. You can trust me, and we are here for you. *We* care for you," she stressed, insinuating the broken-hearted Emilie, hoping he'd captured the essence of her words.

"Thank you, my lady. I'll be alright. Please," he began, nervously running his hand through his chaotic hair, "take care of her for me, and…" He broke off, not able to admit to himself that she might be someone else's by the time he saw her next. "And please ensure her happiness." He could no more look her in the eyes than he could look at his own reflection in the mirror. His every glimpse only further reminded him of loneliness, and the request only further echoed a painful finality. The storm raging within could at any moment overpower his sensibleness, and as he did not wish to crumble before the elder woman, he brusquely excused himself and stormed away.

His puzzling presentation and somber words heightened her sense of urgency, directing her footsteps toward the hallway leading into the front foyer, which then led to the hallway into the dining room. Moving quickly, with razor-sharp focus, her eyes were suddenly pulled toward a lone gray figure standing against a backdrop of white.

There in front of her, visible through the large window framing the front door, stood a forlorn form holding a medium-sized suitcase.

Emilie stood as still as a shadow, face sternly onward, pale and blank.

Unable to contain herself, Lady June burst through the front door and without the slightest hesitation heaved Emilie into an embrace so full of love that she was sure this was what it felt like to have a daughter of one's own. She knew that nothing could be said to sway Emilie's resolve to leave Derbyshire, and so, instead of trying to convince her to stay, she resolved to go.

"Emilie, where are you going?" she began.

"London," came the vacuous reply.

"Where will you be staying in London?"

"I don't know."

"What will you be doing there, have you any idea?"

"I have not."

"Have you any acquaintances with whom you shall pass time?"

"No."

Taking a deep breath in, Lady June began, "Emilie, now listen to me. I am coming with you. Hush now, I don't want to hear it. You will stay with me in London for as long as you need to. I understand your position and wish only to help. You will hear no objections from me on any issue. You are intelligent to know where to go, what to do, and with whom to go. Do we have an agreement? Are you alright to wait for me while I pack my belongings?" she asked, looking into sunken eyes. "Do I have your word that you won't leave without me?"

"Lady June, I appreciate this so very much. Thank you. I needed this. Please, excuse my indolence... I shall wait for you, I assure you," she insisted, knowing full well of Lady June's concern for her rationality, given last night's scenario. After another prolonged search of the young woman's disposition, June hurried off to pack.

Shortly the two women were fully packed into June's carriage, bundled with toasty blankets, and on their way to London.

"Ladies," the driver began, awakening one and startling the other, "we are halfway to London. Shall we stop for a break, or would you prefer to keep going?"

"Halfway, you say? Yes—"

"No!" Emilie snapped. And then, "I'm so sorry. Please, I'd prefer to keep going," she finished, eyes pleading.

"Yes, Rupert, let's do as the young lady says. Do get us home as soon as you're able," June requested, intently studying Emilie's withdrawn features. This carriage ride was not unlike her first one months ago, when she—full of hopeful determination to become someone—was convinced that moving to Kent was the right thing to do. In the silence of this ride, June could see her wrestling with unforgiving memories that would not yield, ones that wounded her identity with deceptive taunts and challenged her spirit with weaknesses. She was not seeing straight.

"Emilie, what's on your mind?" she began. "How can I help? I hate to see you suffer so."

"You're already helping, and for this I am grateful," she countered, quickly turning away. Hardness, which June had not yet seen upon her young features, blanketed her light sweetness like heavy cement. The past week, marked with the highest heights and lowest valleys, had shaken everything she had known about the world.

Emilie was changing—*had changed.*

Slowly releasing tightly kept breath, June desperately hoped that London would remedy this broken heart.

Chapter 20

" *D*on't look Emilie," giggled Julia, "but there's a handsome young man over there—I said, *don't look!* He's been staring at you most ardently since we've arrived," she reported with hushed mischief. Laura and Anne couldn't help themselves and turned to look most interestedly at the man of the moment. They both giggled in approval, forcing Emilie to roll her eyes and insist on absolute disinterest.

"Girls, I told you, I'm not looking for a man—absolutely *not* interested. I'm perfectly content..."

"Yes, yes, you've said that before," interrupted an impatient Julia. "But you might change your mind if you'd see him. The bearded gentleman can't be much older than us, looks quite well off, and I daresay has not stopped staring at you since you've sat your pretty little self down. You *must* give an indication, Emilie, *anything*. At least give a glance. Wouldn't he be a marvelous date for the ball?"

"Julia, no, I'm not looking. Girls, *girls*—" she pleaded, but her three friends were more interested in the unfolding drama than in heeding her pleas. This was just the sort of thrill that would turn their perfectly average lunch hour into an absolutely delightful exploit. These were new friends whom she had met upon beginning work for London's local abolitionist branch.

"I daresay," began Laura, "that is not an indifferent man, and certainly not one I'd be indifferent toward if he were looking my way. However, who do you suppose that young lady is that he sits with? She most certainly comes from noble blood."

"But why would he be staring at Emilie, Laura?" interjected Anne, looking at the three with the complexities of such a situation hanging thickly overhead. The mystery man appeared to be entranced by their friend, using every free moment to stare her way. However, he was having lunch with a young lady who seemed most interested in him. Energetic discussion ensued about whether she was a relation of the man, perhaps a long-lost sister, or better yet a mistress, but due to their absolute shortage of knowledge of his circumstance, they were unable to get far at all.

Emilie, who had had enough of the contemplations and presumptions of the three romantics who shared her lunch table, finally requested to end the topic. "Anne, let's please switch seats," she said firmly.

"Whyever would you want to do that?" retorted a disbelieving Anne, unable to fathom how Emilie could be so dry.

"Well I can't eat while an unknown man stares at me, now can I?" she responded half-smiling, but fully willing her to get up and move.

"Oh Emilie, will I ever understand you?" she stated, reluctantly rising to oblige.

Emilie arose, head high and eyes most intentionally not looking his way, showing impeccable self-control. From the corner of her eye she saw the vague silhouette of a bearded man with a charming, intently engaged young woman. What man could be sitting with one woman while staring at another?

Then the unthinkable happened.

Julia and Anne—first to see—exchanged a wide-eyed glance as the dreaded words came flying out of their mouths. "He's coming over!"

"Oh dear," giggled Laura excitedly as she squeezed Emilie's hand under the table and snuck a brief look his way. "Emilie, prepare thyself," she affirmed deviously to the uproarious pleasure of Julia and Anne.

Emilie wondered how young women working for the abolitionist movement could be so frivolous. Had they been this way before she'd met them, or did she just bring it out in them? She tried to recall the last time she had laughed or giggled, but could not; shattered hearts don't laugh much.

She felt his nearness then.

"Good day, sir," initiated Julia deviously, with head propped up on clasped fingers as Anne and Laura measured his very being, grinning from ear to ear. Emilie sat stone cold. Laura squeezed her hand tighter, indicating how very handsome he was this close.

His voice changed everything. The walls protecting her heart had been doing their job until now. "Good day, ladies," he began, first respectfully addressing Julia, Anne, and Laura, then finally landing a gentle glance on Emilie. The moment exploded as his voice reverberated inside her head, evoking tears which to her horror could not be stopped. Her changed disposition perplexed the three.

"I beg your pardon, do you two know each other?" asked Julia as Emilie jerked a tear away.

"No," Emilie stammered, finally squaring off with him, looking directly into his eyes. Her heart pleaded to know the reason for his betrayal, but her pride forbade her from acquiescing to his presence. *No more tears.*

"My lady, may we…?"

"*No*, I do *not* know this man," she forced through clenched teeth, words final as the grave. Suddenly rising to leave on legs more faulty than expected, she backed into a servant who spilled water onto the floor, causing a scene that reflected the very turmoil within. Now everyone looked on. She could not surrender.

"Please, forgive me," she whispered to the servant, voice and body trembling, turning to flee faster than her composure failed.

"Pardon me, ladies, for the intrusion," stated the dejected mystery man, taking full responsibility for what had just happened, bowing low and forlornly turning to go.

"But sir," Julia beseeched, "do tell us your name that we may at least convey your kind respects to our friend. This is not like her at all."

"Phineas. My name is Phineas McGray, and...I know," he finished, successfully confounding the three women who now wondered what had transpired between the two. Wilberforce had planned a meeting tonight since his return to London, and they fully expected to find Emilie there; they wanted to not only understand this exchange, but also to comfort her.

Four weeks had come and gone, and aside from a letter from Derbyshire inquiring of her whereabouts, Emilie's past had acquired an ethereal sort of dimension. It had happened, but so long ago.

January had taken on a dual nature. The welcome and camaraderie of new friends became a wellspring that lightened her heavy heart, but the hushed silence of snowfall and of the solitary confinement of particularly bitter cold days weakened her against the invasion of particularly bitter memories.

The pace she set and the movements of the day had a singular goal in mind—to forget his face. The sight of it stirred memories from the past that either elicited tears or awakened longing, neither of which she wanted. She remembered Momma's fondness of Phineas, his care the day of the funeral, and the notebook. Then the dance. The dream. Finally the dinner, and with it perplexing betrayal. Cruel thoughts and unwanted feelings flooded her consciousness as she stumbled out of the restaurant, seeking frantically for a place to hide.

Down the icy stone steps she descended toward the public square where stood a frozen fountain, several newspaper stands, one or two more eateries, and scattered groups of people mingling and intermixing either for leisure or work. Into the busyness she slipped, another unknown face hiding behind a beautiful mask with saddened eyes. She moved along hurriedly toward the abolitionists' office. Perhaps she would find solace speaking with Lady More or Lady Thornton about more fitting subjects.

Suddenly a distressed cry came from behind, cutting through every bit of her commiserative state. A stately noblewoman out satisfying her indulgences, as evidenced by the multiple bags now scattered on the dirty winter ground, shrieked in utter disgust at an elder negro woman who had bumped into the servant girl who carried them. She spat indignantly at the older woman, threatening her next several months' pay for the damage she'd caused.

"You dirty imbecile, how could you? Can't you see two feet in front of you?" On and on she spewed, until a sizable crowd of on-lookers had gathered. She had hoped to attract enough attention to involve the police patrolling the grounds.

The young black girl stood still with eyes down and hands clenched white before her.

Emilie knew this would not end well for her either.

After getting over the initial shock of the situation, the elder offender caught in the woman's line of wrathful fire quickly dove to the cold ground to pick up the expensive bags with expensive items. Aging bones slowed her.

Emilie felt the same indignation arising within as she had felt during her conversations with Albert or Lady Clarence. Her cheeks flushed and heart began to beat faster. All else faded into the background. Without the slightest forethought, she moved her way past the thickening layers of gawking men and women and dropped to the ground near the one frightened and pale.

She gave the stunned woman's hand a tight squeeze and worked quickly to gather the bags, returning them to the young girl whose hands were clearly not large enough to carry the load. She gave the elder woman a hand up and fixed her shawl.

Then the fierce lioness came out like never before. Emilie addressed the crowd.

"Ladies and gentlemen," she began, eyeing every person who was more confounded now than before, "please be on your way, nothing to see here. Mishaps happen every day. Come now, go about your business," she continued confidently as one by one they dispersed, looking back at her every so often. She stood protectively between the elder woman and the crowd.

"Madame," she then addressed the woman who stood dumb-founded, hand covering a dramatic mouth aghast with disbelief, "we do not want trouble for an innocent soul, not today. Please, all of your belongings are gathered and in one place. I implore you to be on your way as well."

"Well, I never. *Hmph!*" she retorted, head held high and eyes ever widening in disbelief. Her pride had suffered a blow, and shame was quickly encroaching. Emilie faced her sternly, not letting up until she began to move along. "I *never!*" she huffed once more as she turned to leave, young servant girl trailing obediently behind.

"And madame," Emilie called, "next time please ensure your helper—" Turning toward the little girl, she asked, "And what's your name, young lady?"

"Sarah," came the timid response.

"Please ensure that Sarah's arms are large enough to carry your shopping bags," she requested, winking at the little girl, but facing the woman directly in full seriousness.

At this, the woman's round countenance turned an inflammatory red while her stout body picked up its pace.

The elder woman stood timidly by, watching her moment of favor occur in a most unprecedented way. "Miss," she began with trembling face, "how can I ever repay you?"

"What is your name?" Emilie countered kindly.

"My name is Lenora, or Lenny, as they call me at the house," she answered, not knowing if she should speak or listen, as this was such an unusual experience.

"I'm Emilie. Very pleased to meet you, Lenora. Can I help you get back to your residence? Are you hurt?"

"No, dear child, I'm not hurt. I am better than ever. My God has sent you to save me, and I thank Him for it," she spoke with a quivering whisper, taking her hand and holding it close. A tear followed the wrinkled path down her tired, wind-burned face.

The world began to dance to a different melody then. Even the wildly descending snow acquired an otherworldly loveliness playing about the lampstands of a graying London as Emilie made her way to the office. The heaviness that dragged her down was being replaced by an altogether different substance: a purposeful drive that called back an easy smile to her lips.

Long after Lenora had gone, her words continued to resonate in Emilie's soul. In fact, they helped her to choose thoughts that were better for her, ones she knew would eventually heal her heart. Even the unexpected sighting of Phineas earlier today did not ache as much now.

For the first time, Emilie understood what her passion was for. It was for moments like had just happened, when she stepped in to do the right thing for a fellow human being despite what others might do or say. It could be better used out here, where people may never have warmed their hearts by the fire of kindness, living instead in ice castles cold with division and pride.

She saw it clear as day. Her debates with Albert were frustrating because they were impractical and totally beyond the reach of his daily life. Today, however, these people *saw* the attributes of goodness in action. Emilie loved Lenora and Sarah! It thrilled her to speak it and to show the entire world. She loved Mim and Bailey! She smiled as she stepped closer to the buildings in an attempt to shelter from the relentless snow.

A white piece of paper quickly caught her eye and, coming closer to read it, she recognized Sir Forester's face with bright-red words declaring his innocence sprawled all over it. *Lies*, she moaned. *All lies.* The deceit was so repugnant that she tore the paper from its post, crumbled it vehemently, and planned to rid of it by the nearest flame of fire. *He's 'fully insulated,'* she recalled the gloating field workers saying, balling her fingers into an angry fist.

Indignation arose at Forester, who funded hellish cruelty, at Phineas for succumbing, at Sir Fox for never speaking up as long as he lived, and at herself for being such a fool. Life was no fairytale!

"May I be of any help, my lady?" A swiftly recognized but not-yet-familiar voice interrupted her moment. She turned to face the renowned Sir William Wilberforce standing there with hands behind his back, bowing low in formal greeting. She had never been this close to the man before, though she had heard him speak once at a meeting prior to his departure from London. Here he was, addressing her most cordially.

Her eyes widened as she took in the measure of the legend before her.

He, recognizing her speechlessness, comfortably broke the silence. "I find my passion gets me into trouble, too." He nudged at the crumpled poster in her hand and winked most graciously.

She exhaled. Color brazenly ran across her face as self-consciousness prevailed.

"What blasphemous words impacted you so, Miss...?"

"Emilie Forthyn, sir," she returned with a curtsy.

"Ah yes, Emilie... Your reputation quite precedes you, young lady," he commented lightly, with a sideways nod of his head. Emilie couldn't grasp whether this was complimentary or meant as a jab of some sort. She still couldn't see the victory where she felt failure. "Pray tell, however, what troubled you so about that poster?"

Wilberforce had heard about her risky expedition to the fields of Kent as her stories, now heroic tales, were actively circulated amongst the abolitionists. She was a young version of himself, a kindred spirit whom he was instinctively measuring while they stood and spoke. Seeing her youthfulness, he wondered if she was self-absorbed like many of her contemporaries, or if destiny had truly gotten the best of her, igniting an unquenchable fire the world so desperately needed. He sensed she was an equal, but would vanity steal her momentum?

"What *didn't* bother me about it, sir?" she responded. "Since moving to Kent, I have struggled to see how the slave trade—overseas or here—is dealt such a favorable hand. I have seen them, sir, and spoken to them. I cannot wipe their tears from my eyes. I cannot erase death's sounds, either. It's unjustifiable. So to see *this man*," she cried, shaking the wretched ball of paper in her hand, "so easily justified when I *know* that…that…" She faltered, looking nervously away. She had not spoken of this knowledge to anyone besides Lady June.

"You know…*what?*" he probed, crossing his arms loosely over his chest. Righteous indignation blazed within his eyes. Wilberforce carried burdens that people could not even fathom the weight of. The battle had aged him. Yet his love for God and man made in God's image fueled him to press on.

She couldn't face him. "Nothing, sir," she fumbled, toying with the miserable paper ball. Afraid of giving hope where things may fail, she held her tongue. She did not yet know how to release what could create a false narrative. Lady June would help her to understand the timing of such words.

"Hm, I see," he replied, overcome with a purely quizzical expression. It was said that he was a very animated individual from his youth, and that his love for life was always visible on his features. This was true. He had wanted to hear what was on the tip of her tongue because he felt that it may somehow speak to his personal feelings about Forester's case, but not willing to push her, a different expression replaced pensiveness. Wilberforce knew that he was always free to be contented. He dropped his arms and smiled. "Miss Emilie, it seems that we may both be headed in the same direction. Are you also going to this evening's meeting? Might I accompany you to the office?"

His appearing entirely genuine, she could not resist. She thought back to Derbyshire, about the contrariness of the atmosphere toward much of what she believed in and spoke about, and felt entirely relieved to experience the undivided attention of one who embodied her very passion; it was intoxicating. Real-life heroes, it turned out, had wrinkles, stained shoes, and grumbling stomachs; their good-naturedness predisposed any good soul to their company. "Why yes, sir. I'd be delighted!" she exclaimed, then blushed again at her juvenile outburst.

"Lovely, Miss Forthyn! Now tell me, what else have you learned since moving to Kent? I would love to hear more of your insights, hm?"

"Oh no, sir, I couldn't burden you with more talk. I understand that you are to speak tonight? I'd much rather hear about something from your trip. It may well help you to clarify your speech if you begin now," she insisted.

"Ah yes, yes, I do believe you're right. Now, where are my notes?" He began to dramatically search his pockets with a worried look upon his face.

Now Emilie began to fret, swearing that she'd expended too much of his precious time, preventing him from preparing for the evening. What would everyone miss out on because of her selfishness?

Suddenly he stopped and burst into clear, melodious laughter. Emilie stared.

"Miss Emilie, nothing would please me more than to hear of your escapades at Derbyshire Manor. The people there are not the softest crowd, from what I hear. My notes are my lived experiences. It is not difficult to speak about things which you eat, drink, sleep, and breathe," he said with the noblest grin she had ever seen.

She was in awe of this man. He carried the burdens of an entire people upon his shoulders, yet he laughed and smiled and showed genuine care for her, having met her just a few minutes prior. She could compare him to no other. The closest man was... She stiffened. Her face fell.

He caught on without delay. "What is it, Miss Forthyn?"

"Sir...what do you do when...one you esteemed or trusted..."—she hesitated, choosing her words carefully—"changes?" she finished quickly, looking straight onward as they walked down the sidewalk.

Wilberforce, a man of insight, deduced the reason for this young lady's downcast heart rather easily and desired to protect her dignified privacy with his response. "Miss Emilie, that is a good question," he began, offering her sidelong support as they walked side by side down the wintry sidewalk. "And its answer is simple. You

168

ask yourself if they have proven themselves to be trustworthy over your years of friendship. If so, perhaps there is more to their story? Is there reason to judge them based on what knowledge you have? Is your knowledge complete, or limited? I've learned that things aren't always as they seem at first glance, and sometimes even at second glance. Do you see?" He could tell she was reviewing memories and words spoken, and so gave her some time in silence.

"Yes," she finally said. "I do see, but what if the offense is so grave that you can't even begin to comprehend the rationale behind their change?" Her eyes pleaded for understanding as she stopped, finally facing him. He could see her young, trusting heart.

"Ah yes, this indeed seems grave. At times like these, we must learn to trust who we know the person to be. Have you known him for many years?" he questioned accurately.

"Yes sir, since childhood," she replied forlornly, eyes now shimmering.

"And this is why it pains you so, no doubt," he added. "But if I may offer one final word—and a bold one, at that—as if I would to a daughter, may I?"

She nodded approval.

"Trust the Almighty that if you two are meant to be, nothing will prevent it." He looked into her eyes then, searching for the trust within that had been broken by unjust and painful experiences, waiting for meaning to wash over her.

Her eyes tightened then as the burden of having to do everything right began to lift. Upon his face were inscribed years of trials, errors, failures, and victories that he continued to move forward through. For the first time, she recognized that this was not as much about her as she had thought. Her life would fall into place when the time was right and when she was ready, but for now, as things were, she had to live for the moments every day brought forth. She would love, learn under new mentors, and grow. She longed to be for someone else who Wilberforce was for her.

Hopelessness became less dark as failures began to be released.

Looking back over the past months, her eyes were suddenly opened to see every place where a far greater hand than hers had upheld her. Yes, she was not walking through this alone.

She had heard of Wilberforce's life-changing encounter with God and wondered if he had not just given her a taste. A radiant smile began to dawn upon her face as drooping shoulders lifted.

"Ah yes, there it is," he affirmed gaily. "Emilie, *never forget this moment.*"

She smiled in agreement, promising herself to hold it close to heart, and during the brief remainder of their walk, listened about his favorite song penned by an old, converted slave ship owner and of the weather up north. They also touched upon the qualities of northern beef stew in comparison to London's own, but that only briefly.

"Here we are," he stated brightly as he swung the door open into a bright corridor with voices running up and down the hall from a room at its end.

Emilie, who was now actually hungry, inhaled wafts of soup and fresh bread. "Sir Wilberforce," she began, catching him before he was swept away by friends and leaders eagerly awaiting his arrival, "thank you so much for your kindness. I will never forget your words. Please, if I may be of any help at all, do not hesitate to find me. I have fully committed myself to the work of abolition," she finished as he smiled, tipped his hat, and stepped into the main hall. The noise escalated twofold as the man of the hour was welcomed.

Emilie retreated into a quiet space where she could think over the words just given her. *If it's meant to be, it will be.* Quite honestly, hope to her raw heart was like the blazing noonday sun to a painful sun blister, but with the letting go of certain failures that clung to her like sticky tar, she did feel intrinsically lighter, and after a day like today, where she'd rescued the broken, fought off the breaker, and almost broke herself, hope likely was the best thing for her.

God, as brief as her history with Him was, clearly showed faithfulness to Sir Wilberforce. He changed him and gave him a purpose, one that would impact millions of people if pursued faithfully.

Couldn't He do the same for her? Sitting alone at the corner of a small table, she settled within herself that she, too, would pursue God and His design for her life. It just made sense.

She caught sight of Lady June in the far corner of the room, speaking with Hannah More, purple hat feather moving enthusiastically with every move of her head; the woman caught her eye and waved. Emilie smiled warmly and waved back.

"Emilie—you've come! We've been looking for you. May we join you?" Julia came near with Anne and Laura not far behind, one carrying a bowl of soup, the other bread and a napkin.

"Dearest Emilie," began Laura, "please don't be cross with us about what happened earlier today. Are you?" She handed Emilie the soup and encouraged her to eat. Anne gave her the bread. They sat around, anticipating her response.

As embarrassed as Emilie was about lunch, their genuine concern was a refreshing reminder of friendship. She couldn't help but feel the stark contrast between this and her experience at Derbyshire. She shuddered at the thought of going back. But what would happen with Savonne Manor? This was her inheritance. What would Momma say?

Momma.

It had been a long time since she had even thought of her beloved parents. Would Momma understand the decision to leave Derbyshire, or would she be disappointed that Emilie was not able to amend the age-old rivalry standing like a curse between families? There was much to think about.

The girls gently questioned Emilie about Phineas, being cautious not to be overly pushy or frivolous. In response, Emilie plainly explained that he was a childhood friend that had changed over the years, not wanting to give on more than that. She trusted them but not yet herself, reserving more personal details indefinitely. They indicated their understanding but unanimously felt that there was more. The subtle looks exchanged during Emilie's recitation of childhood facts and memories informed each one that the relationship between Emilie and this Phineas went far deeper. But they dared not push.

After almost an hour of excited greetings, elated chit-chat, and a light dinner, all assembled were ready to hear Wilberforce's address. They had been waiting for days to hear news of what was being said around all of England about Forester and the movement.

Wilberforce did not disappoint. He recounted his firsthand experiences with various slave traders, trade beneficiaries, political leaders, and undercover abolitionist posts of the extent of Forester's involvement in the trade and of his power over the traders. He described how desperate they were to ensure Forester's acquittal; he clearly had the upper hand. It was also mentioned that Forester's tracks, if there were any, were likely very professionally covered.

"So, ladies and gentlemen, as you can plainly see," he underscored, leaning forward on the creaking wooden podium, "we stand before an enormous giant of sorts. Our job continues to be investigative, supportive, and exhortative. If you hear anything, bring it in. If you see anything, bring it in. Let's continue building our repertoire of evidence. I tell you, our African brothers and sisters—their pleas and prayers—are being heard. Today we are much closer than even yesterday."

Then, in an epic turn of events, Wilberforce turned his attention to Emilie. "Miss Emilie," he began, drawing every eye to face her, "your stories—the ones you shared here at one of our meetings some time ago—must be put out there for the public eye to see. We must write them down, create pamphlets," he conjectured while being interrupted by another.

"Draw pictures, show the huts," the woman interjected.

"And definitely use names and quotes to bring life to the faces," augmented a third.

"Yes, yes, precisely. Bring these people and their stories to life. Miss Emilie, are you open to this? Can we ask you, not disclosing your name, of course, to release these stories to the public at large? We understand the inherent risk. You can take some time to think about it."

Emilie never thought that her stories would go beyond this room. She expected an indirect sort of effectiveness to come about. To release them beyond these walls would incur a greater scrutiny of that day's events, inviting more questions to be asked of her and of Mim. The field masters would surely not live that down easily. The risks loomed before her.

But the benefits of having every English man, woman, boy, and girl holding these stories in their hands would surely outweigh any risk. What was her comfortable life compared to the lives of millions of suffering others? If Phineas succumbed to fear or the lure of fame or whatever it was, she did not have to. Lincoln's words came to mind, that sometimes a good thing must be tried multiple times before evil surrenders. Perhaps reading story after story, Lenora's to be included as of today, would ignite the awakening of land they had been fighting for.

For reasons unknown to her, Emilie rose to her feet, her striking figure captivating everyone present as she emanated an authority far beyond her own perception. "Sir Wilberforce," she began, initially trembling, though gaining confidence with every thought, "if the dark ills we see before us we fail to address with the light of goodness, then we are as good as walking corpses. A living soul bears witness to every beautiful and delightful thing in life, experiencing a nearness to its creator with every new encounter. My soul has been so deeply crushed under the weight of the evil known as the trade of human life that I wonder if I shall ever recover. I had heard of it when I was younger, but I experienced it just recently, as you all know. If I cower in fear now, if I allow the fear of man to silence *their stories*, gifted to me by those precious souls, I'm as good as a walking corpse. So, sir, ladies and gentlemen, I will do everything in my power to justly bring these stories to life."

At her final words, the room erupted into applause as many stood to honor the courageous one before them.

Wilberforce smiled, applauding her loudest.

At the end of the meeting, Lady June walked over to see how she was doing. "How are you, my love?" she asked, expressing how she had been missing their morning tea together.

"As you can see, Lady June, I'm doing well. However, *if only you knew*"—she paused then as a foxy look of disbelief crossed her face—"whom I bumped into today," she finished as both brows shot upward. Her look dared Lady June to take a stabbing guess.

"Oh, dear!" the woman exclaimed. Then, "John Learson?"

"No," she led on, encouraging more guesses.

"Lady Clarence?" June continued curiously.

"Try again," encouraged Emilie, who for the first time in weeks felt light and winsome. She attributed this to her newfound sense of purpose.

"Emilie, *no...*?" Mouth agape, June knew it was bound to happen in the city.

"Ahhh, yes, Lady June. *Yes*, quite right. We had a friendly encounter during my lunch hour. Apparently he, being engaged with another young lady, was staring my way the entire time I was engaged with Julia and the girls. Upon our meeting face to face I whimpered like a babe, stumbled into a waiter who then spilled water onto the floor, and fumbled out the door like a drunken madwoman. It was a sight to behold, Lady June. I almost wish you had been there," she finished the facetious tale in horror.

Lady June took her face into both her hands and gave a tender squeeze. "Oh my darling, where would I find amusement without you in my life? I'd be a boring old spinster locked up all the way on 49th Street, drinking straight tea and eating crackers, alone." She smiled, chuckling as the exchange went on. She was catching glimpses of *Emilie Forthyn*, and this thrilled her. Unsure of how this could be, considering that she had just bumped into Phineas, she allowed the unknown to take care of itself. Her girl was surfacing.

Before they parted ways, she took Emilie's hand and ensured that all was truly well. "Are you really alright, Em? You've had quite the grand life in Kent, and now here. Is there anything I can do for you? When I encouraged you to leave Suffolk, I had no idea all of these things would happen," she stated penitently.

"Lady June, there *are* things I'd like to speak with you about. No, please don't worry, nothing serious. I'm fine, I promise you. How about breakfast this Saturday? With the usual?" she asked as Lady June leaned in forehead to forehead, appreciating their relationship.

"Most definitely. You can count on it, darling!"

As they were parting for the remainder of the meeting to catch up with personal acquaintances, Emilie remembered to ask the question she had been carrying since coming to London. "Lady June," she briefly began, knowing there were others she needed to connect with before heading home for the evening, "I can't stop thinking of Mim. Isn't there any way to see her? Are you aware of any connections to Wimberton's residence? I would so cherish any small opportunity to reconnect with her," she continued, hoping for an answer of any sort at all.

"Ah yes, Emilie, your dear Mim. Wimberton owns two estates south of London. From what I hear, he has been overrun with servants and slaves and has been quite bothered by his lot. I'm not sure how he came to be in this place, though. Perhaps others, like Mim, have also been returned and he has poorly accounted for them. He is a harsh man, so I certainly would advise against stepping foot onto his property. His rifle has been known to chase people away. But as for Mim," she continued gingerly, measuring how much she could say in the current moment, "as far as I know, things might be looking up for her soon, but that's all I can say."

"Lady June! Can it be? I wonder what's to happen? Is another residence taking her in? Has someone recognized her excellence and offered to take her in? Oh, I must know what's to happen," she insisted, eagerly awaiting a fuller response, but Lady June was mum.

"I am sorry, my darling, I can say no more than this. But do trust me when I say that things will be better for her, and sooner I hope rather than later." And with this she left Emilie to mingle with others. Disclosure of this sort required the right timing.

Emilie spent the evening planning with Julia, Anne, Laura, and a few others, also connecting with Lady More, who had heard from a bystander about the marketplace square event having to do with old Lady Lenora. She admired Emilie's strength and encouraged her to keep up the good work.

With the evening tapering to a close and carriages being pulled up, Emilie reconnected with Lady June as they both waited for their ride. "I wonder how Mick and Oliver are doing...?" She lingered on the spoken thought, deciding that she would write them a letter tomorrow. She never did give them the appropriate farewell before leaving Derbyshire and did not want them to worry. Lady June's letter penned weeks ago probably needed an update. Then came thoughts of everyone else at Derbyshire and of her imminent decisions about Savonne. But the more time passed between here and there, the easier this decision seemed to become. At this she smiled. She was almost ready to declare what she wanted.

Was it possible to change yet stay the same?

Chapter 21

Convenience, Emilie quickly learned, was a great requirement in life and truth, as honest as it was, seemed to possess an utterly inconvenient potential. Deception, of course, played its hand most advantageously capitalizing upon even the honest man's anxieties, ensuring maintenance of the status quo. And given that London's annual winter ball was taking place this Saturday, Forester's case was begging to be solved—conveniently.

Was the man guilty or not? The people, seeing quietly confident abolitionists around every corner, were becoming uneasy about potential ramifications. The majority rebuked the plausibility of such an elite member of society condemned to prison; they hoped that convenient justice would prevail. Suspect practices were not bothersome so long as life remained the same, untouched.

Wilberforce alone was a force to be reckoned with. Observing his ways, Emilie, too, was becoming an inconvenient young woman in society. She expressed her doubts about Forester openly knowing that truth was on her side. The fields of Derbyshire were proof.

Convenience was neither her measure of a matter nor her goal; her words were scattered freely like seeds on open soil, resulting in what seemed like miniscule changes here and massive ones there. Fruit was fruit.

This particular week in February of 1806 refused to be normal. Young and old alike ran about in huddles of two or three, hiding their honest opinions with plastered smiles as greetings. Everyone was on edge. Even the dogs apprehended change by irrational barks and unusual whimpers. Uncertainty hung over the nation like a suffocating gray tarp, and all were trapped.

On Monday, the judge announced that extra time was needed to course through more of the documents. Sketches were released every few hours and hung outside the courtroom door for desperate ones to peer at, often leaving them more despondent than before they had looked. A fearful imagination can wreak havoc on perception.

Men in starchy attire and powdery white wigs would pour in and out of the building throughout the day, taking frequent smoke breaks, but being legally prevented to speak about anything substantial and case-related. Sometimes they would stand out in the cold in clusters of five or six, discussing in low voices the various possibilities of what they had witnessed that day. Each had a tense brow and rigid walk.

Much was at stake.

On Tuesday it began to be seen that the men laughed more. This surely indicated a sway of direction—was it for or against the man?

Wednesday emerged like any other day. The affluent shopped, the middle class worked, and the lower class toiled. The negro served or slaved. The air was pregnant with the significance of the coming verdict.

She knew the second the heavy courtroom door was opened what it was. The prosecution came out first—enraged, curse words and directives freely flying. She heard one young apprentice fume about the injustice of the decision to the other apprentice, who shook his head in vehement agreement. They scurried eagerly behind their teachers, papers and appearance vividly disheveled, listening intently to what the seasoned attorneys were articulating in low voices.

The sight of Sir Forester exiting the hall of justice was like a dark vision. Her gut turned and she was rendered speechless in describing it. His wrinkled bald head grinned extremely, displaying perfectly white teeth as his satisfied team congratulated him on a job well done, shaking his hand, clapping his back, then slipping back into the darkened building to wrap up. But his eyes, they flitted to and fro, working to convince the masses that he was one of them, an honest laborer for the land. He waved like a renowned icon but seemed more interested in escaping the public eye than standing under its scrupulous gaze. His carriage picked him up within a brief minute and swept him away. The people clapped and waved toward his darkened carriage, hoping to see an appreciative man responding to their cheers. He simply stared straight ahead under the protection of shadows, avoiding them altogether.

Phineas was nowhere to be found. Emilie presumed he stayed behind to clean, as that was the job of the apprentice. She did not really care where he was.

They, too, were left to pick up a mess, though a far bigger one.

"This is what 'being insulated' means, Lady June," Emilie commented later that day as they walked around the public square after lunch.

"I suppose so, Em," she replied dismally, "though I don't understand how, with what you told me, not a single piece of evidence was presented to get him. Such a curious scenario, don't you think? I thought for sure that the judge would recognize fault. I wonder if the jury was paid out? I wouldn't be surprised if all of their loans were dismissed. Emilie, honestly, I wouldn't be surprised at all," she expressed convincingly.

"I know it. I wonder how the office feels right now? Shall we head back, Lady June?"

"Yes, let's. We must regroup," she finished as the two turned up 37th Street toward the old building.

They walked in on a meeting that had just begun, with concerned faces everywhere.

Wilberforce stood by the fireplace, foot atop its stone, hand rubbing chin. A pensive brow betrayed his attempts at normal engagement. "Ladies and gentlemen, we must reorganize. Nothing is lost unless we allow it to be. Our work must continue even more actively now," he began brightly in exhortation. Then, letting his guard down, "I can't—" he stated, shaking his head. "I simply can't understand how this happened." His words were supported by shakes of the head and deep groans of agreement.

Emilie, feeling suddenly enlightened, walked to the front and began encouraging the group about the importance of seeing correctly.

"If we see failure, we will fail," she began. "If, however, we recognize that God's truth, goodness, and justice are on our side, then we *can't* fail. We *shan't* fail! Please, lift up your heads and look from a higher perspective. Historically, does truth win? *Yes, it does*. Though sometimes not openly or right away. This moment in time is pregnant with breakthrough, I feel it, so please, let's not give up," she finished, looking over at Wilberforce. The light still presided within him, although currently a quiet ember instead of a dancing flame.

Agreement energized the room, as one by one the abolitionists reset emotions and refreshed vision; she was right, it was going to be alright. They would keep working and moving forward.

Emilie threw herself at creating pamphlets. She planned to release one story per week so that each one would have the opportunity to do its work on hardened hearts. Chipping away was her operative plan. She would begin with ol' General's life.

Work buried her. From morning to early evening she would stay in the office working tirelessly to write, rewrite, copy, design, and draw, then pass on to the printing press. The finished result was so satisfying! It was even more exhilarating to hand the finished product to an unsuspecting person out on the streets, knowing this may be the final push toward their awakening.

In this way Thursday and Friday flew by.

"Emilie, we're planning to leave early today," began Julia, "to begin preparations for the ball tomorrow. How about you do the same?"

"Yes," Laura chimed in, "you've already done so much, why don't you take a break? I'm sure Lady June would love you home earlier tonight. It'll be good for you to get your mind off of this and onto pearls and perfumes, don't you think?" she pushed gently. They knew that a focused Emilie was not to be deterred, however they tried.

"You're probably right, girls," she began as they feigned astonishment. "I do need a break. I don't even know what to wear tomorrow."

"Wear something pastel. It's in season," began Anne.

"And put on your dancing shoes!" continued Julia, a fixture at the annual winter ball.

"Oh, I don't know if I'll be dancing tomorrow, girls. I don't know anyone who will be there. A ball in London is a fancy affair and one I've not prepared for. And I don't just dance with anyone," she added firmly.

"Perhaps someone you know *will* be there?" Laura teased, referring to Phineas.

"Then I most definitely will *not* be dancing," she shot back faster than her mind could stop her. She glared at Laura briefly, then turned back to her work.

Julia and Anne threw cross looks at Laura, to which she spread her hands remorsefully. She didn't mean to touch that nerve.

"Alright, girls," Emilie continued with her back to the group, "I guess I'll stay for a bit longer and then go. See you tomorrow."

It was a quarter past two when the ladies left. The building quieted down, giving Emilie the environment to focus her tired mind. As she rubbed her brow, she heard the door creak open and shut quietly. She paid it no mind, as people often stopped by the office for reasons of their own. Then came quiet footsteps. Uncertain ones, not confident ones of belonging.

Whoever it was, she was almost done and would be gone shortly.

"Hello there," she began with her back turned to the entrance of the room. "I shan't be here long. I'll clean up after myself when I go."

"Emilie," spoke the gentle stranger.

The voice was not unknown, bringing the world to a standstill. Resting both hands against the table, before turning around she reminded herself what this man represented. Her head commanded her heart to disengage, but she couldn't stop her perceptive heart from really *listening* to what the voice sounded like.

It sounded broken.

But she was broken. By *this man*. His brokenness was deserved. A traitor deserves to feel the severity of his failure.

"Emilie," he began again, "may we talk?"

She straightened her spine tall and proud, clenched her fists, and turned around. "What can I do for you, sir?" came the cold, rushed reply.

They stood an old, dark room apart. She gave no indication to permit him to come closer. If things were different, even this room would be the perfect place to dance again, like once so long ago. But things were different.

Phineas stood at the entrance a different man. He had gained a respectable reputation amongst the nobles, yet he was not arrogant. Hordes of the most powerful men had given him their trust, yet he was neither haughty nor content. Why the paradox? He chose his steps and earned rewards. Then why the melancholic eyes? The mystery tugged at her heart, infuriating her.

Was she wrong about him? Was he coerced into this?

"I've come to tell you that I'm leaving north after the ball," he continued calmly, "and I've come to say goodbye."

"I suppose your success precedes you and they'll be waiting for you with open arms wherever it is you're going," she shot back. She was hurt and angry. These were words meant to damage.

"I suppose," he returned.

"Phineas, I don't know why you'd think that I care about your going…?" she verbalized with finality.

He lingered for another second. She was in pain, and he knew it. Her beauty had matured and her confidence had grown. She was too proud to let go. Plus, she was at this point severely passionate about her work in which, as he had heard around the whole of London, she greatly excelled.

An unconscious slight smile crept across his pitiful face as he remembered her younger years. She never wanted to be left behind, running after him and her brothers to the ends of the fields and getting caught up in whatever adventures they stumbled upon. She never cried or whimpered, but instead trusted her gut and offered support. He always saw her greatness, loving her youthfully then.

And now, more glorious than before, she stood courageously before him upholding truth and justice. Even if it killed her.

She wasn't really denying him. She was denying what she believed he now stood for.

A hopeful flicker of possibility escaped past the iron curtain of darkness as his brows raised slightly in contemplation. *Maybe, just maybe, if she knew.* Her behavior, however, was quick to extinguish it.

"Phineas, I don't have time for this," she interjected impatiently, crossing her arms over her chest. "You must go now." She turned her back to him and began to pick up. Papers went flying and pencils were dropped. There was no longing in her eyes as there once was. She wanted him gone. He was no longer a lover, but a stranger with secrets.

After one final look at the one his heart loved, he turned and walked quietly away.

The door creaked open, then gently shut.

Silence.

The sobbing echoed louder than ever in the damning silence.

Chapter 22

"No, definitely not that one," stated Lady June. "Try the red one on, Em. Tonight is all about elegance, and that one is perfect. You know," she continued, "your words were very encouraging earlier this week. Quite a few people told me how inspired they were after you spoke."

"I'm glad someone was. I wish I believed them myself," she stated despondently, referring privately to her personal life.

Lady June had, of course, noticed her changed disposition since yesterday, but was unwilling to address it until Emilie showed the desire. This was her moment. "What happened yesterday, darling? You've barely eaten since coming home from the office. What's on your mind?"

"Nothing important, Lady June. Just another encounter with him. Why can't he just leave me alone?"

"Yes, why *can't* he leave you alone?" she mused. "I've been wondering that, too."

Emilie ignored the emphasis. For her it was over before it began.

Shortly after, she decided on a flowing cream-colored empire dress with a deep blue sash and accenting silver embroidery. It was fitting for a winter ball. She wore Momma's necklace, matching earrings, and silver gemstones in her hair.

Tonight she hoped to resurrect joy. She wanted to feel beautiful again.

An hour later they were before the front entrance of the grandiose Excelsier Gala. Opulent women and charming men poured in endlessly. If the Foxes' dinner was impressive, this was in a realm all its own. Every single detail boasted of the highest elegance and of the most masterful touch. Music laced in and out of rooms magnificently, deepening her appreciation of the beauty before her. Apparently they were of the last arrivals, as the grand room already overflowed with people sipping on champagne, laughing, and watchfully observing.

Coming to the top of the stairs, she stopped.

Before her opened a vast space with hundreds of faces, very few of which she knew. She scanned the room, hoping to recognize some, spotting the Foxes; John and Fiona; Julia, Anne, and Laura; two of the attorneys from the case; and even the woman from the public square whom she'd ordered on her way. She saw splendidly dressed servants working to keep the people happy.

Tonight this represented the world, all under one roof.

Beginning her descent, she caught the eye of many attendees.

She was, after all, absolutely radiant this evening, with dress and perfectly paired jewelry accentuating her naturally effortless beauty. She was neither haughty nor demanding, carrying herself instead with the decorum of a passionate heart learning to be wise, full of self-awareness and strength. And proper, indeed.

Many a gentleman made his way to take her hand, with John incontestably getting there first, expressing how overjoyed he was to see her again. Possessiveness defined his every action and word—as if she already belonged to him.

She smiled and curtsied, mentioning how lovely the evening was. Whether subconsciously or not she scanned the room for another face, one she hoped not to find, though the thought of encountering him made her feel faint.

What was she thinking? *Keep to your senses*, she told herself. How could she be so weak? The vast disconnect between heart and head was exhausting.

"Emilie, I was hoping to see you tonight," John began. "I've missed you at Derbyshire. It's not the same without you. Will you be returning? Have you received my letters? You there, please give this young lady a drink," he directed a servant walking by.

"Yes, of course, sir." And then turning, "My lady, if you will," he affirmed, bowing low and offering a golden tray with lavish glasses of sparkling wine, one of which Emilie graciously took, appropriately thanking the young servant. John was exactly as she had remembered him, directing people in his own service and assuming Emilie wanted a drink without ever having asked her. He had not changed. His world was full of servants and those meant to be served.

"I have not yet decided what to do, John," she continued. "I'm becoming quite rooted in London. I never thought I'd say this, but I'm beginning to grow rather fond of the city."

"What do you think of how Forester's case turned out? I thought of you throughout its duration."

"I think there's more to the story, but what, I don't know. The evidence is not there. Justice prevailed based on what evidence was there, John. Can we know with full certainty that everything was done with integrity? I don't know. So much was at stake on both sides."

"Yes, I wondered that day how the abolitionists were doing. This must have been such a blow for them...for you. Emilie, what I'm trying to say is, I care for you. I've changed. I'm willing to change more if you'll help me. I've grown mad without you by my side. More than anything in the whole world, I'd love to have you share in my life, to go through things like this together. Please, don't look away. Tell me, is there a chance that you would be willing to make me the happiest man alive?" he pleaded, now facing her, holding her arms with his hands, searching her face.

She looked down at the spritzing glass, swirling the drink around. Marrying John would mean *this* would become her life. As much as he tried to convince her of his change, all remained the same. She didn't despise him, she just didn't love him, and she could never love his life. "John, my heart is so thankful for your continued kindness since the first day when we met," she began, searching for words that would more effectively spare him.

He clung to every word as if it were breath or water.

Suddenly, as she delicately prepared John for a letdown, she caught a brief glimpse of one she knew. He was occupied in conversation against a distant wall with young men she had never seen—relaxed, even laughing. *Phineas*, she breathed, *there you are*. An ache revived deep within.

"Yes, Emilie, what are you saying?" John interfered suddenly, catching her off guard.

"John, I cannot accept you," she released. "Please forgive me. I do not believe that I am the one to make you happy. I'm far too strong-willed and stubborn. You promise you'll change, but I never will. Friendship is all I have to offer," she finished, feeling the bareness of her skin where his hands dropped off.

His face contorted in confounded misery. He was let down. He was so sure of this. "Emilie, will time change anything? I can give you time, if that's what you want. Do you..."

"No, time has not and will not change anything, John," she acknowledged gently. "There is another for you, my dear friend." And with that she curtsied softly, smiled, and walked into the crowd.

It was easier to navigate the room from the top of the stairs, when she could see its entirety, but now on the floor she felt like an ant amidst a thousand blades of moving grass. She did not recognize a single person. Phineas was not where he was a few moments back, leaving her entirely disoriented.

Anne! Catching a glimpse of her redheaded friend, she immediately set out after her. Hordes of annoyed people frowned upon her as she made her way through and past them, toward her destination. Then suddenly out of nowhere, and before she could change trajectory, a large woman that looked to be of great importance stepped right into her line of movement. It was inevitable. Emilie bumped right into her backside.

"I say, what's this about?" the woman shrieked, and turned at once to see who had disturbed her equilibrium. "*You?*" she howled.

It was the woman from the public square who'd have had Lenora's head on a platter if it were feasible.

Emilie quickly regrouped and regained her senses. "I beg your pardon, ma'am. It was wholly unintentional. I do hope you're alright." She stood humble but strong. She was not a bruised reed to be broken.

"Hmph, what's your name? Who are you?" the lady demanded from atop raised nose.

"My name is Emilie Forthyn, ma'am, daughter of the late Sir and Lady Forthyn of Suffolk, niece of Sir and Lady Fox of Derbyshire, friend of Lady June of London, and advocate for the poor and defenseless," she finished boldly, looking directly at the woman, who rolled her eyes at the juvenile before her. Her golden feather drooped over like a wet street cat.

"I've got my eye on you, Emilie Forthyn," she threatened. "I don't know what you're about, but I don't like it. Now go on your way before I find someone who'll put you in your place."

Emilie shuddered momentarily. Then, as if seeing beyond the outward appearance of the corpulent woman, Emilie felt absolute pity at her inner paucity. The woman was so fat with luxury and excess that her soul was suffocating. Hence she was mean, angry, and entirely self-absorbed. *I feel so sorry for you*, Emilie thought.

Her response was kind. "Would it be helpful if I brought you a glass of wine, ma'am?"

"No! *Leave*," she wailed, and quickly walked away. She felt utterly uncomfortable under Emilie's gaze.

There was Anne. Emilie walked over to her and happily received a hug.

"There you are, Em. We've been waiting for you. The girls went to take some punch. Have you ever seen so many charming gentlemen under one roof before?" She was drunk off the thrill.

"Yes, there are many," Emilie replied objectively. "Anne, I just had a run-in with that woman I told you about, remember? From the square?"

"Oh no, that couldn't have been pleasant. What happened? Did she want your gold?" Anne giggled uncertainly. Emilie's account of this woman was frightening.

"No, but she did say that she'd find someone to put me in my place if I didn't leave her alone." Emilie mimicked the woman, and the two burst out chuckling. "I shan't have trouble doing that, ma'am," Emilie retorted with a good laugh. Emilie did not feel threatened. On the contrary, she hoped to get to know the woman, perhaps to help her see the beauty in truth.

Julia and Laura had returned with stories of gentlemen they had bumped into while getting punch, and the four circled around to chat.

A tap on the shoulder interrupted their flow as Lady Clarence appeared, requesting Emilie's attention. "Hello Emilie, how have you been these weeks?" she began. "We must talk regarding Savonne and your inheritance. Have you given these any more thought?"

"Yes, Aunt Clarence, I have been thinking, and I will soon be ready to discuss my position toward the bequeathal. I do hope you and your family are well, Aunt Clarence. The girls are looking most radiant tonight."

"Yes, they are looking precisely that way," she began smugly. Then, rather sharply, "has John made you an offer of marriage tonight?"

Emilie was stunned. It bothered her that Lady Clarence was utterly unrestricted in crossing Emilie's personal boundaries. She refused to acquiesce to the woman's control. "Lady Clarence," she began, "that is my personal business that I shall discuss with you only if I deem necessary. About your other questions, I shall return a clear response soon, once I am fully assured of my decision," she finished, curtsied, and turned to walk away.

Lady Clarence grabbed her arm powerfully. "You ungrateful *girl*," she spat with enough civility so as to not draw attention. "I have shown you nothing but kindness, opening up my home, feeding you, bringing you into society, treating you like one of my own. How *dare* you speak to me thus? I expect an answer before the weekend is out. Do you hear me?"

"Lady Clarence, I appreciate every bit of your *kindness*," Emilie returned emphatically, reminding her aunt of the marvelously bitter things that occurred in Derbyshire, "but I will not be controlled, ma'am. Good day to you." Emilie curtsied and turned toward her friends.

It was getting easier and easier to turn away from that life. Her decision was coming into focus.

Chapter 23

The glamour of the evening rose to even greater heights as the dancing ensued. Couples spun and twirled, mesmerizing the onlookers. Gold, silver, and iridescent colors blurred into a marvelous work of art as bright eyes and smiles flowed about the room.

Many a bachelor had asked Emilie to dance; she declined every one. John danced with Carleighla, a sore expression upon his face. Albert with Fiona. She wished that Mick and Oliver were here. They would have taken to the floor without the slightest hesitation. She caught sight of Phineas a few more times, wondering every time what he was thinking. He looked more and more like himself with every glimpse. She despised him, she told herself. But when their eyes once met, she nearly lost her breath.

Lady June stepped out to dance with a distinguished older gentleman who appeared to fully enjoy her company. She was splendid, looking ageless with every turn.

Sir Fox took Violette to dance, and Lady Fox stood a distance away with a cluster of noble ladies. She could tell they were gossiping based on how they glared at various others around them.

As she enjoyed the dynamics of the night, suddenly and most unexpectedly something entirely catastrophic occurred. It stopped everything. Including the music.

Before she understood what and how, an African servant had tripped and fallen right directly at her, spilling upwards of ten fine glasses of red wine onto the bottom portion of her dress, smashing everything to the fine marble floor. That sound broke the night.

Enormous eyes surrounded her, staring and blinking, breath heaving, no one twitching a muscle. The man stood pale as a ghost, frozen in time and space. In his fifteen years of service, he had never done this before. Lady Clarence stood afar off, iron eyes scrutinizing Emilie's response. The woman from the square, face red and sweaty, stood directly behind the servant, wringing her hands; she, too, watched keenly.

Emilie, aware of the severity of this debacle and understanding that every single eye centered on her in this moment, saw an opportunity. She had a captive audience. Based on the looks and whispers of scorn directed the servant's way, she knew what they wanted her to do.

Her moment of decision had arrived. It was like expecting glory to come in a golden carriage when instead it crept up on a mud-stained donkey. She laughed inside. Whatever the vehicle and as unexpected as this circumstance was, her goal was one. Mind clear, emotions in check, she'd show them what goodness was.

"Good sir," she began, looking the man in the eyes, "it appears we have a mess on our hands."

His eyes widened, despair gripping his soul. Everyone watched on, hoping he would get his just share. The lording of power over the perceived weak gave many immense satisfaction.

Emilie stood there, stains soaking through her dress, shattered glass perilously close, watching the people. "I suppose," she began, "that this was not planned, yes?" She turned around, searching faces, glass shards scratching eerily along the marble floor beneath her dress. "And if it were an unplanned, unexpected event, then there is no reason to find fault, yes?"

"Let him have it," a voice yelled from the crowd.

"Yea, give him what he deserves, that low-life beggar that he is," added another.

The woman from the square wouldn't take her eyes off Emilie, as if gloating over the mishap. It was a replay of what had happened in the square when Lenora knocked her bags to the dirty ground, except this was by far worse. "Young lady, you look startled," she sneered. "What are you to do?"

"Absolutely nothing," Emilie countered firmly. "Ladies and gentlemen, this was clearly an accident. I'm choosing to be understanding. As should you. If someone would please bring something to clean this with, we'll be on our way." Shards lay all around, preventing her from moving forward.

"Oh, *come on*, Emilie." Lady Clarence had now come close, speaking in a hushed voice, hiding behind a concerned face. "Stop trying to make a hero of yourself, pretending you're someone else. Just like your mother used to do. You're a disgrace, a confused fool. You're one of us, and that's how the negro will see you. It's the way of the world. Isn't that right, Lady Forester?"

Forester? Emilie spun to see the name's owner, only to find herself face to face with the woman from the square, face red and lips tightly twitching.

Her spirit raged. Crystal clarity had come. It was time to raise her voice once and for all.

"Dear people of England," she began, voice mounting, commanding full attention. "I can *no longer* watch one man forsake another. You see this man as a lesser human being, as one who *deserves* scorn," she said, standing before the colossal hall, "but people, does he not have two eyes? Is he able to speak with his mouth? Does his heart beat like yours does? What about his lungs? Are they any different than yours or mine? Is he—are they—able to bear and nurture children? For God's sake, people, how is he any different from you or I?" She stopped, letting the question pound throughout the silent hall, cutting deeply into calloused hearts. "I *refuse* to close my eyes and silence my heart so that *you* might live a convenient life. Enough already!"

The crowd began to shuffle uncomfortably, stepping back to give Emilie and the man space. As she knelt to remove glass shards from the bottom of her dress, a hand moved in to help.

Phineas. *Always Phineas.*

He knelt with the two, moving quickly to free her from the glass. Other servants trickled in. The man, finding an ally in Emilie, introduced himself as Charles and swore quietly under his breath that he was pushed from behind. "I swear to you, miss, it was that woman. I felt her arm jolt me from behind," he insisted. One look at Lady Forester convinced Emilie that he wasn't far from the truth.

She avoided Phineas's gaze. He worked quietly by her side, listening to the hushed conversation.

The room began to return to a superficial normal. The violins resumed their now strained sonata. Julia, Anne, Laura, and Lady June ran over, asking about her well-being and ensuring that she was supported.

"I'm fine," she assured them. "I'd really just like to go home now."

"Your words, Emilie Forthyn, need to be inscribed on a monument and placed in the center of our world. Everyone needs to see, hear, read, and feel them every single day of their lives," claimed Lady June, obviously moved by their timeless wisdom. "Yes, my darling child, let's now go home."

Emilie got up, and when she looked, Phineas was gone.

Charles walked over to thank her for her kindness, taking her hand and holding it in both of his. He, too, was touched by her words. They were like rays of hope.

As she made her way to the stairs to leave the ball, men and women stared. Never had they heard anyone say the things she had. She reminded them of Wilberforce, but in her own right. The words landed upon their hearts and left an impact, convicting their beliefs and practices. Deep down, they knew she was right.

Thus the night was changed and she was tired. It was time to go home.

Then suddenly, "Excuse me, miss," came a brusque voice from behind. "Are you the author of the abolitionist pamphlets being circulated around the whole of London?"

"I'm sorry, and who is inquiring?" Emilie responded, turning to face a large man with an eerily familiar voice.

"Only one curious about how you acquired those stories. They sound an awful lot like an experience I had out in the fields of Derbyshire of Kent, where a filthy scoundrel got caught stirring up trouble on my fields. You wouldn't happen to know how and where you got them, now would you?" he baited, watching her every move, preparing for the kill.

"I don't know what you're talking about, sir, and I would appreciate it if you would go your way," she declared, gripping tighter onto Lady June, but holding calmly together.

"William," came an authoritative voice. "I thank you, sir. I've got it from here."

Emilie stood between two men. Guttural unsettledness pulsed throughout her body while beads of perspiration slipped down her back, rendering her speechless. The latter man introduced himself as the chief constable of London and inquired about her name and living arrangements.

"Hm, we've received a particular complaint about nefarious activity on the fields of Kent. Miss Forthyn, I'd like to take you in for questioning. William, I've got it from here. You may go now."

"I-I'm not sure what you're talking about, sir...?"

Seeing her failing disposition, he decided to put the matter off until the following week. "Don't fret, young miss. I'd just like to talk to ya. One of my watchmen suspects that you may know something about a recent field crime. It's protocol to take you in for questioning. Now, I see you've had a busy night. Take care and go on home and come to the central police office on Wednesday."

She feebly agreed and turned to ascend, holding onto Lady June for support but maintaining outward composure, as she knew she was being watched.

At the top of the stairs, she heard hurried footsteps approaching. Lady Clarence was rushing to catch up. Emilie took a deep breath, bracing herself for the woman's usual vexation.

"Emilie, you toy with my nerves," she began anxiously, leaning against a banister for dramatic portrayal. "Tell me this very instant about your intentions toward Savonne and your acquired portion. If you walk away now without answering me, you'll forfeit everything. I will cancel the bequeathal in the name of unmet requirements. Tell me now, will you take over the inheritance according to our family's expectations, or not? Will you honor your late grandfather's desire for both you and your mother to have it?"

"Lady Clarence, I am honored by this offer, but the bequeathal requires things of me I cannot give. I am unable to turn my heart to agree with its foundations. For these reasons, I give you the keys to the house and the inheritance. I agree with my mother—it is not for us. And now I bid thee farewell, Aunt. May we meet one day under better circumstances," finished Emilie, decidedly turning and walking away, leaving Lady Clarence dumbfounded.

"She gave it away..." she pondered to herself, astonished. Emilie's convictions wrecked her heart.

Lady June side-hugged Emilie tight and said that she could stay with her for as long as she desired.

"Until I get married, you mean?" Emilie grinned sheepishly.

"Even then, if you'd like. Emilie, you've got a bright future in store, this I'm sure of."

"No parents, no home, no inheritance, no husband. Lady June, it's not looking too bright right at the moment."

"Emilie, looks are ever so deceiving," she chuckled, knowing in her heart that everything was about to change for her darling girl. "Oh, before I forget—we have a guest tomorrow."

"Lovely! Are they an acquaintance? Is it a 'he' or a 'she?'" Emilie winked lightheartedly. She was laughing again. Tonight's stand liberated her in ways she did not know were possible.

She felt entirely, happily, delightfully free.

Now if only she knew what this interrogation was about.

Chapter 24

" **A**lright, slave, go pack up. You're being relocated," the mal-odorous drunkard barked. "Don't worry," he continued, "no worse than here. Might even be better. They offered a price I couldn't refuse. You're invaluable to me, don't get me wrong," he said, pulling her young frame inappropriately against himself, "but that pretty sum could buy me two pretty girls, maybe even three."

Shockwaves pummeled throughout Mim's mind and body.

"Quit your staring. Go grab your things, before I change my mind."

Mim was stunned. She had walked into the parlor anticipating his usual physical advances and heavy words, but instead he stood before her facing the window that overlooked the road. Sir Wimberton was the most deceptively charming, morally bankrupt man she had ever known. The new normal was unspeakably dreadful, but at least predictable. But who was he waiting for?

"Sir, may I ask where I am going?" she chanced cautiously, eyes fixated on his boots, hands anxious but strong.

"Oh, shut up. Don't act so ornery. A place is a place, just like a slave is a slave. It's all the same. One owner's trash is another's treasure. That's all." He shrugged his broad, sweaty shoulders. The anticipation of the scheduled transaction had worked him up into an anxious frenzy. Mim was good, that he knew, but not quite as good as the sum he demanded. But the fools obliged. And not a penny less. He was now anxious, lightly drunk, and giddy all at once. What if they changed their mind and knocked down the price?

At exactly the determined time, a stately carriage appeared on the horizon.

"Go grab your things, fool. I told them nine o'clock, now don't make a liar out of me," he roared, throwing the nearest object he could find in her direction.

Mim was faster than his drunken delay, however, escaping down the hall quicker than he could utter more obscenities.

Shortly, Wimberton stood on his snowed-in front porch with Mim by his side.

A kindly looking man stepped around the carriage and addressed them both. "I am Rupert of London's Esquire Estates. I have come on behalf of my estate owner to purchase this young lady for the aforementioned sum (as discussed at length prior) this very morning. Unless something has changed, I would like to be on my way as soon as is possible. Here, sir, is a document we have drafted requiring your signature. If you are prepared to fully relinquish all rights to this young girl in absolute perpetuity, please sign here." Rupert pointed to the last line, pulling a silver pen from his fancy coat.

"Where's the money?" Wimberton pushed back.

"The money comes after the signature, sir," Rupert repelled comfortably.

Now aggravated, Wimberton jerked the pen from the unyielding man and signed.

"Here you go, sir," stated Rupert, formally handing over the bag to Wimberton, who plopped down on the top stair to count his gains. Greed and fat escalated his breathing.

"Now miss, if you please, we must be on our way," stated a confident Rupert, offering Mim his left arm while opening the carriage door with his right. He knew the amount was correct, as he had counted it himself.

Mim briskly tore from Wimberton's side and jumped toward the carriage, which was velvety and warm. This moment had to be her rescue. It was no less divine than Emilie not getting caught that day so long ago.

As much as she was able, however, she levelled her expectations to neutral. She knew absolutely nothing about this new place. But somehow, even with the unknowns, she felt one step closer to freedom. As the carriage picked up its pace, she, tattered body wrapped in a warm blanket provided for her, peered outside at the snow-laden resting landscape.

Come what may, nothing could be worse than what she had already lived through.

A curious robin peeked into the window as if entreating someone to come out and play, but the howling February wind intimidated even the bravest of boys. Most cherished the opportunity to stay in and recover after the most unusual ball last night, contemplating conversations within themselves they had rarely entertained before. Whether the heart was impacted or nerves were struck, they could not truly tell, as they felt both enlightened and ashamed all at once.

Emilie, awakened by the smells and sounds from the kitchen far below, turned onto her back, and tried to remember why it was she felt as she did. Catching sight of her devastated dress brought memories and thoughts like a torrential downpour.

That was *Lady Forester*! What a scandalous turn of events.

And Savonne. She was no longer bound to its legacy, with every tie to her past now severed. The freedom to build her own legacy was entirely and utterly thrilling.

Walking over to the window, she noticed the robin bouncing up and down the windowsill. "That's how you must feel, little fella," she chittered to the big-breasted bird. "And you know nothing else. How delightful…"

She smiled. Her spirit felt caught up in a most exquisite story where at first very little appeared appealing, but the longer one looked and pondered and ruminated, the more they would see its absolute beauty. She had to keep letting go. She had to trust.

Even if she felt lonely. Freedom often felt that way.

But today she would not let loneliness stop her from making and entertaining a new acquaintance. She prepared herself and hurried to the dining room to find Lady June perusing *The London Times* and enjoying a savory tea sandwich.

"Good morning, my fair lady." She walked over and gave the woman a peck on the cheek. "Is that caviar?"

"Quite right. Alain snagged a purchase early this morning. I don't know how he does it," she giggled elatedly. "Emilie, our guest should be here any minute. Have you thought of plans for today?"

"Well that depends on who it is and how long they're staying," she began, insisting that Lady June disclose immediately what now seemed to be in the hiding.

"Ah, there they are. I see the carriage. Now stay put, my dear, have a marmalade scone," she prescribed, actually dropping one onto her plate as she made her way toward the east-wing door. "Esther, please make sure the young lady stays put, if you will. This must be done perfectly." Lady June, in a state far more energized than her usual, hurried off toward the front door, making an audible fuss all the way down the hall.

Emilie squirmed and wiggled in her chair for what seemed like an entire hour, waiting for the unexpectedly important newcomer. The tea cooled down and scone lay untouched as she tapped her finger and played with her napkin. A scuffle was suddenly heard down the hall, with more than one set of footsteps making their way toward the dining room.

Emilie sat upright, stood, then sat again. She fixed her dress and fidgeted with her hair, standing again as the sounds were now right outside the door. She picked up the napkin.

Lady June burst in with the grandest, most delighted expression ever to cross her face, swelling with emotion. "Miss Emilie, would you please join me in welcoming Esquire Estates' newest helping hand?" she requested, waving to the mysterious newcomer standing in the shadows.

Mim, the carrier of secrets of the past, walked in.

Tightly kept emotion ripped loose as tears overtook their boundaries. Emilie saw the healed scar across her face and bruises on her arms and began to shake with dark grief. Everything she had desperately longed to forget welled up without question or request for permission. She did not expect to see Mim ever again, feeling that the bitter experiences of that day would never let go, that closure would forever forsake her.

But here stood the closest thing she had had to a best friend, the one who took the beating for her, saving her very life.

Both had changed since their last encounter.

"Mim, my dear Mim!" Emilie cried as the two fell into a tender embrace.

"Yes, Miss Emilie, here I am. I've been invited to stay. This is the happiest gift I could have ever asked for. And I didn't even ask. Thank you, Lady June, for your kindness. I can just laugh and cry all day and then do it all over again. I'm so happy." Her tear-stained face emanated joy.

"Yes, Mim, as am I. Please, please call me 'Emilie' from now on. We are best friends. I have so much to say, so many questions to ask," Emilie began, sitting her down in the chair next to her own. "Are you quite well, my friend? I mean...*are you?*" She took both her hands, holding them atop the table.

Her eyes searched Mim's, looking for that same fierceness and passion from before, praying that they had not been taken from her. She probed deep, looking for her friend. The guilt she carried around could only be relieved if she knew that Mim was safe. She heard Lady June making requests to prepare Mim's living quarters and clothing, insisting that the young lady be treated with the utmost kindness and respect. Rupert was also praised for his excellent dealings with Wimberton.

"Miss Emilie—I mean, *Emilie*," Mim began rather abashedly, "I've told you before that hard times, bad times, will not steal me away. It's in my blood—in my people's blood. I've lived through everything, and my bones are still alive. Things could have been better, yes, but the worse they became, the more determined I got to get free. Heaven must have had enough of my determination," she said with a sheepish grin.

"But...that day... I can't forget, Mim. Old General and you, you were beaten and he was killed. Your scar stares at me and reminds me. I'm so sorry. This was all my fault, and I can't get free—" She couldn't finish; the sobs rose upward and out. Heavy, anguished tears rolled down her face as she and Mim embraced. They had lived through hell together. She desperately longed to be free from the self-loathing that never left her side.

"And here we are. Both of us. Don't you see? Nothing has stopped us, Emilie. The very hand of God has kept us up until this moment. And no, I could never be angry with you. That was not your fault. We chose to go together for the sake of my people. And Miss Emilie, I still wait to see what you have done with the stories."

Emilie exhaled, seeing that her friend was indeed her old self. As she often was, she was right again.

The revolting heaviness lifted.

They sat talking at the table until early afternoon, but not fast enough, it seemed, as the tears and trembling laughter kept coming. Lady June was satisfied that Mim would now be a part of her estate. Her plan to rescue the girl had worked. One day she hoped that Mim would be fully free. She would include that in her work contract. She would pay her an excellent servant's wage so that one day she could support herself.

"Miss Emilie, now that everyone has gone, I've been waiting to ask you one question," Mim led on gently. Emilie knew what was coming. "Is Sir Phineas well?"

Emilie took a deep breath in and looked away at dried flowers in a crystal vase at the opposite end of the table. Another point of inner contention. "He is well, Mim, in fact better than ever, I'd say. Yet I cannot say more, as we no longer talk."

"Hm, I was sure that he would offer you a proposal," she stated, unable to hide her disappointment. "What happened? Is it someone else?"

"To be honest, Mim, I don't know what happened. One day he just...changed. The Phineas I knew, the one who believed in the same things we believe in, was no more. I could not speak with him the same way ever again. Remember Forester's case? The banker whom the abolitionists charged for illegally withholding their money?"

"Yes, I do. Sir Wimberton wailed day after day that if the case 'flopped,' as he called it, then he'd lose everything."

"Yes, well the case did not as you say 'flop.' Instead, the man went free. Phineas was on his side the entire time. He publicly supported him. But some of us secretly believe that Forester really is guilty and that his crimes were covered up. Mim," she continued, "that day when you were taken and I hid inside the cabin, I heard two men walk by, talking about the case. They jested about it, saying that Forester was insulated against the plaintiff and that the abolitionists would not get him. This has led us to believe that there was a cover-up, though only Lady June and I know about this for now. So, to see Phineas supporting this man...it's unthinkable. No matter what happened before, I could never marry a man who supports what I detest."

As was her usual manner, Mim listened intently, hearing both the spoken words and the ones in-between the lines. "But what if this is all one big misunderstanding, Mi—Emilie? Phineas is a good man. I remember him. I have a hard time believing that a good man becomes bad like that. He was never like that, Emilie."

"Oh Mim, you have not changed! My dear friend, how glad I am that we are together. Even if we may disagree on this one thing." Emilie patted her hand and stood to change the subject. Mim's pragmatic insight uncovered a familiar heartache that Emilie did not wish to address at the moment. "Mim, would you like to take a walk to the office where I work? It looks as if the wind has died down."

"Is that allowed?"

"Why yes. This is the best group of people you can imagine, Mim. Ask Lady June, she is a regular there. Their sole mission is to end the slave trade. They will love you, I'm sure of it. Won't you come? Perhaps we'll even bump into Sir Wilberforce, the one I've told you about."

"Yes, Emilie, I will," she stated with head held high. The chains of former days were beginning to loosen.

They separated to quickly wash up and to change into warmer clothing before leaving the estate. Lady June without the slightest hesitation approved of giving Mim the entire day off. She wished them well as they stepped into the frosty chill of late afternoon. Snow flurries hurried about.

On their way through the public square, they walked past a young courier with an urgent message and freshly printed newspapers.

"Case verdict overturned!" he shouted. "New evidence urges the reexamination of recent verdict. Verdict overturned! Take a look for yourselves."

Wondering what case he was referring to, Emilie paid for a paper, only to find Forester's face on its front cover. The case verdict was being challenged!

Reeling from the potential implications, she and Mim raced in silence to the office. Once there, they met a few others who also wondered what this meant. Even Wilberforce was making his way to the office for a meeting. Mim was introduced to everyone there and treated with the utmost respect. They painfully acknowledged her visible and invisible scars. She had never been treated like this before.

Hundreds of questions permeated the atmosphere as the gathering grew in size and intensity. When Wilberforce arrived, they had at least determined that new witnesses came forth with evidence to subvert the verdict. Some had heard that farmers from the north were speaking up convincingly, while others believed that Forester's French enemies were releasing the damning evidence.

One thing was certain: this was a window of opportunity to get the result they knew was there.

The passionate momentum for equality for all men moved Mim to tears. She sat near Emilie and shed these tears. She had found a safe place.

Chapter 25

*M*onday reeled in faster than people could handle. So much was happening. The ball was a curious anomaly which left a foreign aftertaste in the whole of society. Forester's case was under re-examination. Horrendous stories of the inhumane experiences of slaves—of those not thought twice about prior—were reaching ears and hearts. Their world was tilting.

1806 was off to a rocky start.

The following day, things became loud. Bigger clusters of people congregated outside the hall of justice that just last week had released this same man absolutely free of charge. They, knowing full well the implications of an exoneration, rendered him the honor due a saint. If they were honest with themselves, however, it was always about them.

The same attorneys and jurors would storm out of the hall for a cigar break, showing indiscernible scowls and wrinkles upon strained faces. The people ranted and grimaced in the cold, awaiting their own doom, as it were. All was the same except for new apprentices on both sides, as the previous group was dismissed at the completion of last week's closure. These were thrilled at the opportunity, as a re-examination of such a monumental case was a far less common experience than a regular case.

By Wednesday the crowd had grown in size and the frustration likewise mounted. Mim chose to stay at Esquire Estates that day, appreciating the risk of a potentially angry mob. Emilie, however, felt free to partake in the experience with her friends and several of the abolitionist men, knowing that she would be safe.

At noon the sun rose higher, bathing the exceedingly charged atmosphere with a heavenly ambiance, as if erasing the gloom of the previous Wednesday. There was a lift internally, too, though no word had been released.

Then, as historically had never been done, the massive door was pushed open and the justice of the peace himself came out.

"My fellow citizens," he began immediately in a loud, musty voice, "today I most genuinely acknowledge your patience and civility under these most unusual circumstances. Thank you, noble ladies and good sirs. Now as we all know, last Wednesday Sir Forester was fully exonerated from any and all claims of civil or criminal misdoings. This was fair and just based on the evidence that we had and most scrupulously examined."

He paused, wondering how to begin the next part. Clearing his throat, he then leaned to his left to whisper something to the court clerk, nodding a brief yes, then resuming his posture to continue.

"Today, I have a different report of this very same case," he began coarsely. "The man Sir Bartholomew Forester, based on new evidence that has reached my eyes, has been found guilty of all charges. This court renders its judgment impartially and in good faith based on real-life evidence. Please, I beseech you, go home in peace my friends, take a good look at this case and what may be learned from it today. And I implore you to uphold justice in your everyday dealings so as to prevent such monumental events from reoccurring." He finished and stepped quickly back inside the dark courtroom.

Emilie whirled inside and couldn't wait to share the news with Mim and Lady June, but first she was expected at the constable's. She composed her elated emotions for the time being and turned towards the heavy metal door of London's police headquarters. She entered the office and was instructed to wait while he finished with another appointment. No more than five minutes went by when his door swung open and a disheveled man smelling of smoke limped out. She stood. The constable waved to her to come inside, requesting that she shut the door.

"Good day to you, Miss Forthyn. Thank you for arriving as requested. I'm Constable Jack Payne and I've invited you here today because certain individuals have felt rather certain that if you are the author of one of these," he emphasized, picking up a pamphlet, "then you are privy to an experience having occurred at Derbyshire of Kent where, according to such individuals, at least one intruder was found to be trespassing upon their property. There was a fatality, miss. Now, I'm not one to say anything unless I read you your rights."

After the reading, he continued, "Now, are you or are you not implicated in the aforementioned crimes against Derbyshire of Kent?"

"Sir, I come from Derbyshire," she began carefully. "Sir and Lady Fox are my relatives. I would never do anything to distress them or anyone working for them." In her heart, she knew this to be true. The circumstance which caught the girls was a grievous turn of events that neither could have foreseen or speak of without endless pain. She initially planned to evade the answer, fearing that submitting truth would lead to imprisonment, but Momma's words of the respectableness of a woman walking in integrity seemed to lay a weighty hand upon her shoulder, encouraging her to dare to be even *this* bold.

"That day, Constable, I and another went to the fields to speak with the African workers about their lives lived in England. The pamphlet you hold contains true stories of their lives. They deserve to have these stories told, sir. The fatality you speak of," she continued, now holding back tears, "was a man not unlike yourself. He was an army general in Africa who loved his family and his people. England tore this from him. The 'watchman,' as you say it, he was the one who beat him to death that day. I know because I heard it all as I lay hidden in the cabin. I recognize his voice. My friend was also beaten, though her youth prevented death from taking her. Sir," she continued as tears streamed down her face, "if I have to, I will own up to those pamphlets and deal with the ramifications. But as you see, some things are worth fighting for. General DeLeon is worth this."

She could see mixed emotion come and go across his face, as if he were wrestling with the speaking or withholding of certain words. Then he decidedly spoke. "Miss Forthyn, I have the power to imprison you this very day for trespassing on private property, damaging private property, and the inciting of a riot. Hell, I can even throw in the implication to a homicide. There's much I can do," he said, eyeing her response, "but here's what I *will* do." At this point he leaned forward on his cluttered desk, lowered his voice, and urged her to come closer. "I know a certain someone—who shall remain eternally nameless, per his personal request—who has undergone exceeding pains to protect himself, you, and countless others. In fact, he'll likely be out of the country before the month ends. I shan't say more other than to say that you are covered."

Aside from an avalanche of relief, Emilie was stunned. She was speechless.

The constable continued, "I needed to bring you in to satisfy the requirements of legal protocol and, more than anything, for optics. That is all. I know what you did was to further the cause of abolition. I also know that my watchmen care more about their dogs than they do their slaves. I am certain that you did not commit a crime worthy of incarceration." And with that, he tipped his hat to her and insisted that she be on her way.

As she turned to leave, he spoke up. "Miss Forthyn, keep up the good work and make sure this stays between us. I don't need rumors about my pardons for abolitionists."

"Yes, sir, I will. And thank you," she, still in awe of the gracious pardon, humbly replied, walking toward the door. Aside from thinking of how close she had gotten to being locked up, she wondered about this mysterious protector who had told the constable about her. How did he know about the day on the field? Other than

Mim and Lady June, no one else knew. She was also intrigued that the constable appeared to side with their cause, though he did not directly say so. She was thankful for good men in high places. As she hurried home, she pondered about her lot in life and prayed to one day meet this mysterious man.

At home, Lady June insisted that the young ladies beautify themselves, as "you never know who you'll run into," after which they headed by carriage to the office, where what seemed like hundreds of jubilant faces poured into the building. The victory had emboldened many covert abolitionists.

Questions about the new evidence were upon the lips of all in attendance, but no one knew how or by whom it got to the judge. It was, as it were, by divine intervention.

As Emilie walked over to take a drink, she noticed Wilberforce, Hannah More, and a few others talking in hushed voices not far from the table with food and drink. Their smiles and discreet words tugged at her to listen.

"Yes, we knew we were in the right," Sir Granville declared quietly. "Our bank and loan accounts just didn't add up, but that wasn't enough."

"Mm...always loopholes," Wilberforce added, then more words spoken inaudibly, though no less animated.

She tipped her ears a hair more.

"...a spy, as it were," Lady More interjected with wide eyes while Wilberforce deliberated about the newfound evidence. "Yes, indeed...a young man from the country, I just heard from Smith..." She lowered her voice more as the small group turned inward.

A young man from the country. Emilie froze, water halfway to her mouth.

The world tilted further as more words fell upon her ears.

"The police chief recruited him, having heard of his reputable character... I daresay his name was Finley? No, no, it was Phineas, but we can't breathe a word," she finished again, insisting that his identity be kept a secret for fear over his life. "It is believed that he's recently left London."

"What a brave man," Wilberforce stated zealously. He eagerly wished to make his acquaintance but knew the dangers of such exposure.

In one moment, everything suddenly made sense.

Everything changed.

First she went ice cold, then broke into a feverish sweat. Trembling overtook her body as her legs began to give way.

"Oh dear. Somebody, get Emilie a chair!"

She heard scuffling feet and moving furniture and then felt a solid surface beneath her.

"Emilie, are you alright? What's happened? Is there a doctor in the house?" Lady More raised her voice above the noise of the movement.

The pain of failure hit so powerfully that she could not possibly prevail against the downward entanglement. She was drowning in the greatest sorrow of her lifetime. How could she explain that to a doctor? To them? "No, no, I assure you, I'm fine. Just got a little lightheaded, that is all. I have not eaten all day. Please, I don't need a doctor. I think I shall go home and rest up for a bit," she finished, imploring that they let her go. The heartache was too grave for the public eye.

The man she loved was forever gone.

His trembling caresses and pleas for her trust the night of the dinner echoed loudly in her mind as every blind spot laughed cruelly at her loss. She couldn't possibly tell the world of her feeble and foolish heart as the cause of her current ailment!

He needed me. I failed him when he needed me.

Every piece fell into place like an ugly puzzle. His unexpected departure to London, the behavior at the dinner party, and of course his last words.

He had to leave after the ball so as to prevent any suspicion of his name. Forester was a powerful man. Everything had to be done just right in order to work. A single misstep could prove fatal.

Phineas had been playing a part in an immensely complicated drama, and she had missed her role entirely.

Feeling sick to her stomach and now pale as a sheet of new cotton, she again requested to be taken home by carriage. She assuaged Lady June's concerns by making up words about her stomach feeling ill all day today.

"Are you sure you don't need me to come with you, darling? I don't mind, I promise. Or perhaps Mim should go?" the elder persisted with worry.

"No, Lady June, please stay here and enjoy your evening. I'll need someone to tell me all about it tomorrow," she claimed as easily as she could. "I'll be alright, I promise. I must just need to sleep it off. Please look after Mim for me. Let her enjoy the evening, too. I shall see you tomorrow," she finished with a contrived smile and turned to catch the carriage. She prayed the woman would leave her alone—and to her surprise, she did.

The infinite impossibility of her error was more than Emilie could bear. Clambering into the cold carriage, she lay her head back, closed her eyes, and envisioned the Phineas she once knew but now didn't. He was a different man now, changed irrevocably by the past months.

He was a hero, and she did not deserve him.

He had the glorious legacy of saving countless lives through potentially deadly sacrifice. She had a self-righteous, self-loathing, broken heart.

Getting herself to bed was all she could do. She locked the door and collapsed on her bed, dress and jewelry on, weeping once again for all that could have been.

He would forget her now.

She was so ashamed.

For all her talk about truth, she couldn't even see it herself.

Chapter 26

*W*hat does one do when fragmented images of days past cannot be unseen? How does one live with insurmountable failures taunting relentlessly day after day?

Emilie threw herself at work. Redemption would come, or at least she prayed it would, when she had done enough for the people around her. She strove to become their savior. Every one of her coworkers and friends saw a burst of energetic endeavoring to bring her African brothers and sisters help and hope.

The stronger the ache thrashing about within, the harder she labored. She busied herself with writing new pamphlets and organizing charity work to the poor and needy, even organizing a novel biweekly food drop-off to the workers of the fields. She was now tenderly called 'friend' by Sam, Judica, and Thomeus, and 'daughter' by Rosa and Persy, and many others would briefly whisper short versions of stories for her to write about. She collected signatures in support of such work and diplomatically spoke with the estate landlords. They could not refuse her bold truth and raw honesty. With Forester out of the way, England was beginning to sort things out.

"Emilie," Wilberforce one day began, "have you heard about the trade school we plan to open this spring?"

"No, sir, I'm afraid I've been far too occupied to listen," she replied with regret, at which moment Wilberforce studied her disposition without a word.

He let out a breath and hesitantly pursued his line of questions. For the first time since Forester's indictment, he took the time to really look at his young protégé. He knew what pain looked like, and this was unmistakably it. Based on its intensity, he guessed it had something to do with the friend she had spoken of on their first encounter. He made a note to speak with her about him soon. For now, however, he pressed on. "Then I assume you have neither heard about the vote nor its outcome?" He smiled the question.

"No, sir, I had no idea I missed a vote," she responded. "What was being decided?"

"Well, with plans to open up the trade school in April, we began to think about its leadership and how it would be run. Lady More, myself, Sir Granville, Sir Hughes, Lady Wilson, and a few other trusted leaders put forth a few names of those whom we considered to be candidates for this very esteemed position."

"Yes, there are a few I'd have recommended myself had I known about it!"

"Ah yes, there are many. There was, however, but one that received a unanimous recommendation. That's what I'm here to speak with you about, Emilie."

"Sir, I will happily support whoever gets chosen. Is it Sir Pepperton? His dedication puts everyone to shame, myself included! Or I'd also think that Lady and Miss Furlton could do a fine job organizing and instructing the students. They have the most amiable qualities of good character and studiousness."

Before she could keep going, however, Wilberforce took out a stack of papers which presumably held the name of the new director. "Emilie, read these, please." He handed the folded papers to her and stood back to watch with tethered impatience.

She took the stack, wondering why he was giving these to her until she saw the first name scribbled upon it.

Emilie Forthyn.

And the second. *Miss Forthyn.*
The third. *Miss Emilie.*
The fourth. *Miss E. F.*
And so on.

Every single paper was hers. Eyes sopping, failure heavy, and with an overwhelming feeling of unworthiness, she collapsed into the nearest chair and began to weep.

Wilberforce, expecting a different response, knew that today Emilie's burden had reached an unmanageable weight. This burden had shrewdly changed her disposition. He sat with her then and listened while she shared what she felt at liberty to. He encouraged her to receive grace for what she perceived to be failures and to be inspired by her relentless, selfless, and passionate pursuit of what was true and just.

"Emilie, had these things not been important to you, you would easily have accepted this friend's betrayal and continued to have his relationship. But you did not. Not just anyone could have made that same decision. You must see that your decision was a very difficult one to make, especially based on what information you had at that time. Many a person has left the cause of goodness for their own gain, whether it be for love, wealth, reputation, or power. You chose immense loss because of what you knew in your heart to be true *at that time.* Only God knows all. That's why I walk with Him. Because He teaches me about life and its many intricacies. I say this because I know what loss and failure are. Had it not been for Him, I may have given up a long time ago. Be encouraged, my dear friend, you are not alone in this." He squeezed her shoulder and offered her a handkerchief.

She thanked him and, now feeling better, picked up the stack of papers and cried out through a recovering smile, "What do I do with these?"

"You say 'yes,' my young history-maker!"

Continuing to wipe tears which could very well have been happy ones by now, she did just that. She accepted the invitation to become the director of the trade school for all people, African and English, young and old alike.

When she claimed that she had very little to offer, Wilberforce merely smiled and said that she had more than most.

As both Lincoln and ol' General had said, change was coming. They could feel it in their bones. Now she could, too. She embodied the light that chipped away at darkness and the beauty that pervaded ugliness. Truth was getting stronger by the day. Darkness had started to defend itself. Love was on the move.

Chapter 27

"Our twelfth student just enrolled!" exclaimed an ecstatic Julia. The response to the school exceeded everyone's expectations. It seemed that once normal resistance had acquired the same melting point as snow. The public, estate landlords included, no longer felt the pungent bitterness of days past, when all deeply resented the abolitionist movement. Every incremental change serendipitously increased their acceptance of it. If entirely honest, they would admit that they actually appreciated the turn being taken. These admissions were yet rare, though.

It was now April 15th and the School of Good Trades had been operating for exactly one week with Emilie at its helm. She worked tirelessly to bridge the colossal chasm between England's upper echelon and those far below, with the hope of providing more individuals the opportunity to attend the school. Thus far a few had yielded. Others (like the Foxes) wanted nothing to do with Emilie's dream of educating their slaves and servants. She was not deterred, however, and neither were the ones who worked with her. The results they were already seeing only inspired them onward.

Walking home alone mid-week in the indecisive April air, Emilie considered the kaleidoscope of her life. She had heard that Savonne Manor was signed over to Carleighla and that John had proposed to her shortly after (precisely the day after). Carleighla had, of course, readily accepted. Emilie pondered her recent run-in with the Foxes, who, if not for Sir Fox, would have zealously turned a blind eye. Sir Forester duly lost his banking position. It was a relief to know that no matter how powerful the man, a few good constables had brought justice to pass (and rumor had it that Lady Forester had moved to France, though no one could be quite certain of that). Emilie was further pleased with the budding romance between Sam and Mim and willed that their joy would not be quenched by anything at all.

At home, Lady June appeared to have been awaiting her arrival. As Emilie removed her shoes and overcoat in the entryway, she caught sight of her dear friend properly seated at her desk with papers strewn about. She had been writing.

"Lady June, good evening. How has your day been? Any visitors today? Has Sir Griffiths called?" Emilie walked over, giving her a gentle squeeze.

"I promised your mother and father that I would look after you," she began abruptly, eyeing the paper before her, clearly on her own train of thought. "Emilie, you have been like a daughter to me, and I swore to your parents that even if you were under Clarence's roof one day that I would never forsake you. I see your sorrow, my love, and I wonder if I might have done something more to protect you. Hush now," she said softly, silencing protests. "I'm going to share with you something I've never told anyone. Have a seat, my love. I know you have given up on love. But please, don't make the same mistake I made at your age. I, too, gave up on love. I, like you, experienced the severest form of pain when the man I loved with all of my heart, the one who promised me the world, left one day and never came back. I, also not unlike you, threw myself at my passions, things that I could do, ways I could change the world. And although they were all good things, I never have experienced the fullness that life offers. You've been the closest thing to that. But having a man who loves me every waking moment, children, then grandchildren who grow up by my side, and the satisfaction of knowing that I will never be alone—these I lack. I did not give love a second chance, beloved, and today I lack what things may have brought me immense happiness. Emilie, this is my biggest regret. Don't misunderstand me, I have lived a marvelously full and happy life, but there could have been more. So please, from the bottom of my heart, don't give up on love. Don't accept the lesser offer, though it may seem justifiable. That is my request of you."

As their eyes met, their hearts conjoined in loving union. They understood one another well.

"Lady June, I don't know what to say... Thank you—for this, for everything. I don't know where I would be right now if it weren't for you."

"Oh poof, Miss Trade-School Director! It's been nothing, Emmy dear. You didn't need me one bit. You've brightened up this drab old place. I think you're doing *me* the favor of being here." She grinned, eyeing Emilie, looking for an opportunity to address her next couple of points.

Emilie could tell she wasn't finished. "Lady June," Emilie continued gently, "the promise you seek, however, I cannot yet make."

"I know, child. But I still ask it of you." Her face was lovingly stern for a moment, then broke into her typical unabashed grin. "And another thing, darling. First of all, promise me you'll visit your brothers this very week. And stay for at least one week. You deserve a break. They've written requesting that I ask you."

Emilie was not expecting this. She had quite forgotten about her brothers in the midst of her busy schedule. "I suppose it would do me some good to go back. I haven't been since the funeral, and I do miss them."

"Good. And secondly, it's time I told you that I have officially included you in my legal will to inherit everything I have. I'm getting along in my old age and would not ever want to give my wealth to anyone else. You get a percentage now and the rest when I go. There is not a soul more deserving."

At this Emilie was rendered speechless. Never in her wildest dreams had she thought this would happen. She was used to working for her well-being, but this! She tried, as per the appropriate etiquette, to politely decline the grandiose offer, but her words came out so incoherent that Lady June only laughed at her innocent captivation. She had chosen her beneficiary well.

"I'm a stubborn old lady and will not accept 'no' for an answer, Emilie, so don't waste your breath. It's time you took your rightful place in the world. Remember on our first ride to Kent you struggled to understand how being served and led about by others made you a lady? I remember your fiery disposition that day. Today you must understand that a true lady is not defined by what others do for her, but by what she does for others. Sometimes an heiress can do more than a working-class young lady can—this is the way of our society. I'm giving you that power. Position is not something to use casually, and it is a grave responsibility to carry the title. But I fully trust that you will do just that. I have watched you many years now and recognize the strong woman inside. Come, come, today's the day."

Suddenly Mim burst in, cheeks rosy, a strong woman in her own right. "Pardon me!" she began apologetically, but then seeing the paper on the desk and recognizing what Lady June was doing, walked right over to Emilie, slipped an arm around her back, and placed chin on shoulder. "Say 'yes,' Emilie. We need you to be strong and powerful."

"One signature and it's yours, no matter whether you come or go," said Lady June. "It becomes a part of who you are."

Both ladies gave Emilie a moment to think, then Lady June offered her the pen.

Hand trembling, Emilie signed two copies of her right to ownership of everything belonging to the respectable noblewoman Lady June Dorothea Davis of Esquire Estates. She looked at the two women and smiled. She was an heiress. This was the substance of fairytales.

"We hope you enjoy Suffolk, Emilie," Mim mentioned excitedly.

"Thank y—Wait, how did you know I was going?" Emilie questioned, knowing that Mim was not around when she and June had discussed her going.

"Oh," Mim stumbled, looking dreadfully at Lady June. "I-I did hear you outside the door here. I was talking to Esther. You are going, yes?"

"Yes, indeed I am," Emilie replied with a growing suspicion that these two had been conspiring about her.

"That's good, my friend. The north air will do you good. Many will be happy to see you! I must work now," she replied quickly, escaping Emilie's scrupulous gaze.

"Shall we stop for a break, Miss? We have one hour and a half remaining."

"No, George, let's please keep going. The faster we arrive, the better."

"Sure thing, miss."

I am an heiress.

Riding north through the English countryside, she marveled at how everything had changed. Once a young, grieving woman southbound toward a life of genteel nobility, now a remarkably different person. The winding river sparkled gaily along as if reminding Emilie of past dreams, or of one dream in particular. The notebook was packed carefully away. Many parts of her heart felt the same.

She recalled her first exposure to slavery's brutality. It had occurred on this road, except in the opposite direction. Had she made a difference in this man's life? What about in the life of the oppressive master? Had the light reached beyond London?

Laying her head back and closing her eyes, she thought of moment after moment with Phineas. He embodied the qualities of the best sort of man: selflessness, integrity, and strength now refined by fire. He was kind and generous. How different would things be right now if she had listened to the still voice within, rather than yielding to fear?

What did she fear?

She feared losing herself and the image she had envisioned of a heroine. All had to be perfect, a fairytale, like the stories she grew up on. She had to be perfect.

But life was an imperfect entity. There were painful blisters from walking unfathomable distances in poorly fitting shoes, ominous snow storms that one had not prepared for, and broken hearts that drew out one's light and laughter, amongst many other ails. Words that should have never been spoken were far too often spoken. Young men were asked to take on responsibilities that they never should have been asked to take on, and young women were stifled in a box they were never created for.

Humanity was as imperfect as a child's work of art or nature's untouched landscape. But nothing brings more joy than a little girl's heartfelt masterpiece created for her mother or father, who will no less than parade her as the next Reynolds. And who could compete with the fiercely proud mountains, lands, and waters of England where even the masters are challenged to no end to recreate a sorrowfully lesser replica?

Had perfection become her enemy? She wondered now if she would have given Phineas a chance had she not been so proud of her idyllic vision of a true lady of England. She cut him off just like that.

Had she become a lady? Was she now of marriageable quality? Would she find the man Constable Payne spoke of? Unanswerable questions swirled around her mind, energizing unwelcome waves of hopelessness. She evaluated every motive she had had related to herself and Phineas and wondered if she could ever forgive herself.

Looking out the window, she began to recognize the scenery. There was the Hasgroves' dilapidated fence and the Wilsons' drying laundry. Further onward she saw the McGrays' smoke plume, and her heart cringed. She did not ever wish to encounter them again. Then finally, with more emotion than she ever expected, they turned down Abbey Lane.

Home sweet home.

The Forthyn estate stood like a crippled elder with tidy clothes and makeup; it was old but well-groomed. She breathed in the sweet air of early spring and allowed the sun to bathe her face. She had been frowning too much.

Ethan was first to spot her, waving to her from the barn, indicating that he would run over as soon as Belle was in her stall.

Then Miss Fist burst out the front door. "Oh, Miss Emilie! Is it really you? You look so sweet and healthy. Allow Teddy and William to take your things. Come, come inside. You're right on time for fresh mince pie. I knew we'd have visitors today. Always trust your gut, as they say." And at this she ran into the kitchen to fuss all over again about Emilie's arrival.

Emilie couldn't help but smile. How good it was to be back.

Trust your gut, she mused. The poignancy of the advice was sharpened by her very failure to do so, and this cost her dearly.

She never did respond in writing to Mick and Oliver about her coming, so she did not expect them to expect her. They would be home in one hour or so, anyway. The house was swept and tidy. Father's violin stood propped up atop the old oak bookshelf. Momma's teacups and saucers were placed perfectly in the china cabinet near the big window. The perfect use of that corner was for tea time; she remembered that well.

Peace came for the first time in months. The familiar surroundings were like Momma's embrace or Father's pat on the shoulder.

"Miss Fist, I shall be outside in the rose garden. Please, do call me in when my brothers arrive. No no, don't worry, I'm not so hungry right now. Thank you."

Past the garden she went towards her parents' grave. Alone out in the open, she looked up to heaven and allowed tears to freely flow. How she had been fighting these past months. They would have understood her. Greater peace cascaded all around her, as if a gift from above. She breathed it in and out, laying her pain down onto the ground.

One thing you taught me was to learn from my mistakes. I'm learning.

The rose garden was wild with naked sticks and thorns. Last summer's roses were incredibly lush and fragrant, and she hoped this year's crop would surpass them.

It was so long ago when she was the young daughter of the fairly common Sir William Forthyn, owner of a newspaper company and lover of all things good. Today she was an heiress to an immense fortune that had caught her entirely by surprise.

She still *felt* the same.

Sitting on the old swing, she closed her eyes to imagine what life would have been like had she not gone to Kent. The journey had been so dichotomously bittersweet that she couldn't make it out. Had she gained more than she had lost? Was wealth greater than love?

The swing creaked gently back and forth as she stared ahead at the curling plume of smoke above the McGrays' humble estate.

Then suddenly, as if from a dream, she heard a voice. A familiar sound.

"Sir and Lady Forthyn would be proud of you, you know."

Pivoting at a dizzying speed, she suddenly looked upon the face of one who stood with hands in pockets, leaning against the rose trellis.

"Phineas," she croaked, voice small, heart acutely aware.

"Miss Emilie," he acknowledged, tipping his hat.

They remained silent for a moment in time, allowing the past season of life to catch up to their mouths, for there was much to be said. She looked on with wide-eyed torment. He, with calm resoluteness.

At first as she spoke, so did he. The energy to convey what each had inside was so ferocious that they quite aptly stumbled upon their words and manners. They were like young lovers who dared not yet speak of love. They, however, were quite unaware.

"Emilie," Phineas finally collected himself and began. "When last we spoke, I had told you that I planned to leave north… Well, today my plans have changed."

All Emilie could do was listen. She did not feel deserving of his attention or relationship. She was like a wilted rose with fading color and fragrance. Kind of like the petals in the notebook he gave. Those were dead now.

He, believing that he understood her downcast face, continued on. "For reasons I am not able to disclose to you, I have decided to move farther away than northern England."

"Phineas—" she began, "I know your reasons." She looked up at him with a pained expression.

By this he was taken aback. Then, his face brightened. "*What* do you know, Emilie?"

"I know, Phineas, that you were asked to go undercover to facilitate the takedown of Sir Forester. That you risked your life for millions to further the abolitionist agenda. That you are moving away to protect yourself from Forester's vicious accomplices, who may seek you out for retaliation." She paused then, tears filling up her eyes. "I also know that everything I have done to you is absolutely, entirely, and fully irreparable. My behavior is unforgivable. That is why I shall never ask for it. Phineas, you are a hero. I have heard your hushed praises coming even from Wilberforce. So many lives have been and will continue to be changed because of you. Now, please, you *must* go. I can't bear it any longer."

Phineas, the one she had known and grown to love more than words could describe, gave a cock-eyed grin. "How hard you are on yourself, Miss Forthyn," he said with a good-natured smile. He was more relaxed now. Love would take her self-erected walls down. He was only thrilled that she knew. Being unable to share with her his burdens had been one of his greatest challenges. Watching her break and hurt was more than he could bear at times.

He crossed the distance of thawing ground between them and knelt before her, taking her hands in his own. "You need not be so hard on yourself, Emilie Forthyn," he said again, lifting her downcast chin so as to see her face. Sorrow had unmistakably left its mark. His heart ached that he was the reason. "You and I both have had our share of pain," he continued, longing for his Emilie to return. "Today I have come to tell you that I'm leaving much farther away, and I-I thought that…perhaps you would come with me," he said hopefully.

She stiffened, pulling cold hands away. Fierce desire took the back seat as shame and unforgiveness paraded haughtily around her soul.

"I cannot Phin. How could I?" she pleaded, body contorted to be as small as possible. This season of life had been a hard one. "How can I when I judged and condemned you, spoke poorly of you, hated you...*failed* you? How can I ever trust myself again? How can *you* trust me?"

"Emilie, if what you need is my forgiveness, then here, take it. I forgive you. Emilie, *I love you*, more than words can—"

"Stop, you *must* stop. I cannot bear it. I'm determined to never forgive *myself*."

"My darling, my love, you must!"

"It is because I love you that I cannot. You need someone far better than me. I can offer you nothing but my failures..."

Tears streamed down her face as she fought. Finally she dropped her head in her hands and gave in. Phineas's embrace felt like home. She loved him. He offered no words now, allowing her to grieve the loss of a part of herself, just like that day so long ago when Momma and Father were buried.

Whether minutes or hours had gone by, neither could tell. She finally lifted her head and gave a weak string of a smile. As he held her, she grieved over and released pain. Unyielding memories suddenly lost their power. His forgiveness was real and love relentless. She knew he meant them.

Hair flying and eyes caked with dry tears, she finally looked at him as she once did. "Phineas, I love you," she said, allowing the words to seal her heart.

Dreaming about the day these words would rest upon her lips, he stood and gave himself over to sweet elation, dancing a sweet jig right there before the swaying rose bushes. He moved toward her, pulling her up from the swing, twirling her around. She marveled in wonder that this man would change her world as he had. Then, without a word, he fell to one knee and spoke words that redefined her story.

"Emilie Forthyn, will you make me the happiest man alive and become my wife?"

"Yes, Phineas McGray. Yes, I will." And she raised him upward, stepping into his embrace.

Holding her close, he thought of what it took to get here—he'd almost lost her. He kissed her then, so wholly enraptured by the sacred moment they inhabited. This was his bride.

She melted sweetly into his strong arms with every kiss. Together they rested in a place where happiness resided and peace prevailed.

Then, out of nowhere, questions started to tumble in.

"Phin," she asked curiously as they strolled around the rose garden, "who was that woman at the restaurant at the square? That beauty sitting across from you?"

"Ah, yes. If I tell you, you won't believe me," he chuckled, but continued, "That was the granddaughter of the Earl of Hardwicke. In order to secure a piece of evidence necessary to convict Forester, I had to take her on a few dates. Don't worry," he ensured, placing a peck on her forehead, "she was not my style. Though I did behave in a convincing manner long enough for the job to be done. All I could think of was you, though. Sometimes that helped me play the role," he chuckled again, remembering the lengths he had gone to to successfully fulfill his assignment. "She thinks I've gone back to Durham with plans to leave to Scotland."

"I see," she mused, wondering what it was like to date one of the richest ladies in England. Then, "do you know anything about Constable Jack Payne?"

He twirled her around again, intoxicated by the prospect of a future with her. "Yes, I have been connected with him. Why?"

"He had called me in for an interrogation recently, Phin, about events that happened when I was still at Derbyshire," she said, watching his expression change. "I am wondering about one thing that he had said..."

"Yes?"

"Well, there is first of all something that I must also tell you," she began, taking a sharp breath in to tell the whole of it in as condensed a version as possible. "When you left to London that day, before the dinner party, Mim and I—"

"Went to the fields of Derbyshire?" he delicately placed.

Emilie was speechless. How could he possibly have known? "B-but how did you know? Phin, how did you find out?"

"Emilie, Lady June wrote me a letter explaining everything. I know, my darling. I know the story about your stories. I cannot tell you how proud I am of you. Emilie, I cannot wait to spend the rest of my life with you. We will do it together."

She beamed then, recognizing the man of mystery before her.

"Well then, if Lady June did this, you must know of another thing she just did," she teased, allowing his right hand to twirl her around one more time. "I am an heiress, Phin," she finished with a grandiose curtsy.

"Good," he replied enthusedly. "That shall help fund our honeymoon...in America."

And before she could utter a single word, he wrapped her in his arms and kissed her.

TO BE CONTINUED...